About the author

Poul Anderson is one of science fiction's
foremost talents and has twice won its most
coveted honour – the Hugo Award – for his
short stories *No Truce with Kings* and *The
Sharing of Flesh*. His many science fiction
and fantasy novels include: *A Circus of Hells,
Beyond the Beyond, The Star Fox, The
Byworlder, There will be Time* and *Dancer
from Atlantis.*

Also by Poul Anderson in Sphere Books

THREE HEARTS AND THREE LIONS
WAR OF THE WING MEN

The Broken Sword

POUL ANDERSON

With an Introduction by Lin Carter

SPHERE BOOKS LIMITED
30/32 Gray's Inn Road, London WC1X 8JL

First published in Great Britain by Sphere Books Ltd 1973
Reprinted 1977
Copyright © Poul Anderson 1971

A somewhat different version of this book was
published in America in 1954
Copyright © Poul Anderson 1954

The dedication of the first edition was to my mother
ASTRID ANDERSON
and likewise for this one, save that it is now shared
(and thus is doubly gladdening to me in the bestowal)
with my daughter of the same name

Set in Linotype Plantin

Printed in Great Britain by
Hazell Watson & Viney Ltd
Aylesbury, Bucks

A CHANGELING IN ELFLAND

When Orm of Jutland heard the witch prophesy that his firstborn son would be reared in the Halfworld of the Elves, he did not believe there was truth in the curse. But Imric, the cold, clever, heartless elf-earl, for cryptic reasons of his own saw to it that the curse came true. Fathering a son on a female troll held captive in his dungeons, Imric exchanged the nonhuman babe for the true son of Orm the Jutlander.

Thus, while Valgard the Changeling was raised as Orm's son in the Lands of Men, the true son of the Jutlander, Skafloc, was reared to manhood in the twilight fields and whispering woods of timeless and shadowy Faerie....

The author of this extraordinarily imaginative fantasy novel, Poul Anderson, is a tall, curly-headed, owlishly bespectacled and very youthful-looking man in his middle forties.

Anderson was born in 1926 in Bristol, Pennsylvania, of Danish parentage, which explains his unusual first name. Poul himself pronounces it to sound about halfway between "pole" and "powl"—but I have never met anyone except Poul himself who can quite pronounce it.

His father was an engineer, and as engineers go wherever they are needed, Poul was raised literally all over the place: in Bristol first, then in Port Arthur, Texas, as well as in Washington, D.C., Copenhagen, Denmark, and on a farm in Minnesota. He now lives in Orinda, California, with his wife, Karen and their teenage daughter, Astrid.

Anderson began writing while he was a student at the University of Minnesota, and he sold his first stories while still an undergraduate. This early success may have suggested that instead of becoming a scientist he was actually meant to be one of those very rare people, a born writer. Anyway, as Poul himself tells the story:

"At the University of Minnesota, I majored in physics, graduating with honors in 1948. But apart from a little assisting here and there, I have not worked in the field. What happened was that writing, which had been a hobby for a long time, began to pay off while I was in college with some sales to *Astounding Science Fiction*. I decided to take a year off, living by the typewriter . . ."

That "year off" has been going on now for twenty-two years; for, although he returned to college to follow up his B.S. in physics with some graduate work in mathematics and philosophy, Poul Anderson has been a writer first, last, and (let's hope) always.

His first book, an admirable science fiction novel titled *Brain Wave*, was published by Ballantine Books in May, 1954. It's a measure of the high esteem his friends in the science fiction world hold for Poul Anderson and his books that only *five years* after this first book was published, Anderson was hailed as Guest of Honour at the 17th World Science Fiction Convention, held at Detroit in 1959.

To a very large degree, most of Anderson's work has been in science fiction. In the last sixteen years he has published something like thirty-eight books in the field, by my count. He has won recognition for his swashbuckling and imaginative novels—such as *The High Crusade* (favourably reviewed for the Book-of-the-Month Club)—and for his intelligent and carefully-plotted short stories, three of which have won him Hugo Awards as the best story of the year.

But Anderson refuses to be typed as "a science fiction writer." He has turned to other fields and won considerable respect in them. In historical fiction, an area rather neglected in recent years, Anderson has published two adventure novels —*The Golden Slave* and *Rogue Sword*—and has written a third, a vast epic of heroic action in the age of the Vikings, which has yet to find a publisher.

He has also written children's books (such as *The Fox, the Dog, and the Griffin*, retold from an old Danish fairy tale), and book-length nonfiction (for example, *Is There Life on Other Worlds?*). He is also the author of three mystery novels: *Murder in Black Letter, Murder Bound,* and *Perish by the Sword*, which won him Macmillan's first annual Cock Robin Award in 1959.

But, even taking all his versatility into account, I believe it honestly could be said that Poul Anderson's real love is the romantic adventure fantasy laid in the ancient world. He is one of the early members of the Hyborian Legion, a loosely-organized but devout club of enthusiasts of the famous Conan stories of the late Robert E. Howard; Anderson's translations of saga verse from the Old Norse have appeared in the Legion's fascinating magazine, *Amra*, almost from its founding.

He also belongs to one of the smallest and most exclusive writer's clubs on earth today—S.A.G.A., otherwise known as The Swordsmen and Sorcerers' Guild of America, Ltd.—whose membership is strictly limited to the authors of the Sword and Sorcery genre of fantasy. (So exclusive is S.A.G.A., by the way, that it has only *eight members*: Poul Anderson, Lin Carter, L. Sprague de Camp, John Jakes, Fritz Leiber, Michael Moorcock, Andre Norton, and Jack Vance).

Anderson, his wife and daughter also belong to a most unusual organization called The Society for Creative Anachronism, Inc., a rather enormous group of people interested in Medievalism who regularly hold tournaments and revels in antique costume. The Society began first on the West Coast, but interest has since spread all across the country. The original group organized "The Kingdom of the West," and has since issued charters to a group of interested co-Medievalists in the New York/New Jersey area (known as "The East Kingdom"); and a new kingdom, called most appropriately "The Middle Kingdom" has since begun functioning in the Midwest, centring around Chicago.

These tournaments, by the way, are serious and very beautiful. Of course, the contestants do not fight with weapons of edged steel, but their wooden weapons are strong, heavy and most carefully made, and can lay the unwary or unskilled flat—and very often do; therefore, those who wish to fight in a Society tourney must sign a waiver of liabilities in case of injury. While Society members may adopt various titles of nobility (within certain limits) knighthood itself must be earned in combat on the field of honour. And in the Kingdom of the West, Poul Anderson is known as Sir Béla of Eastmarch. Members may also register coats-of-arms with Society heralds: Sir Béla, for instance, bears the arms *azure*, two suns *or* in pale, with saltier *argent*.

Despite his deep and sincere enthusiasm for the genre, Poul Anderson has not written very extensively in the adult fantasy field. This is probably due to the fact that magazine editors and publishing houses have come to think of him by now as primarily a science fiction writer, as much as it is

7

due to the even more unfortunate fact that until very, very recently there was little chance if any of getting an original fantasy novel into print in this country. The astounding success of Professor Tolkien's *The Lord of the Rings*, and the more recent establishment of Ballantine's Adult Fantasy Series may correct this long-standing prejudice against the genre.

But Anderson *has* produced two brilliant, delightfully swashbuckling fantasy novels—the earliest being the book you presently hold in your hands. *The Broken Sword* was first published in 1954, the same year as Anderson's first science fiction novel, *Brain Wave*. His only other book-length venture into the imaginary world of fantasy—an excellent novel called *Three Hearts and Three Lions*—was serialized in *The Magazine of Fantasy and Science Fiction* in 1953; issued in hardcover form by Doubleday in 1961; and done in paperback by Avon Books in the same year. It has recently been reprinted, and thus it is readily available in one or another of these editions.

The Broken Sword, however, is obscure—all but unknown. It was published at the very beginning of Anderson's career by a rather small publishing house, Abelard-Schuman. In the sixteen years since that small printing first appeared, it has never been republished; and until now it has somehow persistently been overlooked by the paperback editors. But novels as superlatively imaginative and entertaining as *The Broken Sword* have a way of lingering in the minds of their readers. I have been unable to get the fabulous world of Valgard and Skafloc out of my mind since I first read this book; and I have been trying to bring the novel to the attention of publishers for years. I feel very happy that, in my capacity as Editorial Consultant to Ballantine's Adult Fantasy Series, I am at last able to make myself heard with some authority.

Poul Anderson has rewritten and revised *The Broken Sword* for this first paperback edition. It's difficult to improve a book as good as this one, but he has learned quite a lot about the art of writing in the last sixteen years, and his repolishing has added new luster to one of the best fantasies of recent decades.

Incidentally, readers of Professor Tolkien will be amused and possibly even startled to discover in these pages a couple of their old friends from Middle-earth, the dwarves Durin —Anderson calls him "Dyrin"—and Dvalin. I hasten to reassure you that this does not imply that Anderson has "borrowed" from the Tolkien trilogy. That would be an impossibility in fact—unless Poul Anderson had access to a time machine—for when Anderson wrote *The Broken Sword*, the first volume of *Lord of the Rings* had yet to be printed, even in Great Britain. Indeed, *The Broken Sword* appeared in print almost simultaneously with that first volume, for *The Fellowship of the Ring* was published in Great Britain by George Allen and Unwin in 1954.

The explanation is simply that Anderson, being of Scandinavian ancestry and well-read in languages like Old Norse, drew upon many of the same sources that Tolkien himself used—such as the Icelandic sagas. As for Durin and Dvalin, Anderson probably got them from the same place Tolkien did, the famous "Catalogue of Dwarves" in the first book of *The Elder Edda* (*Voluspo*, stanzas 10–15, *et seq.*). At any rate, you will find in this novel many of the same imaginative elements that appear in *The Lord of the Rings*: trolls, dwarves, elves, dragons, and the "broken sword" itself, an old literary motif Tolkien revived in his handling of Aragorn's great sword, Anduril.

Poul Anderson can thus be seen as one of that great Fellowship of fantasy writers whose imaginations have been thrilled and excited by "The Northern Thing": a Fellowship which includes William Morris, E. R. Eddison, Fletcher Pratt, C. S. Lewis, and Tolkien himself.

As you will see once you have read this novel, Poul Anderson is very much at home in even so splendid a company.

—LIN CARTER
Editorial Consultant:
The Ballantine Adult Fantasy Series

Hollis, Long Island, New York.

FOREWORD

Late in the year of Our Lord 1018, Sighvat Thordarson fared through Götaland on an errand for King Olaf of Norway. Most folk thereabouts still worshipped in the old way. The wife at one lonely steading would not let him and his friends spend the night because an *Alfarblót* was being readied. Any well-brought-up man in those days could make a stave at any time; and Sighvat was a skald. Quoth he:

> "That Odin be not angered,
> keep off!" the woman said.
> "We're heathen here and holding
> a holy eve, you wretch!"
> The carline who unchristianly
> cast me from this garth
> gave out that they would offer
> at evening to the elves.

So the tale goes in Snorri Sturlason's *Heimskringla*. Elsewhere we read that the dragon heads were removed from warships when they neared home, lest the elves take offence. In such ways we see these beings for what they were in the beginning: gods.

Of course, by the time men in the North started writing books, the elves had dwindled to mere tutelaries, like the Greek dryads or the *kami* of some river in Japan. The Eddas put various of them in Asgard as attendants of the Æsir. But the word is used for two different races, who hold two of the Nine Worlds. Alfheim belongs to the tall, fair "light elves." Though we are not altogether sure of it, most likely Svartalfheim, whose name means "home of the dark elves," is where the dwarfs live. It is interesting to note how much more important the latter are in what stories have come down to us.

Later folklore diminished the elves further, making them nothing but sprites, shrinking their very size, and forgetting their kinship with the still potent dwarfs. Nevertheless a ghost of Alfheim haunted the Middle Ages and Renaissance —the realm of Faerie, whose inhabitants were of human stature but unearthly in their loveliness and magical skills.

In our day, J. R. R. Tolkien has restored the elves to something of what they formerly were, in his enchanting Ring cycle. However, he chose to make them not just beautiful and learned; they are wise, grave, honourable, kindly, embodiments of good will toward all things alive. In short, his elves belong more to the country of Gloriana than to that house in heathen Götaland. Needless to say, there is nothing wrong with this. In fact, it was necessary to Professor Tolkien's purpose.

But twenty-odd years ago, a young fellow who bore the same name as myself harked further back—the whole way to the ninth century—and saw elves and gods alike as having quite another nature. It was, in Europe at least, a raw era. Cruelty, rapacity, and licentiousness ran free. The horrors that the vikings brought to Britain and France were no worse than those Charlemagne had already visited on the Saxons or those the First Crusade would perpetrate in Jerusalem; they could not be. Twentieth century civilization has doubtless fallen from humanistic grace, but it has a long way to go before it strikes that absolute bottom which (God help us) may after all be the norm in history.

Since men tend to see their gods and demigods in their own image, this writer therefore showed elves and Æsir as amoral—when crossed, altogether ruthless. It squared with what we can read about them in Edda and saga.

And he amused himself with a bit of rationalization in the grand old *Unknown Worlds* manner. It seemed only natural that the dwellers in Faerie would be technologically advanced beyond their human contemporaries. Assume, if you will, that there really were races once which could do magic— that is, mentally control external phenomena by some means as yet unknown to our science. (But see the recent work and speculation on "parapsychology.") Assume that they could live indefinitely, change their shapes, and so on. Such an alien metabolism might have its own penalties, in an inability to endure the glare and actinic light of the sun or in disastrous electrochemical reactions induced by contact with iron. Why should these handicapped immortals not compensate by discovering nonferrous metals and the properties of their alloys? Might the elven ships sail "on the wings of the wind" because of having virtually frictionless hulls? Though the kind of castle we generally think of today did not exist in the Europe of King Alfred, the Faerie people could have been building them for a long while. In the same way, other apparent anachronisms would be simply the achievements of races older than man. But an aristocratic warrior culture, particularly with the conservatism induced by long lives, would not be likely to develop science very far. We should not look for gunpowder or steam engines in the ruins of Faerie.

The Broken Sword was slow to find a publisher, who gave it only a single printing. Now, thanks to Lin Carter and Ballantine Books—and to Professor Tolkien, whose noble work is what has made popular the entire genre of heroic fantasy—it can be brought back.

Yet this chance holds for me a dilemma. I am not being affected in referring to the author as someone else. He was. A generation lies between us. I would not myself write anything so headlong, so prolix, and so unrelievedly savage. My vein is more that of *Three Hearts and Three Lions*. This young, in many ways naïve lad who bore my name could, all unwittingly, give readers a wrong impression of my work and me. At the same time, I don't feel free to tamper with what he has done. If nothing else, that would be unfair to those who have heard of his book and think they are buying it.

Well, I've compromised. First, there is this new foreword to explain the situation. Second, without changing the story, I did allow myself a number of textual emendations. I like to think that the author would have been glad to take the advice of a man more experienced—also in techniques of medieval combat! I did not rewrite end to end; as said, that appeared unethical. Hence the style is not mine. But I have trimmed away a lot of adjectives and other wordbrush, corrected certain errors and inconsistencies, and substituted one Person (in one brief though important scene) for another who didn't really belong there.

Thus what you have here is in fact *The Broken Sword* as originally conceived and written. It has simply been made more readable. I hope you enjoy it.

As for what became of those who were still alive at the end of the book, and the sword, and Faerie itself—which obviously no longer exists on Earth—that is another tale, which may someday be told.

Poul Anderson
who in the Society for Creative
Anachronism is known as
Sir Béla of Eastmarch.

I

There was a man called Orm the Strong, a son of Ketil Asmundsson who was a yeoman in the north of Jutland. The folk of Ketil had dwelt there as long as men remembered, and held broad acres. The wife of Ketil was Asgerd, who was a leman-child of Ragnar Hairybreeks. Thus Orm came of good stock, but as he was the fifth living son of his father he could look for no great inheritance.

Orm was a seafarer and spent most of his summers in viking. When he was still young, Ketil died. The oldest brother, Asmund, took over running the farm. This lasted until Orm, in his twentieth winter, went to him and said:

"Now you have been sitting here in Himmerland with the use of what is ours for some years. The rest of us want a share. Yet if we divide the grounds five ways, not to speak of dowering our sisters, we will sink to smallholders and none will remember us after we are dead."

"That is true," answered Asmund. "Best we work to-gether."

"I will not be fifth man at the rudder," said Orm, "and so I make you this offer. Give me three ships with their gear and food stocks, and give whatever weapons are needed by those who will follow me, and I will find my own land and quit all claim on this."

Asmund was well pleased, the more so when two of the brothers said they would go with Orm. Ere spring he had bought the longships and outfitted them, and found many of the younger and poorer men of the neighbourhood who would be glad to fare westward. In the first clear spell of weather that came, while the seas were still rough, Orm took his ships out of the Limfjord, and that was the last which Asmund saw of him.

The crews rowed swiftly north until they had left behind them the moors and deep woods under the high sky of Him-merland. Rounding the Skaw, they got a good wind and raised sail. With sternposts now turned to the home country, they likewise put up the dragon heads at the prows. It piped in the rigging, strakes foamed, seagulls mewed about the yardarm. Orm in his gladness made a stave:

White-maned horses
(hear their neighing!),
grey and gaunt-flanked,
gallop westward.
Wild with winter
winds, they snort
and buck when bearing
burdens for me.

By starting thus early, he reached England ahead of most vikings and had rich plundering. At the season's end he laid over in Ireland. Indeed, he never again left the western isles, but spent his summers gathering booty and his winters trading some of that wealth for more ships.

At last, though, he came to wish for a home of his own. He joined his small fleet to the great one of Guthorm, whom the English called Guthrum. Following this lord ashore as well as at sea, he gained much; but he also lost much when King Alfred won the day at Ethandun. Orm and a number of his men were among those who cut their way out. Afterward he heard how Guthrum and the other surrounded Danes had been given their lives for taking baptism. Orm foresaw at least a measure of peace coming between his folk and Alfred's. Then he would not have so free a pick of what was in England as he still did.

Therefore he went into what would later be called the Danelaw, looking for his home.

He found a green and fair freehold that reached back from a little bay where he could keep his ships. The Englander who dwelt there was a man of wealth and of some might, who would not sell. But Orm came back by night, ringed his house with men, and burned it. The owner, his brothers, and most of his carles died. It was said that the man's mother, who was a witch, got free—for the burners let any women, children, and thralls who wished go out—and laid the curse on Orm that his eldest son should be fostered beyond the world of men, while Orm should in turn foster a wolf that would one day rend him.

With many Danish folk already dwelling thereabouts, the Englander's remaining kin now dared do naught else than accept weregild and land-price from Orm, thus making the farm his in law. He raised a big new house and other build-ings, and with the gold, the followers, and the fame he had, was soon reckoned a great chief.

When he had sat there a year, he felt it were well if he took a wife. He rode with many warriors to the English ealdorman Athelstane and asked for his daughter Ælfrida, who was said to be the fairest maiden in the kingdom.

Athelstane hemmed and hawed, but Ælfrida said to Orm's face: "Never will I wed a heathen dog, nor indeed can I. And while you can maybe take me by force, you will have little joy of it—that I swear."

She was slim and tender, with soft ruddy-brown hair and bright grey eyes, while Orm was a huge bulky man whose skin was reddened and mane nearly white from years of sun and sea. But he felt she was somehow the stronger, so after thinking for a while he said: "Now that I am in a land where folk worship the White Christ, it might be wise for me to handsel peace with him as well as his people. In truth, most of the Danes have done so. I will be baptized if you will wed me, Ælfrida."

"That is no reason," she cried.

"But think," said Orm slyly, "if you do not wed me I will not be christened, and then, if we may trust the priests, my soul is lost. You will answer heavily to your God for losing a human soul." He whispered to Athelstane, "Also, I will burn down this house and throw you off the sea-cliffs."

"Aye, daughter, we dare not lose a human soul," said Athelstane very quickly.

Ælfrida did not hold out much longer, for Orm was not an ill-looking or ill-behaved man in his way; besides, Athel-stane's house could use so strong and wealthy an ally. Thus Orm was christened, and soon afterward he wed Ælfrida and bore her home. They lived together contentedly enough, if not always peacefully.

No church was near; vikings had burned those that formerly were. At Ælfrida's wish, Orm got a priest to come join the household, and for atonement of his sins planned to build the priest a new church. But being a careful man with no wish to offend any of the Powers, Orm continued offer-ing to Thor in midwinter and to Frey in spring for peace and good harvests, as well as to Odin and Ægir for luck at sea.

All that winter he and the priest quarrelled about this, and in spring, not long before Ælfrida's child was born, he lost his temper and kicked the priest out the door and bade him begone. Ælfrida reproached her husband sharply for this, until he cried that he could stand no more woman-chatter and would have to flee it. Thus he left with his ships earlier than he had planned, and spent the summer harrying in Scotland and Ireland.

Scarce were his craft out of sight when Ælfrida was brought to her bed and gave birth. The child was a fine big boy who after Orm's wish she called Valgard, a name old in that family. But now there was no priest to christen the child, and the nearest church lay a good two or three days' journey away. She sent a thrall thither at once.

Meanwhile she was proud and glad of her son, and sang to him as her mother had to her—

Lullaby, my little bird,
of all birds the very best!
Hear the gently lowing herd.
Now the sun is in the west
and 'tis time that you should rest.

Lullaby, my little love,
nodding sleepy on my breast.
See the evening star above
rising from the hill's green crest.
Now 'tis time that you should rest.

Lullaby, my little one.
You and I alike are blest.
God and Mary and their Son
guard you, who are but their guest.
Now 'tis time that you should rest.

II

Imric the elf-earl rode out by night to see what had happened in the lands of men. It was a cool spring dark with the moon nearly full, rime glittering on the grass and the stars still hard and bright as in winter. The night was very quiet save for sigh of wind in budding branches, and the world was all sliding shadows and cold white light. The hoofs of Imric's horse were shod with an alloy of silver, and a high clear ringing went where they struck.

He rode into a forest. Night lay heavy between the trees, but from afar he spied a ruddy glimmer. When he came near, he saw it was firelight shining through cracks in a hut of mud and wattles under a great gnarly oak from whose boughs Imric remembered the Druids cutting mistletoe. He could sense that a witch lived here, so he dismounted and rapped on the door.

A woman who seemed old and bent as the tree opened it and saw him where he stood, the broken moonlight sheening off helm and byrnie and his horse, which was the colour of mist, cropping the frosty grass behind him.

"Good evening, mother," said Imric.

"Let none of you elf-folk call me mother, who have borne tall sons to a man," grumbled the witch. But she let him in and hastened to pour him a horn of ale. Belike what crofters dwelt nearby kept her in food and drink as payment for what small magics she could do for them. Imric must stoop inside the hovel and clear away a litter of bones and other trash ere he could sit on the single bench.

He looked at her through the strange slant eyes of the elves, all cloudy-blue without whites or a readily seen pupil. There were little moon-flecks drifting in Imric's eyes, and shadows of ancient knowledge, for he had dwelt long in the land. But he was ever youthful, with the broad forehead and high cheekbones, the narrow jaw and straight thin-chiselled nose of the elf lords. His hair floated silvery-gold, finer than spider silk, from beneath his horned helmet down to the wide red-caped shoulders.

"Not often of late lifetimes have the elves gone forth among men," said the witch.

"Aye, we have been too busy in our war with the trolls," answered Imric in his voice that was like a wind blowing through trees far away. "But now truce has been made, and I am curious to find what has happened in the last hundred years."

"Much, and little of it good," said the witch. "The Danes have come from overseas, killing, looting, burning, seizing for themselves much of eastern England and I know not what else."

"That is not bad." Imric stroked his moustache. "Before them, Angles and Saxons did likewise, and before them Picts and Scots, and before them the Romans, and before them Brythons and Goidels, and before them—but the tale is long and long, nor will it end with the Danes. And I, who have watched it almost since the land was made, see naught of harm in it, for it helps pass the time. I would fain see these newcomers."

"Then you need not ride far," said the witch, "for Orm the Strong dwells on the coast, distant from here by the ride of a night or less on a mortal horse."

"A short trip for my stallion. I will go."

"Hold—hold, elf!" For a while the witch sat muttering, and her eyes caught what light came from the tiny fire on the hearth, so that two red gleams moved amidst the smoke and shadows. Then of a sudden she cackled in glee and screamed, "Aye, ride, ride, elf, to Orm's house by the sea. He is gone a-roving, but his wife will guest you gladly. She has newly brought forth a son, who is not yet christened."

At these words Imric cocked his long, pointed ears forward. "Speak you sooth, witch?" he asked, low and toneless.

"Aye, by Sathanas I swear it. I have my ways of knowing what goes on in that accursed hall." The old woman rocked to and fro, squatting in her rags before the dim coals. The shadows chased each other across the walls, huge and misshapen. "But go see for yourself."

"I would not venture to take a Dane-chief's child. He might be under the Æsir's ward."

"Nay. Orm is a Christian, though an indifferent one, and his son has thus far been hallowed to no gods of any kind."

"Ill is it to lie to me," Imric said.

"I have naught to lose," answered the witch. "Orm burned my sons in their house, and my blood dies with me. I do not fear gods or devils, elves or trolls of men. But 'tis truth I speak."

"I will go see," said Imric, and stood up. The rings of his byrnie chimed together. He swept his great red cloak around him, went forth and swung on to the white stallion.

Like a rush of wind and a blur of moonlight he was out of the woods and across the fields. Widely stretched the land, shadowy trees, bulking hills, rime-whitened meadows asleep under the moon. Here and there a steading huddled dark beneath the vast star-crusted sky. Presences moved in the night, but they were not men—he caught a wolf-howl, the green gleam of a wildcat's eyes, the scurry of small feet among oak roots. They were aware of the elf-earl's passage and shrank deeper into the gloom.

Erelong Imric reached Orm's garth. The barns and sheds and lesser houses were of rough-hewn timbers, walling in three sides of a stone-paved yard. On the fourth, the hall raised its gable ends, carved into dragons, against the star clouds. But Imric sought the small lady-bower across from it. Dogs had smelled him, bristled and snarled. Then before they could bark he had turned his terrible blind-seeming gaze on them and made a sign. They crawled off, barely whimpering.

He rode like a wandering night-wind up to the bower. By his arts he unshuttered a window from without, and looked through. Moonlight shafted over a bed, limning Ælfrida in silver and a cloudiness of unbound hair. But Imric's gaze was only for the new-born babe nestled against her.

The elf-earl laughed behind the mask of his face. He closed the shutters and rode back northward. Ælfrida moved, woke, and felt after the little one beside her. Her eyes were hazed with uneasy dreams.

III

In those days the Faerie folk still dwelt upon earth, but even then a strangeness hung over their holdings, as if these wavered halfway between the mortal world and another; and places which might at a given time appear to be a simple lonely hill or lake or forest would at another time gleam forth in eldritch splendour. Hence those northern highlands known as the elf-hills were shunned by men.

Imric rode toward Elfheugh, which he saw not as a tor but as a castle tall and slender-spired, having gates of bronze and courtyards of marble, the corridors and rooms within hung with the loveliest shifty-patterned tapestries of magic weave and crusted with great blazing gems. In the moonlight the dwellers were dancing on the green before the outer walls. Imric rode by, through the main portal. His horse's hoofbeats echoed hollowly, and dwarf thralls hurried forth to attend him. He swung to the ground and hastened into the keep.

There the light of many tapers was broken into a flowing, tricky dazzle of colours by mosaics gilt and bejewelled. Music breathed through the chambers, rippling harps and keening pipes and flutes with voices like mountain brooks. Patterns in the rugs and tapestries moved slowly, like live figures. The very walls and floors, and the groined ceiling in its blue twilight of height, had a quicksilveriness about them;

they were never the same and yet one could not say just how they changed.

Imric went down a staircase. His byrnie clinked in the stillness. Of a sudden it grew dark about him, save for the rare light of a torch, and the air of the inner earth filled his lungs with chill. Now and again a clash of metal or a wail resounded through the wet rough-hewn corridors. Imric paid no need. Like all elves, he moved as a cat does, swift and silent and easy, down into the dungeons.

Finally he stopped at a door of brass-barred oak. It was green with mould and dark with age, and only Imric had the keys to the three big locks. These he undid, muttering certain words, and swung back the door. It groaned, for three hundred years had gone by since last he opened it.

A woman of the troll race sat in the cell beyond. She wore only the bronze chain, heavy enough to anchor a ship, which fastened her by the neck to the wall. Light from a torch ensconced outside the door fell dimly on her huge squat mighty-muscled form. She had no hair, and the green skin moved on her bones. As she turned her hideous head toward Imric, her snarl showed wolf teeth. But her eyes were empty, two pools of blackness in which a soul could drown. For nine hundred years she had been Imric's captive, and she was mad.

The elf-earl looked at her, though not into her eyes. He said softly, "We are to make a changeling again, Gora."

The troll-woman's voice was like a thunder, slowly rolling from the deeps of the earth. "Oho, oho," she said, "he is here again. Be welcome, whoever you are, you out of night and chaos. Ha, will none wipe the sneer off the face of the cosmos?"

"Hurry," said Imric. "I must make the change ere dawn."

"Hurry and hurry, autumn leaves hurrying on the rainy wind, snow hurrying out of the sky, life hurrying to death, gods hurrying to oblivion." The troll-woman's crazy voice boomed down the corridors. "All ashes, dust, blown on a senseless wind, and only the mad can gibber the music of the spheres. Ha, the red cock on the dunghill!"

Imric took a whip from the wall and lashed her. She cowered and lay down. Quickly, because he liked not the slippy clammy cold of her flesh, he did what was needful. Thereafter he walked nine times widdershins about her where she squatted, singing a song no human throat could have formed. As he sang, the troll-woman shook and swelled

22

and moaned in pain, and when he had gone the ninth time around she screamed so that it hurt his ears, and she brought forth a man-child.

The form could not by a human eye be told from Orm Dane-chief's son, save that it howled wrathfully and bit at its mother. Imric tied the cord and took the body in his arms, where it lay quiet.

"The world is flesh dissolving off a skull," mumbled the troll-woman. She clanked her chain and lay back, shuddering. "Birth is but the breeding of maggots therein. Already the skull's teeth stand forth uncovered by lips, and crows have left its eyesockets empty. Soon wind will blow through all the bones." She howled as Imric closed the door. "He is waiting for me, he is waiting on the hill where the mist blows ragged, for nine hundred years has he waited. The black cock crows—"

Imric locked the door anew and hastened up the stairs. He had no joy in making changelings, but the chance of getting a human baby was too rare to lose.

When he came out into the courtyard he saw that bad weather was brewing. A wrack of clouds drove across heaven, blacknesses from which the moon fled. Mountainous in the east, with runes of lighting scribbled across, a storm stood on the horizon. Wind hooted and howled.

Imric sprang to the saddle and spurred his horse south. Over the crags and hills they went, across dales and between trees that writhed in the rising gale. The moon cast fitful white gleams across the world, and Imric showed as another such phantom.

He raced with his cloak blowing like bat wings. Moonlight glittered on his mail and his eyes. As he rode along the strands of the lower, flatter Danelaw country, surf clashed at his feet and spray blew on to his cheeks. Now and again a lightning flash showed that waste of running waters. Thunder bawled ever louder in the darkness that followed, boom and bang of great wheels across the sky. Imric urged his horse to yet wilder speed. He had no wish to meet Thor out here in the night.

At Orm's garth he reopened Ælfrida's window. She was awake, holding her child to her breast and whispering comfort to him. The wind blew her hair around her face, blinding her. She would suppose it had somehow unlatched the shutters.

Lightning burst white. The thunder that went with it was

23

a hammer-blow. She felt the baby leave her arms. She snatched for him, and felt the dear weight once more, as if it had been laid there. "God be thanked," she gasped. "I dropped you but I caught you."

Laughing aloud, Imric rode homeward. But of a sudden he heard his laughter echoed through the noise by a different sound; and he reined in with his breast gone cold. A last break in the clouds cast a moonbeam on the figure which galloped across Imric's path. A bare glimpse he had, seated on his plunging steed, of the huge eight-legged horse that outran the wind, its rider with the long grey beard and shadowing hat. The moonbeam gleamed on the head of a spear and on a single eye.

Hoo, halloo, there he went with his troop of dead warriors and howling hounds. His horn called them; the hoof-beats were like a rush of hail on a roof; and then the pack was gone and rain came raving over the world.

Imric's mouth grew tight. The Wild Hunt boded no good to those who saw it, and he did not think the one-eyed Huntsman had merely chanced this near to him. But—he must get home now. Lightning seethed around him, and Thor might take a fancy to throw his hammer at anyone abroad. Imric held Orm's son in his cloak and struck spurs into his stallion.

Ælfrida could see again, and clutched the yelling boy close to her. He should be fed, if only to quiet him. He suckled her, but bit until it hurt.

IV

Skafloc, Imric named the stolen child, and gave him to his sister Leea to nurse. She was as beautiful as her brother, with thinly graven ivory features, unbound silvery-gold tresses afloat beneath a jewelled coronet, and the same moon-flecked twilight-blue eyes as he. Spider-silk garments drifted about her slenderness, and when she danced in the moonlight it was as a white flame to those who watched. She smiled on Skafloc with pale full lips, and the milk that she brought forth by no natural means was sweet fire in his mouth and veins.

Many lords of Alfheim came to the naming-feast, and they brought goodly gifts: cunningly wrought goblets and rings, dwarf-forged weapons, byrnies and helms and shields, clothing of samite and satin and cloth-of-gold, charms and talismans. Since elves, like gods and giants and trolls and others of that sort, knew not old age, they had few children, centuries apart, and the birth of one was a high happening; still more portentous to them was the fostering of a human.

As the feast was going on, they heard a tremendous clatter of hoofs outside Elfheugh, until the walls trembled and the brazen gates sang. Guards winded their trumpets, but none wished to contest the way of that rider and Imric himself met him at the portal, bowing low.

It was a great handsome figure in mail and helm that blazed less brightly than his eyes. The earth shook beneath his horse's tread. "Greeting, Skirnir," said Imric. "We are honoured by your visit."

The messenger of the Æsir rode across the moonlit flagstones. At his side, jumping restlessly in the scabbard and glaring like fire of the sun itself, was Frey's sword, given him for his journey to Jötunheim after Gerd. He bore another sword in his hands, long and broad, unrusted though still black with the earth in which it had lain, and broken in two.

"I bear a naming-gift for your foster son, Imric," he said. "Keep well this blade, and when he is old enough to swing it tell him the giant Bolverk can make it whole again. The day will come when Skafloc stands in sore need of a good weapon, and this is the Æsir's gift against that time."

He threw the broken sword clashing on the ground, whirled his horse about, and in a roar of hoofbeats was lost in the night. The elf-folk stood very still, for they knew the Æsir had some purpose of their own in this, yet Imric could not but obey.

None of the elves could touch iron, so the earl shouted for his dwarf thralls and had them pick it up. Led by him, they bore it to the nethermost dungeons and walled it into a niche near Gora's cell. Imric warded the spot with rune signs, then left it and avoided the place for a long time.

Now some years went by and naught was heard from the gods.

Skafloc grew apace, and a bonny boy he was, big and merry, with blue eyes and tawny hair. He was noisier, more boisterous than the few elf children, and grew so much faster that he was a man when they were still unchanged. It was not the way of the elves to show deep fondness for their young, but Leea often did to Skafloc, singing him to sleep with lays that were like sea and wind and soughing branches. She taught him the courtly manners of the elf lords, and also the corybantic measures they trod when they were out in the open, barefoot in dew and drunk with moonlight. Some of what wizard knowledge he gained was from her, songs which could blind and dazzle and lure, songs which moved rocks and trees, songs without sound to which the auroras danced on winter nights.

Skafloc had a happy childhood, at play with the elf young and their fellows. Many were the presences haunting those hills and glens; it was a realm of sorcery, and mortal men or beasts who wandered into it sometimes did not return. Not all the dwellers were safe or friendly. Imric told off a member of his guard to follow Skafloc around.

Sprites whirled in the mists about waterfalls; their voices rang back from the dell cliffs. Skafloc could dimly see them, graceful shining bodies haloed with rainbows. Of moonlit nights, drawn by the glow like other denizens of Faerie, they would come out and sit on the mossy banks, naked save for weeds twisted into their hair and garlands of water lilies; and elf children could then talk to them. Much could the sprites tell, of flowing rivers and fish therein, of frog and otter and kingfisher and what those had to say to each other, of sunlit pebbly bottoms and of secret pools where the water lay still and green—and the rush through the falls in a roar and a rainbow, shooting down to cavort in whirlpools!

Other watery places there were from which Skafloc was warned away, quaking bogs and silent dark tarns, for the dwellers were not good.

Often he would be out in the forest to speak with the little folk who lived in it, humble gnomes with grey and brown clothes and long stocking caps and the men's beards hanging to their waists. They dwelt in gnarly comfort beneath the largest trees, and were glad to see the elf children. But they feared the grown elves, and thought it well that none of these could squeeze into their homes—unless of course by shrinking to gnome size, which none of the haughty elf lords cared to do.

A few goblins were about. Once they had been powerful in the land, but Imric had entered with fire and sword, and those who were not slain or driven elsewhere had been broken of their might. They were furtive cave dwellers now, but Skafloc managed to befriend one and from him got some curious goblin lore.

Once the boy heard a piping far off in the woods, and he thrilled to its eeriness and hastened to the glen from which it came. So softly had he learned to move that he stood before the creature ere it was aware of him. It was a strange being, manlike but with the legs and ears and horns of a goat. On a set of reed pipes it blew an air that was as sorrowful as its eyes.

"Who are you?" asked Skafloc wonderingly.

The creature lowered his pipes, seeming ready to flee, then grew easier and sat down on a log. His accent was odd. "I am a faun," he said.

"I have heard of no such." Skafloc lowered himself cross-legged to the grass.

The faun smiled sadly in the twilight. The first star blinked forth above his head. "There are none save me hereabouts. I am an exile."

"Whence came you hither, faun?"

"I came from the south, after great Pan was dead and the new god whose name I cannot speak was in Hellas. No place remained for the old gods and the old beings of our land. The priests cut down the sacred groves and built churches— Oh, I remember how the dryads screamed, unheard by them— screams that quivered on the hot still air as if to hang there for ever. They ring yet in my ears, they always will." The faun shook his curly head. "I fled north; but I wonder if those of my comrades who stayed and fought and were slain with exorcisms were not wiser. Long and long has it been, elf-boy, and lonelier than it was long." Tears glimmered in his eyes. "The nymphs and the fauns and the very gods are less than dust. The temples stand empty, white under the sky, and bit by bit they crumble to ruin. And I—I wander alone in a foreign land, scorned by its gods and shunned by its people. It is a land of mist and rain and iron winters, angry grey seas and pale sunlight spearing through clouds. No more of sapphire water and gentle swells, no more of little rocky islands and the dear warm woods where the nymphs waited for us, no more of grapevines and fig trees heavy with fruit, no more of the stately gods on high Olympus—"

The faun ceased his crooning, stiffened, cocked his ears forward, then rose and bounded into the brush. Skafloc looked around and saw the elf guard approaching to take him home.

But often he was out by himself. He could stand the daylight which the folk of Faerie must shun, and Imric did not await any danger to him from mortal things. Thus he ranged far more around than the other children of Elfheugh, and came to know the land far better than a human might who had lived there for a lifetime.

Of the wild beasts, the fox and the otter were friendliest to elves, it being thought that there was some kind of kinship, and insofar as these had a language the elves knew it. From the fox Skafloc learned the hidden ways of wood and meadow, trails through sun-spattered shade and myriad tiny signs which told a story to one who knew the full use of his senses. From the otter he learned of the world about lake and stream, he learned to swim like his supple teacher and to sneak through cover which would scarce hide half his body.

But he got to know the other animals as well. The most timid of birds would come sit on his finger when he whistled in its own tongue; the bear would grunt a welcome when he trod into its den. Deer, elk, hare, and grouse became wary of him after he took up hunting, but with some special ones he made peace. And the story of all his farings among the beasts would be lengthy.

And the years swung by, and he was borne along. He was out in the first shy green of spring, when the forests woke and grew clamorous with returning birds, when the rivers brawled with melting ice and a few little white flowers in the moss were like remnant snowflakes. The summer knew him, naked and brown with flying sun-bleached hair, chasing butterflies uphill toward the sky, rolling back down through the grasses for sheer joy; or out in the light nights which were a dreamy remembrance of day, stars overhead and crickets chirring and dew aglitter beneath the moon. The thunderous rains of autumn washed him, or he wove a crown of flame-coloured leaves and stood in sharp air filled with the calls of departing birdflocks. In winter he flitted among the snowflakes, or crouched under a windfall while storm bellowed and trees groaned; sometimes he would stand on moonlit snowfields and hear the lake ice boom in the cold, a toning that rolled between the hills.

V

When Skafloc's limbs began to lengthen more swiftly, Imric took him in charge, only a little at first, but more and more with time until he was being raised wholly as a warrior of Alfheim. Being short-lived, humans could learn faster than the people of Faerie, and Skafloc's knowledge grew with even more haste than his body.

He learned to ride the horses of Alfheim, white and black stallions and mares of an eerie quicksilver grace, quick and tireless as the wind, and erelong his night gallops were taking him from Caithness to Land's End with the cloven air singing in his ears. He learned the use of sword and spear and bow and axe. He was less fleet and lithe than the elves, but grew to be stronger than any of them and could bear war-gear as many days on end as needful; and as for grace, another mortal man would have been a clod beside him.

He hunted wide over the land, alone or in company with Imric and his followers. Skafloc's bow twanged death to many a tall-antlered stag, his spear stopped many a long-tusked boar. There was other and trickier game, chased crazily through the woods and across the crags, unicorns and griffins which Imric had brought from the edge of the world for his pleasure.

Skafloc learned also the manners of the elves, their stateliness and their unending intrigue and their subtle speech. He could dance to harps and pipes in the drenching moonlight, naked and abandoned as the wildest of them. He could himself play, and sing the strange lilting lays older than man. He learned the skaldic arts so well that he talked in verse as easily as in common speech. He learned every language of Faerie and three of man's. He could discriminate among the rare viands of the elves, the liquid fires which smouldered in spider-shrouded bottles beneath the castle, but for all that his taste for the hunter's black bread and salt meat, or the rainy sunny earthy savour of berries, or upland springs, was not blunted.

After the first soft beard was on his cheeks, he got much heed from the elf women. Without awe of gods, and with few children, the elves knew not wedlock; but their nature was such that their women had more wish for lovemaking and their men less than among humans. Thus Skafloc found himself in great favour, and many a good time did he have.

The hardest, most perilous part of his training was in magic. Imric had him wholly in hand for this, once he was ready to go beyond the simple spells that a child could safely use. While he was not able to learn as deeply as his foster father, because of his humanity and short lifespan, he came to be as adept as most elf chieftains. He learned first how to shun and sidestep the iron no elf, troll, or goblin could endure; even when told, and when a gingerly touch on a nail in a yeoman's house had shown, that he would not be harmed by it, he left it alone out of habit. Next he learned the runes for healing wounds and illness, warding off bad luck, or wishing evil on a foe. He learned the songs which could raise or lay storms, bring good or bad harvests, call forth either anger or peace in a mortal breast. He learned how to coax from their ores those metals, unknown to humans, which were alloyed in Faerie to take the place of steel. He learned the use of the cloak of darkness, and of the skins he could don to take the form of a beast. Near the end of his training he learned the mighty runes and songs and charms which could raise the dead, read the future, and compel the gods; but save in time of direst need no one cared to be shaken to his inmost being by these and risk the destruction they could wreak on him.

Skafloc was often down by the sea, he could sit hour upon hour looking out over its restlessness to the hazy line where water met sky, he never wearied of its deep voice or its tang of salty depths and windy reaches or its thousand moods. He came of a seafaring breed, and the tides were in his blood. He spoke to the seals in their grunting, barking tongue, and the gulls wheeled overhead to bring him news from the earth's ends. Sometimes when he was in company with other warriors, the sea maidens would rise from the foam, wringing out their long green hair as they came up on to the strand, and then there would be merriment. They were cool and wet to the touch and they smelled of kelp; afterward Skafloc would have a faint fishy taste on his lips; but he liked them well.

At fifteen years of age he stood nearly as tall as Imric, broad of shoulder and taut of sinew, with long hair flaxen against brown skin. He had a straight, blunt, strong-boned face, a wide mouth quick to smile, large deep-blue eyes set well apart. A mortal without his schooling would have said that a mystery hung over him, veiling itself behind those eyes, which had looked on more than common mankind saw, revealing itself in that leopard gait.

Imric said to him: "Now you are big enough to be given your own weapons rather than old ones of mine, and also I have been summoned by the Erlking. We will fare overseas."

At this Skafloc whooped, cartwheeled out into the fields,

and galloped his horse madly through the lands of men, making magic out of sheer need to do something. He caused pots to dance on the hearth and bells to ring in the steeples and axes to cut wood of their own accord, he sang cows up onto the crofter's roof and a wind into being which scattered his hay over the shire and a rain of gold out of the sky into his yard. With the Tarnkappe about his shoulders, he kissed the girls working at twilight in the fields and rumpled their hair and tossed their men into a ditch. For days thereafter, masses were sung to halt the spate of witchcraft; but by that time Skafloc was at sea.

Imric's black longship sped with her sail taut to a wind he had raised. His crew was of picked elf warriors, for the chance of meeting trolls or kraken was not to be ignored. Skafloc stood by the dragon prow peering eagerly forward; he had been given witch-sight early in his life and could see by night as well as by day. He spied porpoises, silver-grey under the moon, and hailed an old bull seal he knew. Once a whale broached, water roaring off its flanks. Things which mortal sailors only glimpsed or dreamed were plain to the cloudy slant elf-eyes and to Skafloc: the sea maidens tumbling in the foam and singing, the drowned tower of Ys, a brief gleam of white and gold and a hawk-scream of challenge overhead—Valkyries rushing to some battle in the east.

Wind sang in the rigging and waves roared at the strakes. Ere dawn the vessel had reached the other shore, been drawn up on the beach and hidden by spells.

The elves took shelter beneath an awning across the hull, but Skafloc was about during much of the day. He climbed a tree and looked in wonder at the plowlands rolling southward. The buildings here were not like those in England. Among them was the gaunt grey hall of a baron. Skafloc thought with brief pity of the narrow lives that flickered in its gloom. He would not trade.

When night came, the elves mounted the horses they had brought and rode storm-swift inland. By midnight they were in mountain country where the moonlight cast thin silver and thick shadows on crags, cliffs, and the far green shimmer of glaciers. The elves rode along a narrow trail, harness chiming, lances high, plumes and capes streaming. Hoofbeats rang on the stones and echoed back through the wilderness night.

A horn sounded hoarsely from above, another from below. The elves heard a clank of metal and a tramp of feet. When they came to the end of the trail they saw a dwarf troop on guard at a cave mouth.

The bandy-legged men scarce came to Skafloc's waist, but they were broad of shoulder and long of arm. Their dark, bearded faces were angry; their eyes smouldered beneath tangled brows. They held swords, axes, and shields of iron. But against these the elves had prevailed in the past, by spears and arrows, by speed and agility, and by making craftier plans.

"What will you?" boomed the leader. "Have the elves and trolls not wrought us enough ill, harrying our lands and bearing our folk off as thralls? This time our force is larger than yours, and if you come nearer we will slay you."

"We come in peace, Motsognir," replied Imric. "We wish only to buy of your wares."

"I know your trickery, Imric the Guileful," said Motsognir harshly. "You would put us off our guard."

"I will give hostages," the elf-earl offered; and this the dwarf king grudgingly accepted. Leaving several of the newcomers disarmed and surrounded, Motsognir led the others down into his caverns.

Here fires lit the rock walls with bloody shadow-beset dimness, and over their forges the dwarfs laboured unceasingly. Their hammers rang and clattered until Skafloc's head belled in answer. Here were made the trickiest works of all the world, goblets and beakers encrusted with gems, rings and necklaces of ruddy gold intricately fashioned; weapons were beaten out of metals torn from the mountain's heart, arms fit for gods—and indeed the dwarfs had done work for the gods—and other weapons laden with evil. Mighty were the runes and charms the dwarfs could grave, and baffling were the arts they had mastered.

"I would have you make an outfit for my foster son here," Imric said.

Motsognir's mole-eyes searched Skafloc's tall form in the wavering light. His voice rumbled through the hammer-clang: "Well, are you up to your old changeling tricks again, Imric? Someday you will overreach yourself. But since this is a human, I suppose he will want arms of steel."

Skafloc hesitated. The wariness of years was not overcome at once. But he had known what was coming. Bronze was too soft, the curious elf-alloys too light, to make full use of his growing strength.

"Aye, steel," he said firmly.

" 'Tis well, 'tis well," growled Motsognir, and turned to his forge. "Let me tell you, boy, that you humans, weak and short-lived and unwitting, are nonetheless more strong than elves and trolls, aye, than giants and gods. And that you can touch cold iron is only one reason. Ho!" he called. "Ho, Sindri, Thekk, Draupnir, come to help!"

Now the forging went apace, sparks flew and metal shouted. Such was the skill of those smiths that it was only a short while before Skafloc wore winged helm, shining byrnie, shield on back and sword at side and axe in hand, all of blue-gleaming steel. He yelled for joy, swung high his weapons and shrilled the war-cry of the elves.

"Ha!" he shouted as he rammed the sword back into its sheath. "Let trolls or goblins, aye, giants dare approach Alfheim! We shall smite them like the lightning and carry the fire into their own lands!" And he made the staves:

> Swiftly goes the sword-play
> singing in the mountains.
> Clash of steel is calling,
> clanging up to heaven: —
> arrows flying angry;
> axes lifting skyward,
> banging down on byrnies,
> breaking shields and helmets.
> Swiftly goes the sword-play:
> Spears on hosts are raining ;
> men run forth in madness,
> mowing ranks of foemen;
> battle tumult bellows;
> blood is red on axeheads;
> greedily the grey wolf
> gorges with the raven.

"Well spoken, if a trifle boyish," said Imric coolly, "but remember not to touch elves with those new toys of yours. Let us begone." He gave Motsognir a sack of gold. "Here is payment for the work."

"Rather had I been paid by the freeing of your thralls of our race," said the dwarf.

"They are too useful," declared Imric, and left.

At dawn his troop sheltered in a cave, and the next night

rode on to the great forest in which stood the Erlking's castle.

Here was a weaving of witchery that Skafloc did not yet know how to unravel. He was dimly aware of high slender towers against the moon, of a blue twilight wherein many stars wavered and danced, of a music which pierced flesh and bone to thrill in the very soul; but not until they were in the throne room could he clearly see anything.

Surrounded by his tall lords, in a throne of shadow sat the Erlking. Golden were his crown and sceptre, and his robes of a purple that blent with the spacious gloaming. His hair and beard were white, and he alone of the elves showed lines of age in brow and cheeks. His face was otherwise as if carved in marble; but fires burned within his eyes.

Imric bowed, and the warriors in his train bent the knee to their king. When the ruler spoke, it was like windsong: "Greeting, Imric, earl of Britain's elves."

"Greeting, lord," answered the chieftain, and he met the Erlking's calm, terrible gaze.

"We have summoned our chieftains to council," said the ruler, "since word has reached us that the trolls make ready to go to war again. It cannot be doubted 'tis us they arm against, and we may look for the truce to end in the next few years."

"That is well, lord. Our swords were mouldering in the scabbards."

"It may not be so well, Imric. Last time the elves drove back the trolls and would have entered their land had not peace been made. Illrede Troll-King is no fool. He would not attempt war did he not think he was stronger than formerly."

"I will ready my domain, lord, and send out spies."

"Good. Perhaps they can learn something useful, though our own have failed." Now the Erlking turned his eyes on Skafloc, who grew cold about the heart however boldly he confronted that flame of a gaze. "We have heard tell of your changeling, Imric," he murmured. "You should have asked us."

"There was no time, lord," argued the earl. "The babe would be baptized ere I could get word here and back. Hard is it to steal a child these days."

"And risky too, Imric."

"Aye, lord, but worth it. I need not remind you that humans can do much which is barred to elf, troll, goblin or

34

the like. They may use every metal, they may touch holy water and walk on holy ground and speak the name of the new god—aye, the old gods themselves must flee some things which humans have the freedom of. We elves need such a one."

"The changeling you left in his place could do all that."

"Indeed, lord. But you know the wild and evil nature of a half-breed like that. He cannot be trusted with magic as this human can. Were it not that men must never be sure their children are stolen, so that they would call their gods to avenge them, elves would make no changelings."

Thus far the talk had been of what everybody understood, in the leisured manner of immortals. But now the Erlking's tone sharpened. "Can this human be trusted? Let him but turn to the new god and he is beyond our reach. Already he grows perhaps overly strong."

"No, lord!" Skafloc stood forth in that proud assembly and looked straight into the Erlking's face. "I am wholly thankful to Imric that he rescued me from the dullblind round of mortal life. I am elf in all but blood, it was elf breasts I suckled as a babe and elf tongue I speak and elf girls I sleep beside." He lifted his head, almost arrogantly. "Give me leave, lord, and I will be the best of your hounds —but if a dog be driven out, he will become a wolf and feed on his master's flocks."

Some of the elves were aghast at this forwardness, but the king nodded, and smiled a grim smile. "We believe you," he said, "and indeed earlier men adopted into Alfheim proved stout warriors. What worries us about you is the story of the Æsir's naming-gift. They have a hand in this somewhere, and their purpose is not likely to be our own."

A shudder ran around the gathering and some made rune signs in the air. But Imric said: "Lord, what the Norns have ordered, not even the gods may alter. And I would count it shame to lose the most promising of men because of a dim fear of the morrow."

"That it would be," nodded the Erlking, and the council turned itself to other things.

A lavish feast was held ere the meeting of the elf lords dissolved. Skafloc's head swam with the magnificence of the Erlking's court. When finally he came home, his contempt and pity for humans were so great that for a while he had naught whatsoever to do with them.

Now some half-dozen years went by. The elves showed no change, but Skafloc grew until his outfit had to be altered by Imric's dwarf thralls. He came to stand taller and broader than the earl, and was the strongest man in the realm. He wrestled bears and wild bulls, and often ran down a stag on foot. No other in Alfheim could have bent his bow or handily swung his axe, whether or not it was of iron.

He grew leaner of face, and let a moustache the wheaten colour of his long hair grow on his lip. But he became, if anything, merrier and more unruly than before, a lover of madcap pranks and breakneck stunts, a mischievous warlock who would raise a whirlwind just to lift a girl's skirt, a mighty drinker and brawler. Restless with his own strength, he prowled the land, hunting the most dangerous game he could find. Monsters of the blood of Grendel he sought out and slew in their fens, sometimes suffering frightful wounds which only Imric's magic could heal, but ever ready for a new bout. Then again he might lie idle for weeks on end, staring dreamily at clouds high above, scarce stirring himself. Or in beast shape, with senses strange to man, he would seek forests and waters, to gambol as otter or lope as wolf or wing in the pride of an eagle.

"Three things have I never known," he boasted once. "Fear, and defeat, and love-sickness."

Imric regarded him strangely. "Young are you," he said, "not to have known the three ultimates of human life."

"I am more elf than human, foster father."

"So you are—as yet."

One year Imric outfitted a dozen longships and went a-roving. The fleet crossed the eastern sea, and plundered goblins dwelling along the rocky coasts. Then the crews rode inland and made a raid on a troll town, burning it after they had slain its folk and taken their treasures. Though war was still not declared, such forays and tests of strength were growing common on either side. Sailing north and then east through a weird white land of mist and cold and drifting icebergs, Imric and Skafloc and their warriors at last rounded a cape, passed through a strait, and went on south. There they fought dragons, and harried among the demons of the land. They followed the shore westward again, until it turned south, and then northward anew. Their hardest battle was on a desert strand with a troop of exiled gods, grown thin and shrunken and mad in their loneliness but wielding fearsome powers even so. Three elf ships were burned after the fight, there being none left to man them, but Imric was the victor.

They saw somewhat of humans, but paid no great heed, their interest being in Faerie. Mortal men never spied them save in frightened glimpses. Not everywhere did they war; most realms guested them well and were eager to trade goods, which made for long stopovers. Three years after they set out, the ships returned with a huge load of wealth and captives. It had been a glorious voyage, of which great report went about in Alfheim and the neighbouring lands; and the fame of Imric and Skafloc stood high.

VI

The witch dwelt alone in the woods with only her memories for daily company, and over the years these fed on her soul and left their castings of hatred and vengeance-lust. By trying this and that she learned how to increase her powers a little, until she was raising spirits out of the earth and speaking with demons of the upper air; and they taught her more. To the Black Sabbath on the Brocken she rode, high through the sky on a broomstick with her rags astream in the wind. A monster feasting it was, where ancient hideous shapes chanted about the dark altar and drank deep from kettles of blood; but perhaps the worst of all were the young women who joined in the rites and the dreadful matings.

Wiser the witch returned, with a rat for familiar who took blood out of her withered breasts with his sharp little teeth and at night crouched on her pillow and chittered in her ear as she slept. And so at last she thought she had strength to raise the one whom she had longed for.

Thunder and lightning rolled about her hovel, blue glare and the stink of hell's pits. But the shadowy presence before which she grovelled was beautiful in its way, as all sin appears beautiful to the willing sinner.

"O you of the many names, Prince of Darkness, Evil Companion," cried the witch, "I would that you grant my wish, and for that I will pay your old price."

He whom she had called spoke, and his voice was slow and soft and patient: "Already you have gone far down my road, but you have not altogether become mine. The mercy from

37

above is infinite, and only if you yourself reject it can you be lost."

"What care I for mercy?" asked the witch. "It will not avenge my sons. I stand ready to give my soul unto you if you will deliver my enemies into my hands."

"That I may not do," said her guest, "but I may give you the means to entrap them if your cunning be greater than theirs."

"That will be enough."

"But bethink you, have you not had revenge on Orm already? 'Tis your work that he has a changeling for eldest son, and the ill that that being will wreak on him can be great."

"Yet Orm's true son prospers in Alfheim, and his other children grow apace. I would wipe out his foul seed to the last of the lot, even as he wiped out mine. The heathen gods will not help me, nor surely will He whose name I had best not speak. Therefore you, Black Majesty, must be my friend."

A gaze wherein were little flickering flames more cold than winter brooded long on her. "The gods are not out of this matter," said the quiet, rustling voice, "as you may have heard. Odin, who foresees what dooms are laid on men, makes schemes that are long in the weaving. . . . But you shall have my help. Power and knowledge will I give you, until you become a mighty witch. And I will tell you how to strike, by a way which is sure unless your enemies are wiser than you think.

"There are three Powers in the world which not gods nor demons nor men can stay, against which no magic shall prevail and no might shall stand, and they are the White Christ, Time, and Love.

"From the first you may await only thwarting of your desire, and you must be careful that He and His in no way enter the struggle. This you can do by remembering that Heaven leaves lesser beings their free will, and thus does not force them into its own ways; even the miracles have done no more than leave open a possibility to men.

"The second, which has more names than I myself—Fate, Destiny, Law, Wyrd, the Norns, Necessity, Brahm, and others beyond counting—is not to be appealed to, for it does not hear. Nor can you hope to understand how it exists together with the freedom whereof I spoke, any more than you can understand how there are both old gods and new.

But for the wreaking of the greatest spells, you must ponder on this until you know in your inmost being that truth is a thing which bears as many shapes as there are minds which strive to see it.

"And the third of the Powers is a mortal thing, therefore it can harm as well as help, and this is the one you must use."

Now the witch swore a certain oath, and was told where and how to drink the knowledge she needed, and there the council ended.

Save for this: that as her caller left the hut, she peered after him, and what she saw departing was not what she had seen within. Rather the shape was of a very tall man, who strode swiftly albeit his beard was long and wolf-grey. He was wrapped in a cloak and carried a spear, and beneath his wide-brimmed hat it seemed that he had but a single eye. She remembered who also was cunning, and often crooked of purpose, and given to disguise in his wanderings to and fro upon the earth; and a shiver went through her.

But then he was gone—and she had not really seen him clear—it could have been a trick of the starlight—she would not brood on such uneasy questions, but only on her loss and her coming revenge.

Save that the changeling was fierce and noisy, he could not be told from the true babe, and though Ælfrida puzzled over her little son's ways she had no thought it was not him at all. She christened the child Valgard as Orm wished, and sang to him and played with him and was gladdened. But he bit so hard that it was pain to nurse him.

Orm was delighted when he came home and saw such a fine strong boy. "A great warrior will he be," cried the chief, "a swinger of weapons and a rider of ships and horses." He looked about the yard. "But where are the dogs? Where is my trusty old Gram?"

"Gram is dead," said Ælfrida tonelessly. "He sought to leap on Valgard and rend him, so I had the poor mad beast slain. But it must have given notions to the other dogs, who growl and slink away when I carry the child outside."

"That is strange," said Orm, "for my folk have ever been good with hounds and horses."

But as Valgard grew it became plain that no beast liked to have him around; cattle ran off, horses snorted and shied, cats spat and climbed a tree, and the boy must early learn the use of a spear to ward himself against dogs. He in return was no friend to animals, but dealt kicks and curses, and became a relentless hunter.

He was sullen and close-mouthed, given to wild tricks and refusal of obedience. The thralls hated him for his ill will and the cruel jests he played on them. And slowly, fighting it the whole way, Ælfrida came to have no love for him.

But Orm was fond of Valgard even if they did not always agree. When he had to strike the boy, he could draw no cry of pain however hard his hand fell. And when he had sword-drill and his blade whined down as if to split the skull, Valgard never blinked. He grew up strong and swift, taking to weapons as if born with them, and showed no fear or softness whatever happened. He had no real friends, but they were not few who followed him.

Orm had more children by Ælfrida—two sons, red-haired Ketil and dark Asmund, who were both promising boys, and daughters Asgerd and Freda, of whom the last was nigh an image of her mother. These were like other youngsters, glad and sad by turns, playing about their mother and then later rambling over the whole land, and Ælfrida loved them with an abiding and aching love. Orm liked them too, but Valgard was his darling.

Strange, aloof, silent, Valgard neared his manhood. He was outwardly no different from Skafloc, save maybe that his hair was a shade darker and his skin whiter and that there was a flat hard shallowness to his eyes. But his mouth was sullen, he seldom smiled except when he drew blood or otherwise gave pain, and then it was a mere skinning of teeth. Taller and stronger than most boys of his age, he had small use for them aside from leading them in gangs to work mischief. He would rarely help with the farm unless it was butchering season, but instead went on long lonely walks.

Orm had never raised the church he once planned; however, the yeomen roundabout had joined to do this, and he did not forbid his folk to go to mass there. Ælfrida got the priest to come and talk to Valgard. The boy laughed in his face. "I will not bow to your snivelling god," he said, "or any others for that matter. Insofar as appealing to them does make sense, my father's sacrifices to the Æsir are of more help than whatever prayers he or you give to Christ. For if I were a god, I might well be bribed by blood offerings to send good luck, but a man so pinchpenny that he merely annoyed me with mealy-mouthed prayers I would stamp on

—thus!" And he brought his heavy-shod foot down on the priest's.

Orm chuckled when he heard of it, and Ælfrida's tears were of no avail, so the priest got scant satisfaction.

Valgard liked best the night. Then he would often slip from his bed and steal outside. He could run till dawn with his loping wolfish gait, driven by some moon-magic glimmering in his head. He knew not what he wished, save that he felt a sadness and a yearning for which he lacked a name, a gloom lighting only when he slew or maimed or brought to ruin. Then he could laugh, with the troll blood beating in his temples!

But one day he took heed of the girls at work in the fields with their dresses clinging to their sweat-sweet bodies, and thereafter he had another sport. He owned strength and good looks and a glib elf tongue when he cared to unleash it. Soon Orm had to pay gild for thralls or daughters wronged.

This he did not care much about, but it was another matter when Valgard quarrelled in his cups with Olaf Sigmundsson and slew him. Orm paid the weregild but saw that his son was not safe to have around. Of late years he had spent most of his time at home, and what voyages he did make were for peaceful trade. But that summer he took Valgard in viking.

This was glorious to the boy, who soon won the respect of his shipmates by his skill and daring in battle, though they did not care for his needless killings of the helpless. But after a while the berserkergang began to come on Valgard, he trembled and frothed and gnawed the rim of his shield, he rushed forward howling and slaying. His sword was a red blur, he did not feel weapons biting on him, and sheer terror of his twisted face froze many men till he cut them down. When the fit was over he was weak for a time, but he had heaped corpses high.

Only rough and lawless men cared to have much to do with a berserker, and these were the only sort he cared to lead. He was out plundering every summer, whether or not Orm went; and Orm soon stopped. As his full strength came to him, Valgard won a frightful name. He likewise won gold wherewith to buy ships. These he manned with the worst of evildoers, until Orm forbade him to land his crews on the farm.

The other children of the house were liked by almost everyone. Ketil was akin to his father, big and merry, always ready for a fight or frolic, and often went to sea when he was old enough. But he only went once in viking, quarrelled bitterly with Valgard, and afterwards sailed his own way as a trader. Asmund was slender and quiet, a good archer but no lover of battle, and came to take over more and more the running of the farm. Asgerd was a big fair may with blue eyes and gold hair and cool strong hands; but Freda was growing into her mother's beauty.

Thus matters stood when the witch decided it was time to draw the threads of the web together.

VII

On a blustery fall day, with the smell of rain in the keen air and leaves turned to gold and copper and bronze, Ketil and a few comrades rode forth to hunt. They had not gone far into the woods when they saw a white stag so huge and noble they could scarce believe it.

"Ho, a beast for a king!" shouted Ketil, spurring his horse, and away they went over stock and stone, leaping logs and dodging trees, crashing through brush and crackling the fallen leaves, with wind roaring in their ears and the forest a blur of colour. Strangely, the hounds were not very eager in the chase, and though Ketil was not riding the best of horses he drew ahead of the dogs and the other hunters.

Before him in the evening glimmered the white stag, leaping and soaring, antlers treelike against the sky. For a time rain sluiced icily through the bare boughs ;in the blindness of the chase Ketil hardly felt it. Nor did he feel hours or miles or aught but the surge of his gallop and the eagerness of the hunt.

At last he burst into a little clearing, nigh caught up with the stag. The light was dim, but he launched his spear at the white shape. Even as he made his cast the stag seemed to shrink, to fade like a wind-blown mist, and then he was gone and there was only a rat scuttering through the dead leaves.

Ketil grew aware that he had outstripped his companions and become lost from them. A thin chill wind whimpered through dusk. His horse trembled with weariness. Well it might, for they had come into a part of the forest unknown to him, which meant they were far west of Orm's garth. He could not understand what had upborne the beast, that it had not foundered erenow. And the eeriness of what had happened ran coldly along his backbone.

But just on the edge of the clearing, a cottage stood beneath a great oak. Ketil wondered what manner of folk would live that lonely, and how they did it, for he saw no signs of farming. Yet at least here was shelter for himself and his horse, in a neat small house of wood and thatch with firelight cheery in the windows. He dismounted, picked up his spear, and rapped on the door.

It opened, to show a well-furnished room and an empty stable beyond. But it was on the woman that Ketil's eyes rested, nor could he pull them away. And he felt his heart turn over and then slam within his ribs as a wildcat attacks its cage.

She was tall, and the low-cut dress she wore clung lovingly to each curve of her wondrous body. Dark unbound hair streamed to her knees, framing a perfect oval of a face white as sea foam. Her wide full mouth was blood red, her nose delicately arched, her eyes long-lashed under finely drawn brows. They were a fathomless green, those eyes, with golden flecks and they seemed to look into Ketil's very soul. Never, he thought in his daze, never before had he known how a woman might look.

"Who are you?" she asked, softly and singingly. "What will you?"

The man's mouth had gone dry and the pulsebeat nigh drowned out his hearing, but he made shift to reply: "I am —Ketil Ormsson. . . . I lost my way hunting, and would ask a night's shelter for my horse and . . . myself. . . ."

"Be welcome, Ketil Ormsson," she said, and gave him a smile at which his heart almost left his breast. "Few come here, and I am ever glad to see them."

"Do you live—alone?" he asked.

"Aye. Though not tonight!" she laughed, and at that Ketil threw his arms about her.

Orm sent men to ask of all his neighbours, but none could say aught about his son. Thus after three days he became sure that something ill had happened to Ketil. "He may have broken a leg, or met robbers, or otherwise come to grief," he said. "Tomorrow, Asmund, we will go search for him."

Valgard sat sprawled on the bench with a horn of mead

in his fist. He had ended a summer's viking trip two days before, left his ships and men at a garth he had bought some ways from Orm's, and come home for a while, more because of his father's good food and drink than to greet his kinfolk. The firelight streamed like blood off his surly face. "Why do you say this only to Asmund?" he asked. "I am here too."

"I did not think there was any deep love between you and Ketil," said Orm.

Valgard grinned and emptied the horn. "Nor is there," he said. "Nevertheless I will hunt for him, and I hope 'tis I who find and bring him home. Few things would seem worse to him than being beholden to me."

Orm shrugged, while tears glimmered in Ælfrida's eyes.

They set out next dawn, many men on horseback, dog-barks coming in frost out of mouths, and scattered into the woods according to plan. Valgard went alone and afoot as was his habit. He carried a great axe for weapon and bore a helmet on his tawny mane, but otherwise in his shaggy garments he might have been a beast of prey. He snuffed the crisp air and circled about looking for spoor. At tracking he was inhumanly gifted. Erelong he found faint remnants of a trail. He grinned again and did not sound his horn, but set off at a long easy lope.

As the day wore on, he came west into thicker and older forest where his rambles had never taken him before. The sky greyed and clouds flew low over skeleton trees. Wind whirled dead leaves through the air like ghosts hurrying down hell-road, and its whine gnawed at Valgard's nerves. He could smell a wrongness here, but having no training in magic he did not know what it was that bristled the hair on his neck.

At dusk he had gone far, and was tired and hungry and wroth at Ketil for giving him this trouble. He would have to sleep out tonight, with winter on the way, and he vowed revenge for that.

Hold—Dimly through the thickening twilight he saw a glimmer. No will-o'-the-wisp that; it was fire—shelter, unless it was a lair of outlaws. And were that the case, Valgard snarled to himself, he would have joy in killing them.

Night outraced him to the cottage. A thin wind-driven sleet stung his cheeks. Cautiously Valgard edged to a window, and peered in through a crack between the shutters.

44

Ketil sat glad on a bench before a leaping fire. He had a horn of ale in one hand, and the other caressed a woman on his lap.

Woman—almighty gods, what a woman! Valgard sucked a sharp breath between his teeth. He had not dreamed there could be such a woman as her who laughed on Ketil's knees.

Valgard went to the door and beat it with the flat of his axe. It was some time before Ketil got it open and stood spear in hand to see who had come. By then the sleet was thick.

Huge and angry, Valgard filled the doorway with his shoulders. Ketil cursed, but stepped aside and let him in. Valgard stalked slowly across the floor. Water from the melting sleet dripped off him. His eyes glittered at the woman, where she crouched on the bench.

"You are not very guest-free, brother," he said, and barked a laugh. "You leave me, who travelled many weary miles to find you, out in the storm while you play with your sweetheart."

"I did not ask you here," said Ketil sullenly.

"No?" Valgard was still looking at the woman. And she met his gaze, and her red mouth curved in a smile.

"You are a welcome guest," she breathed. "Not ere this have I guested a man as big as you."

Valgard laughed again and swung to face Ketil's stricken stare. "Whether you asked me or not, dear brother, I will spend the night," he said. "And since I see there is only room for two in the bed, and I have come such a long hard way, I fear me you will have to sleep in the stable."

"Not for you!" shouted Ketil. The knuckles stood forth white where he gripped his spear. "Had it been Father or Asmund or anyone else from the garth, he had been welcome. But you, ill-wreaker and berserker that you are, will be the one to sleep in the straw."

Valgard sneered and chopped out with his axe. It drove the spear against the lintel and split off its head. "Get out, little brother," he bade. "Or must I throw you out?"

Blind with rage, Ketil struck him with the broken shaft. Fury flamed in Valgard. He leaped. His axe shrieked down and buried itself in Ketil's skull.

Still beside himself, he swung about on the woman. She held out her arms to him. Valgard gathered her in and kissed her till their lips bled. She laughed aloud.

45

But next morning when Valgard awoke, he saw Ketil lying in a gore of clotted blood and brains, the dead eyes meeting his own, and suddenly remorse welled up in him.

"What have I done?" he whispered. "I slew my own kin."

"You killed a weaker man," said the woman indifferently.

But Valgard stood above his brother's body and brooded. "We had some good times together between our fights, Ketil," he mumbled. "I remember how funny we two found a new calf that strove to use its wobbly legs, and wind in our faces and sun asparkle on waves when we went sailing, and deep draughts at Yule when storms howled about our father's hall, and swimming and running and shouting with you, brother. Now it is over, you are a stiffened corpse and I gang on a dark road—but sleep well. Goodnight, Ketil, goodnight."

"If you tell men of this, you will be slain," said the woman. "That will not bring him back. And in the grave is no kissing or coupling."

Valgard nodded. He picked up the body and bore it into the woods. He did not wish to touch the axe again, so he left it sticking in the skull when he raised a cairn over the dead man.

But when he came back to the cottage, the woman was waiting for him, and he soon forgot all else. Her beauty outshone the sun, and there was naught she did not know about the making of love.

The weather grew unrelentingly cold, until the first snow whispered down. This winter would be long.

After a week, Valgard thought it would be best if he returned home. Else others might come looking for him, and fights might break up his crews. But the woman would not come with him. "This is my place and I cannot leave it," she said. "Come, though, whenever you will, Valgard my darling. I will always gladly greet you."

"I will be back soon," he vowed. He did not think of carrying her off by force, though he had done that to many before her. The free gift of herself was too precious.

At Orm's hall he was joyously greeted by the chief, who had feared him lost too. None else was overly happy at seeing him again.

"I hunted far to the west and north," said Valgard, "and did not find Ketil."

"No," replied Orm, with sorrow reborn in him, "he must

46

be dead. We searched for days, and at last found his horse wandering riderless. I will ready the funeral feast."

Valgard was but a brace of days among men, then he slipped into the woods anew with a promise to be back for Ketil's grave-ale. Thoughtfully, Asmund watched him leave.

It seemed odd to the youngest brother how Valgard dodged talk of Ketil's fate, and odder yet that he should go hunting—as he said—now that winter was on hand. There would be no bears, and other game was getting so shy that men did not care to go after it through the snow. Why had Valgard been gone that long, and why did he leave that soon?

So Asmund wondered, and at last, two days after Valgard left, he followed. It had not snowed or blown since, and the tracks could still be seen in the crisp whiteness. Asmund went alone, walking on ski through silent reaches where no life stirred but him, and the cold ate and ate into his flesh.

Three days later, Valgard returned. Folk had gathered at Orm's garth from widely around for the grave-ale, and the feast went apace. The berserker slipped grim and close-mouthed through the crowded yard.

Ælfrida plucked at his sleeve. "Have you seen Asmund?" she asked shyly. "He went into the forest and has not come home yet."

"No," said Valgard shortly.

"Ill would it be to lose two tall sons in the same month and have only the worst left," said Ælfrida and turned away from him.

At eventide the guests met in the great hall for drinking. Orm sat in his high seat with Valgard on his right. Men crowded the benches down both the long sides of that room and lifted horns to each other across the flames and smoke of the fire, where it burned in the trench between. Women went to and fro to keep those horns filled. Save for the host family, the men had grown merry with ale, and many an eye followed Orm's two daughters through the hazed, restless red light.

He bore a cheerful mien, as befitted a warrior with scorn for death; none could tell what lay beneath it. Ælfrida could not keep from weeping now and then, quietly and hope-lessly. Valgard sat wordless, draining horn after horn until his head buzzed. He only deepened his gloom. Away from the woman and the alarums of war alike, he had naught to

47

do but brood on his deed, and Ketil's face swam in the dusk before him.

Ale flowed until all were drunk and the hall rang with their noise. And then a knocking on the main door cut loud and clear through the racket. The latch was up, but the sound drew men's heed. Through the foreroom, into the big chamber, trod Asmund.

The firelight limned him against blackness. He stood white and swaying. In his arms he bore a long cloak-wrapped burden. His hollow gaze swept the hall, seeking one man; and bit by bit, a great silence fell.

"Welcome, Asmund!" cried Orm into that quiet. "We had begun to fear for you—"

Still Asmund stared before him, and those who followed his look saw it fixed on Valgard. He spoke at last, tonelessly: "I have brought a guest to the grave-ale."

Orm sat moveless, though he paled beneath his beard. Asmund set his burden on the floor. It was frozen stiff enough to stand, leaned against his arm.

"Cruel cold was the cairn where I found him," said Asmund. Tears ran from his eyes. "It was no good place to be, and I thought it shame that we should hold a feast in his honour and he be out there with naught but wind and the stars for company. So I brought Ketil home—Ketil, with Valgard's axe in his skull!"

He drew aside the cloak, and the fire-glow fell like new-spilled blood on that which was clotted around the axe. Rime was in Ketil's hair. His dead face grinned at Valgard. His staring eyes were filled with flamelight. Stiffly he leaned on Asmund and stared at Valgard.

Orm turned slowly about to confront the berserker, who was meeting that blind stare with his own jaw fallen like the corpse's. But on an instant rage came. Valgard leaped up and roared at Asmund: "You lie!"

"All men know your axe," said Asmund heavily. "Now seize the brotherslayer, good folk, and bind him for hanging."

"Give me my right," Valgard shouted. "Let me see that weapon."

None moved. They were too shocked. Valgard walked down the hall to the foreroom doorway through a breathlessness where naught but the flames had voice.

Weapons were stacked nearby. Passing, he snatched a spear and broke into a run. "You'll not get free!" Asmund cried, and moved to draw sword and bar the way. Valgard lunged. Through Asmund's unarmoured breast the spear went, pinning him against the wall so that he stood there with Ketil still leaned against him, the two dead brothers side by side gaping at their murderer.

Valgard howled as the berserkergang swept over him. His eyes blazed lynx-green and froth was on his lips. Orm, who had followed him, bellowed, grabbed up a sword, and attacked. Valgard whipped forth his eating knife, knocked Orm's blade aside by striking the flat of it with his left arm, and buried his in the chief's throat.

Blood spurted over him. Orm fell. Valgard took the sword. Others were coming. They blocked his escape. Valgard hewed down the nearest. His howling rang between the rafters.

The hall boiled with men. Some sought to get into a safe corner, but others to capture the crazy one. Valgard's blade sang. Three more yeomen toppled. Then several bore a plank from the trestle table before them. With this, by their weight they pushed Valgard well away from the stack of weapons. Folk armed themselves.

But in that crowded space, it did not go fast. Valgard slashed at those between him and the door who bore nothing. They fell aside, several wounded, and he won through. A warrior who had gotten an iron-rimmed shield as well as a sword stood in the foreroom. Valgard smote. His steel hit the shield rim and broke across.

"Too weak is your blade, Orm," he cried. As the man rushed at him, he reached back and wrenched the axe from Ketil's head. In his haste, the other man was careless. Valgard's first blow battered the shield aside. His second took the man's right arm off at the shoulder. Valgard went out the door.

Spears hissed after him. He fled into the woods. The blood of his father dripped from him for a while, until it froze and gave no further help to the hounds set on to his trail. Even when he had lost them, he kept running lest he too freeze. Shuddering and sobbing, he fled westward.

VIII

The witch sat waiting, alone in darkness. Presently something slipped through a rat-hole. Looking down to the shadowed floor, she saw her familiar.

Thin and weary, he did not speak ere he had crawled up to her breast and drunk deep. Then he lay on her lap and watched her with hard little glittering eyes.

"Well," she asked, "how went the journey?"

"Long and cold," he said. "In bat shape, blown on the wind, I fared to Elfheugh. Often as I crept about Imric's halls I came near death. They are beastly quick, the elves, and they knew I was no ordinary rat. But nonetheless I contrived to spy on their councils."

"And is their plan as I thought?"

"Aye. Skafloc will fare to Trollheim for a raid in force on Illrede's garth, hoping to slay the king or at least upset his readying for war—now that he has openly called an end to the truce. Imric will remain in Elfheugh to prepare defences."

"Good. The old elf-earl is too crafty, but Skafloc alone can scarce avoid the trap. When does he leave?"

"Nine days hence. He will take some fifty ships."

"Elves sail swiftly, so he should be at Trollheim the same night. With the wind I will teach him how to raise, Valgard can reach thither in three days, and I'd best allow him another three to busk himself. So if he is to greet Illrede only a short time before Skafloc, I must keep him here— hm, he will need time to get to his own men—well, controlling him will be no great task, since he is now an outlaw fleeing hither in despair."

"You treat Valgard roughly."

"I have naught against him, he not being of Orm's seed, but he is my tool in a stiff and perilous game. It will not be near as easy to ruin Skafloc as it was to kill Orm and the two brothers, or will be to get at the sisters. My magic and my force alike he would laugh at." The witch grinned in the half-light. "Aye, but Valgard is a tool I shall use to make a weapon that will pierce Skafloc's heart. As for Valgard himself, I give him a chance to rise high among the trolls, the more so if they conquer the elves. It is my hope to make Skafloc's downfall doubly bitter by causing the wreck of Alfheim through him."

And the witch sat back and waited, an art that many years had taught her.

Near dawn, when a grey and hopeless light crept over the snows and the ice-leaved trees, Valgard knocked on the woman's door. She opened it at once and he fell into her arms. Nigh dead of weariness and cold he was, with gouts of blood caked upon him and wildness in his eyes and ravaged face.

She gave him meat and ale and curious herbs, and erelong he could hold her close to him. "Now you are all that is left to me," he mumbled. "Woman whose beauty and wantonness wrought this ill, I should slay you and then fall on my own weapon."

"Why do you say that?" she smiled. "What is there bad?"

He buried his face in the fragrance of her hair. "I have slain my father and my brothers," he said, "and am outlaw beyond atonement."

"As for the slayings," said the woman, "they do but prove you stronger than those who threatened you. What does it matter who they were?" Her green eyes burned into his. "But if the thought of doing away with your kin troubles you, I will tell you that you are guiltless."

"Eh?" He blinked dully at her.

"You are no son of Orm, Valgard Berserk. I have second sight, and I tell you that you are not even of human birth, but of such ancient and noble stock that you can scarce imagine your true heritage."

His huge frame grew taut as an iron bar. He clasped her wrists hard enough to leave bruises, and his shout resounded in the cottage: "What do you say?"

"You are a changeling, left when Imric the elf-earl stole Orm's first-born," said the woman. "You are Imric's own son by a slave who is daughter to Illrede Troll-King."

Valgard flung her from him. Sweat gleamed on his forehead. "Lie!" he gasped. "Lie!"

"Truth," answered the woman calmly. She walked towards him. He backed away from her, his breast heaving. Her voice came low and relentless: "Why are you so unlike the children of Orm or any man? Why do you scorn gods and men, and walk in a loneliness only forgotten in the tumult of slaying? Why, of all the women whom you have bedded, has none become with child? Why do beasts and small children fear you?" She had him in a corner now, and her eyes would not release him. "Why indeed, save that you are not human?"

"But I grew up like other men, I can endure iron and holy things, I am no warlock—"

"There is the evil work of Imric, who robbed you of your heritage and cast you aside in favour of Orm's son. He made you look like the stolen child. You were raised among the petty rounds of men, and have had naught to rouse the wizard power slumbering within you. That you might grow up, age, and die in the brief span of humankind, that the things holy and earthly which the elves fear might not trouble you, Imric traded your birthright of centuried life. But he could not put a human soul in you, Valgard. And like him, you will be as a candle blown out when you die, with no hope of Heaven or hell or the halls of the old gods—yet you will live no longer than a man!"

At this Valgard croaked, thrust her aside, and rushed out the door. The woman smiled.

It grew loud and cold with storm, but not till after dark did Valgard creep back to the house. Bent and beaten he was, but his eyes smouldered upon his leman.

"Now I believe you," he muttered, "nor is there aught else to believe. I saw ghosts and demons riding the gale, flying with the snow and mocking me as they swept by." He stared off into a dark corner of the room. "Night closes on me, the sorry game of my life is played out—home and kin and my very soul have I lost, have I never had, and I see I was but a shadow cast by the great Powers who now blow out the candle. Good night, Valgard, good night—" And he sank sobbing on to the bed.

The woman smiled her secret smile and lay down beside him and kissed him with her mouth that was like wine and fire. And when his dazed eyes turned mutely to hers, she breathed: "This is no speech for Valgard Berserk, mightiest of warriors, whose name is terror from Ireland to Gardariki. I thought you would seize on my words with gladness, would hew fate into a better shape with that great axe of yours. You have taken gruesome revenges for lesser hurts than this—the robbery of your being and the chaining into the prison which is a mortal's life."

Valgard felt something of strength return, and as he caressed the woman it rose fiercer in him, together with hatred for everything save her. At last he said: "What can I do? Where can I avenge myself? I cannot even see elves and trolls unless they wish it."

"I can teach you that much," she answered. "It is not hard to give the witch-sight with which the beings of Faerie

52

are born. Thereafter, if you like, you can destroy those who have wronged you, and can laugh at outlawry, you who will be more powerful than any king of men."

Valgard narrowed his gaze on her. "How so?" he asked slowly.

"The trolls make ready for war with their olden foes the elves," she said. "Erelong Illrede Troll-King leads a host against Alfheim, most likely striking first at Imric here in England, that his flank and rear be safe when later he moves southward. Among Imric's best warriors, because iron and holy things trouble him not, as well as because of strength and warlock knowledge, will be his foster son Skafloc, Orm's child who sits in your rightful seat. Now if you sailed quickly to Illrede, and offered him good gifts and the services of your humanlike powers as well as telling him your descent, you could find a high place in his army. At the sack of Elfheugh you could slay Imric and Skafloc, and Illrede would most likely make you earl of the British elf-lands. Thereafter, as you learned sorcery, you would wax ever greater—aye, you might learn how to undo Imric's work and make yourself like a true elf or troll, ageless till the end of the world."

Valgard laughed, the yelp of a hunting wolf. "Indeed that is well!" he cried. "Murderer, outlaw, and inhuman, I have naught to lose and much to gain. If so be I join the hosts of cold and darkness, then I will join them with a whole heart, and in battles such as men have never dreamed will drown my wretchedness. Oh, woman, woman, a mighty thing have you done to me, and it is evil, but I thank you for it!"

Fiercely he loved her; but when later he spoke above the gale it was in a chill and level tone.

"How shall I get to Trollheim?" he asked.

The woman opened a chest and took forth a leather sack tied at the mouth. "You must leave on a particular day that I will tell you," she said. "When your ships are under weigh, untie this. It holds a wind which will blow you thither, and you will have witch-sight to see the troll garths."

"But what of my men?"

"They will be part of your gift to Imric. The trolls find sport in hunting men across the mountains, and they will sense that yours are evildoers whom no god will bestir himself to help."

Valgard shrugged. "Since I am to be troll, let me also be

my blood true in treachery," he said. "But what else can I give that will please him? He must have a glut of gold and jewels and costly stuffs."

"Give him that which is more," said the woman. "Orm has two fair daughters, and the trolls are lustful. If you bind and gag them, so they cannot draw cross or name Jesus—"

"Not those two," said Valgard in horror. "I grew up with them. And I have done them enough harm already."

"Those two indeed," said the woman. "For if Illrede is to take you in service, he must be sure you have broken all human ties."

Still Valgard refused. But she clung to him and kissed him and wove him a tale of the dark splendours he could await, until at last he agreed.

"But I wonder who you are, most evil and most beautiful of this whole world," he said.

She laughed softly, cuddled on his breast. "You will forget me when you have had a few elf women."

"Nay—never can I forget you, beloved, who broke me as you would."

Now the woman held Valgard in her house for as long as she deemed needful, making some pretence of brewing enchantments to restore his witch-sight, and spinning out her accounts of Faerie. However, this was hardly called for, since her loveliness and love-skill bound him more surely than chains.

Snow filled the dusk when at length she said, "You had best start out now."

"We," he answered. "You must come along, for I cannot live without you." His big hands fondled her. "If you come not willingly, I shall carry you, but come you must."

"Very well," she sighed. "Though you may feel otherwise when I have given you sight."

She rose to her feet, looked down at him seated, and stroked the lines and angles of his face. Her mouth curved in an almost wistful smile.

"Hate is a hard master," she breathed. "I had not thought to have joy again, Valgard, but it is a wrench to bid you farewell. All good luck to you, my dearest. And now—" her fingertips brushed his eyes "—see!"

And Valgard saw.

Like smoke in the wind, the well-kept little house and the tall white woman wavered before him. In sudden terror, he willed to see them not with magic-tricked mortal eyes, but as they really were—

He sat in a hovel of mud and wattles, where one tiny dung fire cast a feeble glow on heaps of bones and rags, rusted metal tools and twisted implements of sorcery. He looked up into the dim eyes of a hag whose face was a mask of wrinkled skin drawn over a lolling toothless skull, and to whose shrivelled breast clung a rat.

Wild with horror, he stumbled to his feet. The witch leered at him. "Beloved, beloved," she cackled, "shall we not away to your ship? You swore you would not part from me."

"For *you* I am outlaw!" Valgard howled. He grabbed his axe and struck at her. Even while he smote, her body shrank. Two rats sprang across the floor. The axe thudded into the ground just as they went down a hole.

Foaming, Valgard took a stick and thrust it into the fire. When it was well alight, he touched it to the rags and thatch. He stood outside while the hovel burned, ready to hew at anything which might show itself. But there were only the leaping flames and the piping wind and the snow hissing as it blew into the fire.

When naught but ashes was left, Valgard shouted forth: "For you I have lost home and kin and hope, for you I am resolved to forswear my lifetime and league with the lands of darkness, for you I have become a troll! Hear me, witch, if still you live. I will take your rede. I will become earl of the trolls in England—maybe one night king of all Trollheim —and I will hound you down with every power I then have. You too, like men and elves and whoever gets in my way, you will feel my wrath, and never will I rest until I have flayed alive you who broke my heart with a shadow!"

He wheeled about and loped eastward, soon lost in the snowfall. Crouched below the earth, witch and familiar grinned at each other. This was just as they had planned.

The crews of Valgard's ships were the worst of vikings, most of them outlawed from their homelands and all of them unwelcome wherever they went. Thus he had bought a garth of his own where they might winter. They lived well, with thralls to serve them, but were so quarrelsome and unruly that only their chief could hold them together.

When word of the murders reached them, they knew it would not be long ere the men of the Danelaw came to put an end to them, and they busked the ships and themselves to sail. But they could not agree on whither they should go, now in winter, and there was much dispute and some fighting. They might have sat thus till their foes were upon them had Valgard not returned.

He came after sunset into the hall. The burly hairy men sat draining horn after horn until their shouting deafened ears. Many snored on the floor beside the dogs; others yelled and squabbled, with onlookers more apt to egg them on than step between. To and fro in the shifty firelight scurried the terrorized manthralls, and women who had long since wept out their tears.

Valgard stepped up to the empty high seat—a tall and terrible figure, mouth set in yet grimmer lines than his men remembered, the great axe which had begun to be called Brotherslayer slanted over one shoulder. Quiet spread in waves as folk saw him, until at last only the longfire had voice in that hall.

Valgard spoke: "We cannot abide here. Though you were never at Orm's garth, folk will make what happened into an excuse for getting rid of you. Now that is just as well. I know a place where we can win greater wealth and fame, and thither we sail the dawn after tomorrow."

"Where is that, and why not leave tomorrow?" asked one of his captains, a scarred old fellow by name Steingrim.

"As to the last, I have a business here in England which we will attend tomorrow," said Valgard. "And as to the first, our goal is Finnmark."

An uproar arose. Steingrim lifted his voice above it: "That is the most foolish babble I ever heard. Finnmark is poor and lonely, and lies across a sea which can be dangerous even in summer. What can we win there save death, by drowning or by the sorcerers who dwell in that land; or at best a few earthern huts to huddle in? Near at hand are England, Scotland, Ireland, Orkney, or Valland south of the channel, where good booty may be gotten."

"I have given my orders. You will follow them," said Valgard.

"Not I," answered Steingrim. "I think you have gone mad in the woods."

Like a wildcat, Valgard sprang at the captain. His axe crashed down into Steingrim's skull.

A man yelled, grabbed a spear and thrust at Valgard. The berserker sidestepped, yanked the shaft from his hands, and

56

knocked him to the ground. Pulling the axe from Steingrim's head, Valgard stood looming in the smoky light with his eyes like flakes of sea-ice. He asked quietly: "Does anyone else wish to gainsay me?"

None spoke or moved. Valgard stepped back to his high seat and told them: "I acted thus harshly because we cannot go on in our old loose way. Our lives are lost unless we become like a single man, whose head I alone am fit to be. Now I know my plan looks unwise at first, but Steingrim should have heard me out. The fact is I have word of a rich man's garth built in Finnmark this summer, where anything we could wish is stored. They will not await vikings in winter, so we can take it easily. Nor do I fear rough weather on the way, for you know I have some skill at foretelling it and I snuff a good wind coming."

The gang remembered how Valgard's leadership had been to their betterment. As for Steingrim, he had no kin or oath-brother here. So they shouted they would follow Valgard wherever he went. When the body had been dragged out and the drinking taken up anew, he gathered his captains.

"We have a place nearby to sack ere leaving England," he told them. " 'Twill not be hard, and good plunder is to be had."

"What place is that?" asked one man.

"The garth of Orm the Strong, who is now dead and cannot ward it."

Even those reavers thought this would be an evil deed, but they dared not talk against their chief.

IX

Ketil's grave-ale became also a feast for Asmund and Orm. Men drank silent and sorrowful, for Orm had been a sage leader, and he and his sons were well-liked thereabouts in spite of his being no churchman. The ground was not yet frozen too hard for the carles to start making a howe the day after the murders.

Orm's best ship was dragged from its house into the grave. In it were laid treasures, and meat and drink for a long voyage; horses and dogs were killed and put in the ship; and those whom Valgard had slain were placed in it with the best of clothes, weapons, and every kind of gear, and with hellshoes on their feet. Thus had Orm wanted to be buried, and had made his wife promise.

When the task was done, some days later, Ælfrida came forth. She stood in the dull grey winter light, looking down at Orm and Ketil and Asmund. Her unbound hair fell to their breasts and hid her own countenance from those who stood watching.

"The priest says it would be a sin, or I would slay myself now and go to my rest beside you," she whispered. "Weary will life be. You were good boys, Ketil and Asmund, and your mother is lonely for your laughter. It seems but yesterday I sang you to sleep on my breast, you were so little then, and suddenly you were great long-legged youths, good to look on and a pride to Orm and me—and now you lie so still, with a few snowflakes drifting down on your empty faces. Strange—" She shook her head. "I cannot understand you are slain. It is not real to me."

She smiled at Orm. "Often did we quarrel," she murmured, "but that meant naught, for you loved me and—and I you. You were good to me, Orm, and the world is cold, cold, now you are dead. This I ask all-merciful God: that He forgive what things you did against His law. For you were ignorant of much, however wise with a ship or with your hands to make me shelves and chests or carve toys for the children. . . . And if so be God can never receive you in Heaven, then I pray Him I too may descend to hell to be with you—aye, though you go to your heathen gods, there I would follow you. Now farewell, Orm, whom I loved and love. Farewell."

She bent and kissed him. "Cold are your lips," she said, and looked bewilderedly about her. "Thus were you not wont to kiss me. This is not you, dead in the ship—but where are you, Orm?"

They led her out of the hull, and the men worked long casting earth over it and the grave-chamber built on it. When they were done, the howe rose huge at the edge of the sea and waves came up the strand to sing a dirge at its foot.

The priest, who had not approved of this heathenish burial, would not consecrate the ground, but he did whatever he could and Asgerd paid him for many masses for the souls of the dead.

There was a young man, Erlend Thorkelsson, who was

betrothed to Asgerd. "Hollow is this garth now that its men are gone," said he.

"So it is," replied the maiden. A cold sea-wind, blowing fine dry snowflakes, ruffled her heavy locks.

"Best I and a few friends should stay here a while and get things in order," he said. "Then I would we wedded, Asgerd, and thereafter your mother and sister can come live with us."

"I will not wed you until Valgard has been hanged and his men burned in their house," she said angrily.

Erlend smiled without mirth. "That will not be long," he said. "Already the war-arrow goes from hand to hand. Unless they flee sooner than I think they can pull themselves together to do, the land will shortly be rid of that pest."

"It is well," nodded Asgerd.

Now most of those who had come to the feast went home, but the folk of the garth sat behind, with Erlend and some half-dozen other men. As night fell, a strong wind came with snow on its wings, to howl around the hall. Hail followed, like night-gangers thumping their heels on the roof. The room lay long and dark and cheerless; folk huddled together at one end of it. They spoke little, and the horns passed often.

Once Ælfrida stirred from her silence. "I hear something out yonder," she said.

"Not I," said Asgerd, "and naught would be abroad tonight."

Freda, who misliked her mother's dull stare, touched her and said timidly, "All alone are you not. Your daughters will never forget you."

"Aye—aye." Ælfrida smiled the least bit. "Orm's seed shall live in you, and the dear nights we had are not in vain—" She gazed at Erlend. "Be good to your wife. She is of the blood of chieftains."

"What else could I be but good to *her*?" he said.

There came of a sudden a beating on the door. Above the wind rose a shout: "Open! Open or we break in!"

Men clutched for their weapons as a thrall undid the bar —and was at once cut down by an axe. Tall and grim, guarded by two men's shields held before him, snow mantling his shoulders, Valgard trod in from the foreroom.

He spoke: "Let the women and children come outside and they shall live. But the hall is ringed with my men and I am going to burn it."

A cast spear clanged off one of the iron-bound shields. The smoke-reek grew stronger than it should be.

"Have you not done enough?" shrieked Freda. "Burn this house if you will, but I would rather stay within than take my life of you."

"Forward!" shouted Valgard, and ere anyone could stop them he and a dozen of his vikings had come inside.

"Not while I live!" cried Erlend. He drew his sword and charged at Valgard. The axe Brotherslayer flashed to and fro, knocked the blade aside with a clatter and buried its beak under his ribs. He pitched to the floor. Valgard leaped over him and grabbed Freda's wrist. Another of his men took Asgerd. The rest formed a shield-burg about these two. Helmeted and mailed, they had no trouble winning back to the door, killing three who fought them.

When the raiders had gone forth, the men inside rallied, armed themselves more fully, and tried to make a rush. But they were hewn down or forced back by warriors who stood at every way out. Ælfrida cried and ran to the door, and her the vikings let through.

Valgard had just finished binding the wrists of Asgerd and Freda, with lead ropes to drag them along if they would not walk. The roof of the hall already burned brightly. Ælfrida clung to Valgard's arm and wailed at him through the flame-roar.

"Worse than wolf, what new ill are you wreaking on the last of your kin? What turns you on your own sisters, who have done you naught but good, and how can you stamp on your mother's heart? Let them go, let them go!"

Valgard watched her with pale cold eyes in an unmoving face. "You are not my mother," he said at last, and struck her. She fell senseless in the snow and he turned away, signalling his men to force the two captive girls down to the bay where his ships were beached.

"Where are we bound?" sobbed Freda, while Asgerd spat on him.

He smiled, a mere quirk of lips and said: "I will not harm you. Indeed, I do you a service, for you are to be given to a king." He sighed. "I envy him. Meanwhile, knowing my men, I had best watch over you."

Such of the women as did not wish to be burned alive shepherded the children outside. The raiders used them but afterwards set them free. Other women stayed inside with their men. Flames lit the garth for a great ways around, and erelong the other buildings had caught fire, though not before they had been plundered.

Valgard left as soon as he was sure those within were dead, for he knew that neighbours would see the burning and arrive in strength. The vikings launched their ships and stood out to sea, rowing against a wind which blew icy waves inboard.

"Never will we reach Finnmark like this," grumbled Valgard's steersman.

"I think otherwise," he answered. At dawn, as the witch had told him, he untied the knots that closed her leather bag. At once the wind swung around until it came from astern, blowing straight north-east in a loud steady drone. Sails set, the ships fairly leaped ahead.

When folk reached Orm's garth, they found only charred timbers and smouldering ash-heaps. A few women and children were about, sobbing in the dreary morning light. Ælfrida alone did not weep or speak. She sat on the howe with hair and dress blowing wild, sat unstirring, empty-eyed, staring out to sea.

Now for three days and nights Valgard's ships ran before an unchanging gale. One foundered in the heavy waves, though most of her crew were saved; on the rest, bailing never could end; and uneasy mutters went from beard to beard. But Valgard overawed thoughts of mutiny.

He stood nearly the whole time in the prow of his craft, wrapped in a long leather cloak, salt and rime crusted on him, and brooded over the waters. Once a man dared gainsay him, and he slew the fellow on the spot and cast the body overboard. He himself spoke little, and that suited the crew, for they cared not to have that uncanny stare upon them.

He would not answer the pleas of Freda and Asgerd for word on where they were bound, but he gave them well of food and drink, let them shelter beneath the foredeck, and did not let the men bother them.

Freda would not eat at first. "Naught do I take from the murdering thief," she said. The salt streaking her cheeks was not all from the sea.

"Eat to keep your strength," counselled Asgerd. "You do not take it from him, since he has robbed it from others, and the chance may come to us to escape. If we pray God for help—"

"That I forbid," said Valgard, who had been listening, "and if I hear any such word I will gag you."

"As you will," said Freda, "but a prayer is more in the heart than the mouth."

"And not very useful in either place," grinned Valgard. "Many a woman has squawked to her God when I clapped hands on her, and little did it avail. Nevertheless, I will have no more talk of gods on my ship." For while he did not await help for them from Heaven—it was only that soulless Faerie folk were so deeply learned in magic that a Power they knew was greater yet, and knew they would never understand, sent them into blind panic by its mere names and signs—he did not wish to take needless risks, and still less did he wish to be reminded of what was forever denied to him.

He lapsed into his thoughts and the sisters into silence. Nor did the men say much, so that the only sounds were the *whoot* of wind in the rigging, the brawl of sea past the bows, the creak of straining timbers. Overhead flew grey clouds from which snow or hail often whirled, and the vessels rolled and pitched alone on the running waves.

On the third day, near nightfall, beneath a sky so low and thick as almost to bring dusk by itself, they raised Finnmark. Bleak rose the cliffs from surf that shattered itself booming upon them. Their heights were bare save for snow and ice and a few wind-twisted trees.

"That is an ugly land," shivered Valgard's steersman, "and I see naught of the garth whereof you spoke."

"Make for that fjord ahead," commanded the chief.

The wind blew them into it, until the sullen cliffs blocked it off. Then masts were lowered and oars came out, and the ships splashed through twilight towards a rock-strewn beach. Peering before him, Valgard saw the trolls.

They were not quite as tall as him, but nigh twice as broad, with arms like tree boughs that hung to their knees, bowed short legs and clawed splay feet. Their skin was green and cold and slippery, moving on their stone-hard flesh. Few of them had hair, and their great round heads, with the flat noses, huge fanged mouths, pointed ears, and eyes set far into bone-ridged sockets, were like skulls. Those eyes lacked whites, were pits of blackness.

They went for the most part unclad, or wore but a few

skins, however freezing the wind. Their weapons were chiefly clubs, and axes, spears, arrows, and slings that used stone, all too heavy for men to swing. But some wore helms and byrnies and carried weapons of bronze or elven alloy.

Valgard could not but shudder at the sight. "Has the cold gotten to you?" asked a man of his.

"No—no—'tis naught," he muttered. And to himself: "I hope the witch was right and the elf women are fairer than these. But they will make wondrous warriors."

The vikings grounded their ships and drew them ashore. Thereafter they stood unsurely in the dusk. And Valgard saw the trolls come down on onto the strand.

The fight was short and horrible, for the men could not see their foes. Now and again a troll might happen to touch iron and be seared by it, but mostly they knew well how to dodge that metal. Their laughter coughed between the cliffs as they dashed out men's brains, or ripped them limb from limb, or hunted them up through the mountains.

Valgard's steersman saw his fellows die while his chief leaned unmoving on his axe. The viking roared and rushed on the berserker. "This is your doing!" he shouted.

"Indeed it is," replied Valgard, and met him in a clamour of steel. Erelong he had slain the steersman, and by that time the rest of the battle was over.

The troll captain approached Valgard. Rocks scrunched beneath his tread. "We had word of your coming, from a bat that was also a rat," he rumbled in the Danish tongue, "and give you many thanks for good sport. Now the king awaits you."

"I come at once," said Valgard.

He had already gagged the sisters and bound their arms behind them. Stunned with what they had witnessed, they stumbled blindly along a deep gorge and a barren mountainside, past unseen guards into a cave and thence into the hall of Illrede.

It was huge, hewn out of rock but furnished with magnificence raided from elves, dwarfs, goblins, and other folk, men among them. Great gems gleamed on the walls amid subtle tapestries, costly goblets and cloth bedecked tables of ebony and ivory, and the fires burning down the length of the hall lit rich garments on the troll lords and their ladies.

Thralls of elf, dwarf, or goblin race moved about with trenchers of meat and cups of drink. This was a high feast, for which human and Faerie babies had been stolen as well as cattle, horses, pigs, and wines of the south. Music of the snarling sort that the trolls liked came rattling out of the smoky air.

Along the walls stood guards, moveless as heathen idols, the ruddy light aglint on their spearheads. The trolls at table gobbled and guzzled, quarrelling with each other in a thunderous din. But the lords of Trollheim sat quiet in their carven seats.

Valgard's gaze went to Illrede. The king was vast of girth, with a wrinkled massive face and a long beard of green tendrils. When his inkpool eyes fell on the newcomers, a fear that he sought to hide prickled over the changeling's backbone.

"Greeting, great king," he said. "I am Valgard Berserk, come from England to seek a place in your host. I am told you are father to my mother, and fain would I claim my heritage."

Illrede nodded his gold-crowned head. "That I know," he said. "Welcome, Valgard, to Trollheim, your home." His glance swung to the maidens, who had sat down for want of further strength, forlornly side by side. "But who are these?"

"A small gift," said Valgard firmly, "children of my foster father. I hope they will please you."

"Ho—ho, ho—ho, ho, ho!" Illrede's laughter shocked through the stillness that had fallen. "A goodly gift! Long is it since I held a human may in my arms—Aye, welcome, welcome, Valgard!"

He sprang to the floor, which thudded under his weight, and went over to stand above the girls. Freda and Asgerd looked wildly about them. One could well-nigh read their thoughts: "Where are we? A lightless cave, and Valgard talks to no one, but the echoes are not of his words—"

"You should see your new home," leered Illrede, and touched their eyes. And at once they had the witch-sight, and saw him stooping over them, and their courage broke and even through the gags their screams went on and on.

Illrede laughed again.

X

The elf raid on Trollheim was to be a strong one. Fifty longships were manned with the best warriors of Britain's elves, and veiled and warded by the sorceries of Imric and his wisest warlocks. It was thought that under these spells they could sail unseen into the very fjords of Finnmark's troll realm; how deeply inland they could thrust thereafter would hang on what resistance they met. Skafloc hoped they could get into Illrede's own halls and bring back the king's head. He was wild to go.

"Be not too reckless," cautioned Imric. "Kill and burn, but lose no men in mere adventures. 'Twill be worth more if you get a measure of their strength than if you wipe out a thousand of them."

"We will do both," grinned Skafloc. He stood restless as a young stallion, eyes alight, the tawny hair tumbling down from his headband.

"I know not—I know not." Imric looked grave. "I feel, somehow, that no good will come of this trip, and would fain order it halted."

"If you do that, we will go anyway," said Skafloc.

"Aye, so you will. And I may be wrong. Go, then, and luck be with you."

On a night just after sunset, the warriors embarked. A moon newly risen cast silver and shadow on the crags and scaurs of the elf-hills, on the strand from which they rose, on the clouds racing eastward on a wind that filled heaven with its clamour. The moonlight ran in shards and ripples over the waves, which tumbled and roared, white-maned, on the rocks. It shimmered off weapons and armour of the elf warriors, while the black-and-white longships drawn up on the shore seemed but shades and light-gleams.

Skafloc stood wrapped in a cape, the wind streaming his hair, awaiting the last of his men. To him, pale in the moonlight, with her tresses tossing cloudy and her eyes aglow, came Leea.

" 'Tis good to see you," cried Skafloc. "Bid me farewell and sing a song for my luck."

"I cannot give you goodspeed properly, for I cannot come up to that iron byrnie of yours," she answered in her voice that was like breeze and rippling water and small bells heard from afar. "And I have a feeling my spells will avail naught against a doom that is set for you." Her gaze sought his. "I know, with a sureness beyond proof, that you sail into a trap; and I beg you, by the milk I gave you as a child and the kisses as a man, to stay home this one time."

"That would be a fine deed for an elf chief, in command

of a raid that may bring back his foeman's head," Skafloc said in anger. "Not for anyone would I do so shameful a thing."

"Aye—aye." Sudden tears glimmered in Leea's eyes.

"Men, whose span is cruelly short, rush nonetheless to death in their youth as to a maiden's arms. A few years ago I rocked you in your cradle, Skafloc, a few months ago I lay out with you in the light summer nights, and to me, undying, the times are almost the same. And no different, in that blink of years, is the day your hacked corpse will await the ravens. I shall not ever forget you, Skafloc, but I fear I have kissed you for the last time."

And she sang:

> Seaward blows the wind tonight,
> and the seamen, never resting,
> rise from house to take their flight
> with the gulls, and spindrift's questing.
> Woman's arms and firelit hearth,
> kith and kin, can never hold them
> when the wind beyond their garth
> of the running tides has told them.
> *Spume and seaweed shall enfold them.*

> Wind, ah, wind, old wanderer,
> grey and swift-foot, ever crying,
> Woman curses, who, from her,
> calls forth Man to doom and dying.
> Seamen, kissed by laughing waves,
> cold and salt-sweet, hearts deceiving,
> shall be borne to restless graves
> when the sea their life is reaving.
> *And their women will be grieving.*

Skafloc liked not this song, which smacked of bad luck. He turned and shouted to his men to get the ships afloat and get aboard them. But soon as he himself was waterborne, he lost every foreboding in renewed eagerness.

"This gale has blown for three days now," said Goltan, a comrade of his. "And it has a wizard smell about it. Mayhap some warlock sails eastward."

"'Twas kind of him to spare us the trouble of raising our own wind," laughed Skafloc. "However, if he has been three

66

days eastbound, his ship is of mortal make. *We* travel at a better clip!"

Masts and sails were raised, and the slim dragon-headed craft leaped ahead. Like the gale itself they went, like flying snow and freezing spindrift white under the moon, waves seething in their wake, a long easy bounding over the noisy waters. Swiftest of all in Faerie, afoot or on horse or in hull, were the elves, and ere midnight Finnmark's cliffs loomed in sight.

Skafloc's teeth gleamed forth. Quoth he:

> Elves come early
> east to Trollheim,
> song of spear
> and sword to sing.
> Good are gifts
> they give, for troll-men:
> sundered skulls
> and splitted bellies.

> Trolls shall tumble
> (tumult rages),
> fear of firebrands
> freeing bowels.
> Kin, be kind
> to clamouring troll-men:
> have they headaches,
> hew the heads off.

The elves grinned down the length of the plunging hull, lowered sail and mast, and took to their oars. Into the fjord the fleet steered, busked for battle, but no sign of enemy guards met their eyes. Instead they saw other vessels drawn up on the beach—three mortal longships, whose folk were bloodily strewn across the rocks.

Skafloc leaped ashore, sword out and cloak flapping behind him. "Strange is this," he said uneasily.

"Belike they sheltered here from the gale and were set on by trolls," Goltan replied. "'Twas a very short time ago—see, feel, the blood is still wet, the bodies warm—and so the killers may be at Illrede's hall reporting the matter."

"Why, then, that is wondrous luck!" cried Skafloc, who had not looked to make a surprise attack. Rather than wind his horn, he signalled with his blade. Not he nor the elves gave further thought to the dead men, who were merely human.

The crews sprang into the shallows and dragged their ships ashore. A few stayed there on guard, while Skafloc led the main troop along the inland trail.

Through a gorge they went, where mortals would have been blind, and came out on to a mountainside where snow glittered dazzling and peaks raked the sky. Wind shrieked and cuffed them with cold hands. Ragged clouds blew across the moon's face, as if it blinked. Lithe as cats, the elves made their way over cliff and crag, up the mountain towards the cave mouth that gaped in its side.

Nearing, they saw a band of trolls come out, belike the coast watchers bound back to their posts. Skafloc's cry rose over the wind: "Swiftly, and we can cut them off!"

Pantherish he sprang, the elves beside and around him. Ere the trolls were fully aware, metal howled in their ears, and that was the last sound they heard. But of course the noise reached inside, and when Skafloc's raiders entered, they met growing opposition.

Din of weapons was redoubled in the descending tunnel. The war-shouts of the elves and the booming cries of the trolls rolled in broken echoes. Skafloc and Goltan led the way shield by shield, hewing over the rims. Mostly un-unarmoured and all slower-moving, troll after troll fell beneath those sharp edges.

A warrior thrust at Skafloc with a spear like a young tree. He caught that thrust on his shield, forced the shaft aside, closed in and smote. His iron blade burned through the shoulder to the heart. Glimpsewise he saw a club smashing at him from the left. It could have crushed his helmet and the head beneath. He got his shield in the way. The blow rang on its sheet-iron facing and the shock sent him staggering back. He fell to one knee, but freed his sword and cut a leg out from under the troll. Rising, he swept his glaive in a whistling, twisting curve, and another troll's head leaped from its neck.

At last the retreating defenders came into a large cave. The elves cried their glee at having a space big enough for their best kind of fighting. Longbows came off backs and the grey-feathered arrows stormed up from behind Skafloc's front line and down again among the trolls. As the defenders gave way and their own ranks broke, single combats scattered across the floor. One troll without mail was seldom a match for that leaping, dodging, hewing, stabbing blur which was an elf.

Some of the attackers did die, with shattered skulls or ripped hides, and no few took wounds. But for the trolls it was a slaughter. Nonetheless the royal guards stood fast in the archway that led to their master's feasting hall. When the elves, having finished off everyone else, charged, too few of them could get at that grim line, and there was too little room for their speed and skill to count. They recoiled in confusion, leaving a number of dead and hurt. Nor would missiles be much use against that wall of shields, which were made to cover from just below the eyes to just below the knee.

But Skafloc saw how high the arch was above them. "Let me show you the way!" he shouted. Streaming green troll blood and some of his own red, with dented helm and shield and nicked sword, he laughed as he scabbarded the blade and took a spear. Dashing forward, he pole-vaulted over the foemen's heads into the hall beyond.

Falling, he drew sword again. The landing, with the weight he bore, shocked in his soles and thudded in the ground. He whirled about. The guardsmen having been on duty, were well armoured, but legs and parts of arms must needs be bare. The iron blade brought down three trolls in as many blows.

Others turned to face him. The elves rushed on the suddenly ragged line—broke it asunder and poured into the troll-king's hall!

Skafloc saw Illrede at the far end, clutching a spear but rocklike in his high seat. The man plunged towards him. Two trolls who sought to stop Skafloc sank beneath his weapon. Then a man trod into his path.

For a moment Skafloc stood stiff with astonishment, seeing his own face glare at him behind the descending axe. He got his shield up barely in time. However, the axe was not soft bronze or light alloy, it was steel itself, and not blunted by combat; whereas the shield had taken much beating. The axe struck the rim, clove wood and thin iron, and did not stop until it had laid open Skafloc's left arm.

He tried to keep the axe caught in place while he cut from above. But the stranger sprang back, wrenching free his weapon with a strength that sent Skafloc lurching. Then he moved to the attack. Skafloc cast aside the now useless shield. Iron belled and sparked on iron. Both men wore helm and byrnie, and unshielded, the swordsman was not well matched against the greater weight of the axe. Though Skafloc knew the elven art of thrust, parry, and bind, a blade such as he bore tonight was poorly balanced for that. He made shift to defend himself, but must keep on giving way.

Then the tide of battle came between. Skafloc found himself suddenly pitted against a troll, who gave him a hard fight ere falling. Meanwhile the stranger was embroiled with elves. He cut his way through them, back to Illrede, and the remaining trolls rallied about those two. In a quick, strong push they beat a path to a rear door. Through this they went.

"After them!" roared Skafloc in battle fury.

Goltan and the other elf captains urged him back. " 'Twould be foolhardy," they said. "See, the door opens on lightless downward-leading caverns where we could be too easily ambushed. Best we bar it on this side instead, that Illrede call not the monsters of the inner earth up against us."

"Aye, you are right," said Skafloc grudgingly.

His glance swept the hall, first greedily across the riches therein, then with a measure of sorrow across the bodies of elves sprawled on the blood-slippery floor. Yet he must rejoice at how few they were beside the enemy dead. The troll wounded were being dispatched—the loudness of their groans and cries dropped fast—while the elven hurt were being roughly bandaged until healing magic could be worked for them back home.

Suddenly Skafloc's eyes came to rest in an amazement hardly less than when he had seen his own shape among the foe. Two mortal women lay bound and gagged near the high seat.

He strode over. They shrank from his knife when he drew it. "Why, I am only going to free you," he said in the Danish tongue, and did. They rose, shuddering, clinging to each other. He was surprised afresh when the tall fair-haired one stammered through tears: "B-b-backbiter and murderer, what new evil do you wreak?"

"Why—" Skafloc checked his bewilderment. Though he had learned the speech of men, he had had little use of it and spoke it with the singing note of the elf tongue. "Why, what have I done?" He smiled. "Unless you like being tied up."

"Mock us not, Valgard, on top of everything else," said the golden-haired maiden.

"I am not Valgard," Skafloc said, "nor do I know him unless he is that man whom I fought—but belike you did not see that in the crowd. I am Skafloc of Alfheim, and no friend to trolls."

"Aye, Asgerd!" burst from the younger girl. "He cannot be Valgard. See, he is beardless, he wears different garments, he speaks strangely—"

"I know not," mumbled Asgerd. "Is this death around us another trick? Is he making an enchantment to beguile us—? Oh, I know naught save that Erlend and our kindred are dead." She began to sob, dry racking coughs.

"No, no!" The younger maiden clung to Skafloc's shoulders searching his face, beaming through tears like springtime sunshine through rain. "No, stranger, you are not Valgard though you do look much like him. Your eyes are warm, your mouth knows well how to laugh— Thanks unto G—"

He covered her lips with his palm before she could finish. "Do not speak that name yet," he said hastily. "These are also Faerie folk who cannot bear to hear it. But they will do you no harm. Rather will I see that you are taken to where-ever you wish."

She nodded, wide-eyed. He dropped his hand and looked long at her. She was only of middle height, but each inch was one of supple slender youthful beauty gleaming through the tatters of her dress. Her locks were long and lustrous bronze-brown, sparked with red; her face was a sweet mould-ing of broad forehead and pertly tilted nose and wide soft mouth. Under dark brows, her long-lashed eyes were big, wide-set, bright, a grey that woke some ghostly half-memory in Skafloc's elf-schooled mind. But he could not make out what it was, and it left him.

"Who are you?" he asked slowly.

"I am Freda Ormsdaughter from the Danelaw in England; this is my sister Asgerd," she told him. "And you, warrior—?"

"Skafloc, Imric's fosterling, of Alfheim's English lands," he answered. She shrank back, barely stopping a sign of the cross. "I tell you, do not fear me," he said with un-wonted earnestness. "Wait here while I take charge of our work."

The elves got busy plundering Illrede's hall. Ranging through offside rooms, they found slaves of their own race whom they freed. Finally they went outside. Near the cave mouth they found houses, sheds, and barns which they set afire. Though a strong wind still blew, the weather had mostly cleared, and flames roared bright into a star-frosted sky.

"Meseems Trollheim is nothing to fear," said Skafloc.

"Be not too sure," cautioned Valka the Wise. "We took them unawares. I wish I knew how big the levies have grown and how near to this stead they are camping."

"We can find that out another time," said Skafloc. "Now let us go back to the ships, and we can be home ere dawn."

Asgerd and Freda had stood by, numbly watching from their witch-sighted eyes what the elves did. Strange were these tall warriors, moving like water and smoke, with never a sound of footfall but with byrnies chiming silvery through the night. Ivory pale, with thin high-boned features, beast ears and blankly glowing eyes, they were a sight of terror to mortal gaze.

Among them passed Skafloc, almost as soft-footed and graceful, seeing like a cat, speaking their eldritch tongue. Yet he was a man in his looks, and Freda, remembering the warmth of him, unlike what cool silky-skinned elf flesh had happened to brush her, felt sure he was human.

"Heathen must he be, to dwell among these creatures," said Asgerd once.

"Well—I suppose so—but he is kind, and he saved us from—from—" Freda shuddered and wrapped more tightly about herself the cloak Skafloc had given her.

The man blew his horn for withdrawal, and the long, silent file wound its way down the mountain. Skafloc walked beside Freda, saying naught but often casting his glance upon her.

She was younger than him, with a trace of endearing coltish awkwardness still in the long legs and slim-waisted body. She bore her head high, and the shining hair seemed to crackle in the frosty moonlight—but he thought it would be soft to the touch. As they came down the rugged slope he steadied her, and the little hand was engulfed in his calloused paw.

Then all at once there rang between the steeps the bull bellow of a troll horn, and another answered it and another, echoes snarling back from cliffs and blowing ragged on the wind. The elves stopped dead, ears cocked, nostrils aquiver while they searched the night for trace of their foes.

"I think they must be ahead, to cut off our retreat," said Goltan.

"Bad is that," said Skafloc, "but it would be worse to go blundering down the black gorge and have rocks hurled at us from above. We will make our way beside it instead of through it."

He blew a battle call on the lur horn carried for him. Elves made the first of the great curving lurs and used them still, though men had forgotten them since the Age of Bronze. To Freda and Asgerd he said: "I fear we must fight once more. My folk will ward you if you speak not those names which hurt them. If you do, they must scatter, and trolls standing out of earshot can slay you with arrows."

"It would not be good to die without calling on—Him above," said Asgerd. "However, we will obey you in this."

Skafloc laughed and laid a hand on Freda's shoulder. "Why, how can we but win when such beauty is to be fought for?" he asked gaily.

He told off two elves to carry the girls, who could not keep up when the pace grew swift, and had others form a shield-burg around them. Then, at the head of a wedge formation, he proceeded over the ridge towards the sea.

Lightly went the elves, springing from rock to crag, ring-mail singing and weapons agleam in the moonlight. When they saw the trolls massed black against the wan night-bridge of the gods, they raised a shout, clashed swords on shields, and ran to the fight.

But Skafloc drew a quick breath at the size of the troll force. He guessed the elves were outnumbered some six to one—and if Illrede could raise that horde this fast, what might not his full strength be?

"Well," he said, "we shall have to kill six trolls apiece."

The elf archers loosed their shafts. The slower trolls could not match the moon-darkening clouds which sighed again and again over them. Many sank on the spot. But as ever, most arrows rattled harmlessly off rocks, or stuck in shields, and all were soon spent.

The elves charged, and battle burst in the night. Roaring troll horns and dunting elf lurs, wolf-howling troll cries and hawk-shrieking elf calls, thunder of troll axes on elf shields and clangour of elf swords on troll helmets, stormed to the stars.

Axe and sword! Spear and club! Cloven shield and sundered helm and broken mail! Red gush of elf blood meeting cold green flow of troll's! Auroras dancing death-dances overhead!

Two tall shapes, hardly to be told apart, loomed in the strife. Valgard's axe and Skafloc's sword clove bloody trails through the locked and swaying warriors. The berserker foamed with the rage that had come on him, bawled and smote. Skafloc was silent save for panting breath, but scarcely less wild.

The trolls had hemmed in the elves on every side, and in that press, where swiftness and agility counted for little, troll strength came into its own. It seemed to Skafloc that for each gaping grinning face that sank before him, two more rose out of the blood-steaming snow. He had to stand his ground, while sweat rivered off him to freeze in his breeks, and grip his new shield and strike without end.

Thus it was Valgard who came to him, mad with the berserkergang and with hatred for everything elfly—most for Imric's fosterling. They met well-nigh breast to breast, eyes glaring into eyes through the tricky moonlight.

Skafloc's blade clanged on Valgard's helm and dented it. Valgard's axe chopped splinters from Skafloc's shield. Then Skafloc got in a sidewise cut that laid open Valgard's cheek so that the teeth grinned forth. The berserker howled anew and laid on a thunderous hail of blows, knocking the blade aside, banging on the shield till Skafloc's left arm was ready to drop off and blood drenched the cloth bound over the earlier wound in it.

Nonetheless he watched his chance; and when his foe stuck a leg too far forward, Skafloc hewed down deep into the calf. He might have disabled, had his edge not been blunted from use. As was, Valgard hooted and fell back. Skafloc followed.

A blow as of a falling boulder smote his helm, casting him to his knees. Illrede Troll-King had loomed beside him and swung a stone-headed club. Valgard came back with axe aloft. Though his ears rang and pain was an iron band around his temples, Skafloc rolled aside. The weapon struck ground. Battle-crazed, an elf in the shield-burg took a step out of it to cut down the berserker ere he could free his axe. Illrede's mallet hit and broke that warrior's neck. Valgard lifted his axe and brought it down through the hole in the line, on to the elf behind. But it was into the burden he bore that the axe sank.

The shield-burg closed and moved against man and troll,

who retreated from so many spears. Skafloc got back up and led them away. They left their dead behind. Illrede likewise rejoined his guardsmen. Valgard stayed where he was, alone, for the fit had passed from him.

Swaying on his feet, painted with blood, he stood over Asgerd's body. "I did not mean that," he said. "Indeed my axe is accursed—or is it me?" He passed a hand over his eyes, puzzledly. "Yet . . . they are not my kin, are they?"

Weak after the fury, he sat down beside Asgerd. The battle moved further away from him. "Now there are only Skafloc and Freda to kill, then all the blood I once thought my own is shed," he mumbled, stroking her heavy golden braids. "And it might be well to do it with you, Brother-slayer. Ælfrida too, if she still lives. I could kill—why not? She is not my mother. My mother is a great horrible thing chained in Imric's dungeons, Ælfrida, who sang me to sleep, is not my mother—"

Ill went it with the elves, however valiantly they fought. In their van, Skafloc shouted to them, rallied and ordered and led them. His blade yelled death. No troll could stand before that whirling steel, and with his men he slowly carved a seaward lane.

For a space he faltered, when Goltan fell with a spear through him. "Now I am one friend poorer," he said, "and that is a wealth not gained back." His voice rose anew: "Hai, Alfheim! Forward, forward!"

And so at last a remnant broke through the trolls and retreated to the beach. Valka the Wise, Flam of Orkney, Hlokkan Redlance, and other great elves fell in the rearguard. But meanwhile the rest won to their ships. Some among them, in full sight of the trolls, ran about the slope above, scattering what booty remained. This softened the attack, for Illrede would rather get back his treasures than lose many more folk.

Enough elves were alive and somewhat hale for the undermanning of about half the ships. The rest they set alight with fire spells. Then they launched and boarded and rowed painfully out of the fjord.

Freda, huddled in the bottom of Skafloc's dragon, saw him standing tall and bloody against the moon, making rune signs and uttering words she did not know. The wind shifted aft, became a gale, a storm, and with iron-hard sails and bowbent masts and twanging tackle the ships leaped forward. Faster and ever faster they fled, like the spindrift, like the clouds, like dream and witchcraft and moonlight over the water. Skafloc stood in the spray-sheeting bows and sang his warlock song, unhelmed hair flying and ragged byrnie ringing, a shape out of lost sagas and worlds beyond man.

Darkness came to Freda.

XI

She awoke on a couch of carved ivory, spread with furs and silks. She had been bathed and dressed in a white samite shift. By her bedside stood a curiously wrought table bearing wine, water, clustered grapes and other fruits of the southland. Save for this she could see only an endless deep-blue twilight.

For a time she could not remember where she might be or what had happened. Then recollection rushed back and she fell to wild sobbing. Long she wept. But peace was in the very air she breathed; and when she had wept herself out and taken some of the wine, it was more than heady, it was like a calming hand laid on her heart. She fell into dreamless sleep.

Awakening again, she felt marvellously rested. As she sat up, Skafloc came striding through the blue spaciousness to her.

No sign of his wounds remained, and he bore an eager smile. He wore a brief, richly embroidered tunic and kilt that showed the muscles alive beneath his skin. Sitting down beside her, he took her hands and looked into her eyes.

"Do you feel better?" he asked. "I put into the wine a drug that helps heal the mind."

"I am well, only—only where am I?" she answered.

"In Imric's castle of Elfheugh, among the elf-hills of the north," said Skafloc, and as her eyes grew wide with alarm: 'No hurt shall be done you, and all shall be as you wish."

"I thank you," she whispered, "next after God Who—"

"Nay, speak not holy names here," Skafloc warned her, "for elves must flee from such things, and you are a guest of theirs. Otherwise you free to do whatever you like."

"You are not an elf," said Freda slowly.

"No, I am human, but raised here. I am foster son to Imric the Guileful, and feel more akin to him that to who-ever my real father was."

"How came you to save us? We had despaired—"

Skafloc told briefly of the war and his raid, then smiled afresh and said, "Better to speak of you. Who could have had so fair a daughter?"

Freda flushed, but began telling him her story. He listened without understanding what it meant. The name of Orm carried naught to him, for Imric, to break his fosterling's human ties, had given out that the exchange of babes was made far off in the west country; furthermore, by means that he knew, he had raised Skafloc so as to kill any curiosity about parentage. As for Valgard, Freda knew naught save that he was her brother gone mad. Skafloc had sensed an inhumanness about the berserker, but with so much else to think over—especially Freda—did not search deeply into the matter. He decided that Valgard might well be possessed by a demon. The likeness to himself he supposed must be due a mirror spell; Illrede could have put one on Valgard for any of a dozen reasons. Besides, none of the elves to whom Skafloc chanced to speak of the matter had noticed it. Was that because they had been too busy staying alive, or because Skafloc had mis-seen? Imric's fosterling shrugged off the whole question and forgot about it.

Nor did Freda ponder on the likeness of the two men, for she could never have mistaken them. Eyes and lips and play of features, gait and speech and manner and touch and thought, were so different in them that she scarcely noticed the sameness of height and bone and cast of face. She wondered fleetingly if they maybe shared a forebear—some Dane who spent a summer in England a hundred years ago—and then herself forgot about it.

For there was too much else. The drug she had taken might dull but could not hide the starkness of what had happened. As she talked, the bewilderment and the following wonder that had hitherto kept grief at bay yielded before its onrush; and she ended her tale weeping on Skafloc's breast.

"Dead!" she cried. "Dead, all dead, all slain save Valgard and me. I...I saw him kill Father and Asmund when Ketil was already dead, I saw Mother stretched at his feet, I saw the axe go into Asgerd—now only I am left, and I would it were me who had died instead of—Oh, Mother, Mother!"

"Be of good cheer," said the man awkwardly. The elves had not taught him about mourning such as this. "You are

77

unharmed, and I will seek out Valgard and revenge your kindred upon him."

"Little good will that do. Orm's garth is an ash heap and his blood spilled and lost, save in one gone mad and one left homeless." She clung to him, shuddering. "Help me, Skafloc! I scorn myself ... for being afraid ... but I am. I am afraid of being this alone—"

He ruffled her hair with one hand, while the other tipped her chin back so that she looked into his eyes. "You are not alone," he murmured, and kissed her with butterfly gentleness. Her lips quivered under his, soft and warm and salty with tears.

"Drink," he said, and held out the wine-cup.

She took a draught, and another, and huddled a while in his arms. He comforted her as best he could, for it seemed wrong to him that she should ever know unhappiness; and he whispered certain charms that lifted woe sooner than nature does.

And she remembered that she was daughter to Orm the Strong, who beneath his gusty merriment had always been a man stern with himself. He raised his children to be likewise: "None can escape his weird; but none other can take from him the heart wherewith he meets it."

So in the end, calm, even looking forward to the marvels that Skafloc promised her, she sat straight and told him: "Thank you for your goodness to me. I have myself back in hand now."

He chuckled. "Then 'tis time you broke your fast," he said.

A dress had been laid out for her, of the filmy flowing spider silk worn by elf women. Though Skafloc did her bidding and turned his back while she changed into it, she blushed hotly, for it hid little. Yet she could not help feeling pleasure at the heavy gold rings he put on her arms and the diamond-twinkling coronet he set on her locks.

They crossed the unseen floor and came into a long hallway which did not appear at once but grew like a mist about them into solidity. Shining colonnades lined the marble walls, and the richly hued figurings of rugs and tapestries moved in slow, fantastic dances.

Here and there went goblin thralls, a race halfway between elf and troll, green-skinned and squat but of not unpleasing aspect. Freda shrank against Skafloc with a small cry when a yellow demon-shape stalked past bearing a chandelier. Ahead of him scuttled a dwarf with a big shield.

"What is *that*?" whispered Freda.

Skafloc grinned. "One of the Cathayan Shen, whom we took captive in a raid. He is strong and makes a good slave. However, as his kind can only move in straight lines unless deflected by a wall, the dwarf must lay the shield slantwise across corners for him to rebound off like light off a mirror."

She laughed, and he listened in wonder to the clear peal of it. Always in the mirth of the elf women was a hint of malicious mockery; Freda's came like a morning in blossom time.

The two ate of rare viands, alone at a table where music sighed from the air around them. Quoth Skafloc:

> Food is good for friendship,
> Fairest one, and wine-cups.
> Good it is to gladden
> gullets in the morning.
> But my eyes, bewildered
> by the sight of Freda,
> sate themselves on sun-bright
> southern maiden's beauty.

She dropped her eyes, feeling her cheeks burn afresh, though she could not but smile.

Remorse came upon her. "How I can know cheer so soon after my kin are dead? Broken is the tree whose branches sheltered the land, and wind blows cold across fields gone barren—" She ceased looking for words, saying merely, "We all grow poorer when good folk go."

"Why, if they were good you need not mourn them," said Skafloc glibly, "for they are safe from this world's sorrows, come home to Him above. I should think, in truth, that only the sound of your weeping could trouble their bliss."

Freda clung to his arm as they left the room. "The priest spoke about deaths unshriven—" Her free hand knuckled her eyes. "I love them, and they are gone and I mourn alone."

Skafloc's lips brushed her cheek. "Not while I live," he murmured. "And you should pay no great heed to what some yokel priest has prated of. What does he know?"

They came into another chamber, whose vaulted ceiling was made dusky by its own height. Freda saw standing therein a woman whose beauty was not of mortal flesh. Beside her, the girl felt little and plain and afraid.

"You see I came back, Leea," Skafloc hailed her in the elven tongue.

"Aye," she replied, "with no booty, and more than half your men lost. A fruitless quest!"

"Not altogether," Skafloc said. "More trolls fell than did elves, and the foe was left in disarray, and their captives that we freed can tell us much about them." Arm around her waist, he drew Freda close against him. She came willingly in her dread of the cold white witch that glowered at her. "And look what a jewel I did bring back."

"What do you want with her?" taunted Leea. "Unless your own blood is calling within you."

"Belike." Skafloc was unruffled.

She drew near and laid a hand on his arm, searching his face with her eyes of blue dusk and moonlight. "Skafloc," she said urgently, "get rid of this wench. Send her home if you will not slay her."

"She has no home," Skafloc said, "and I will not cast her out into beggary who has already suffered more than enough." Gibing: "Why do you care what two mortals do?"

"I care," Leea said sorrowfully, "and I see my spaedom was right. Like calls to like—but not her, Skafloc! Take any mortal maid save this. There is doom in her; I can feel it, like a chill in my marrow. 'Twas not simple chance you found her, and she will wreak great harm on you."

"Not Freda," said Skafloc stoutly, and to change the talk: "When will Imric return? He had been summoned to council by the Erlking when I came back from Trollheim."

"He will be here soon. Wait until then, Skafloc, and it may be that he can see clearly the doom I only sense, and warn you."

"Should I, who have fought trolls and demons, fear a girl?" snorted Skafloc. "That is not even raven-croak, it is hen-cackle." And he led Freda away.

Leea stared strickenly after them, then fled through the long halls with tears aglimmer in her eyes.

Skafloc and Freda wandered on through the castle. Her words at first came piecemeal and grave. But the philtres she had drunk and the charms he had cast made eagerness mount through head and heart. More and more did she smile, and exclaim, and chatter, and look at him. At last he said: "Come outside and I will show you something I made for you."

"For me?" she cried.

"And maybe, if the Norns be kind, for myself too," he laughed.

They crossed the courtyard and passed through the high brazen gates. Beyond, sunlight dazzled on blue-shadowed whiteness, and no elves were abroad. The humans walked on into the ice-flashing woods, Skafloc's cloak wrapped around them both. Breath steamed out into unclouded heaven; to breathe back in stung. The surf droned, and a breeze soughed through darkling firs.

"Cold," shivered Freda. The ruddy-bronze of her hair was the only warmth in that whole world. "Outside your cloak it is cold."

"Too cold for you to wander begging on the roads."

"There are those who would take me in. We had many friends; and our land, now mine, I suppose, would make a —" her tongue grew unwilling "—a good dowry."

"Why go forth to seek friends when you have them here? And as for land—see."

They topped a hill, one of a ring about a dell. And down there Skafloc had made summer. Green were the trees beside a little dancing waterfall, and flowers nodded in sweet deep grass. Birds sang, fish leaped, a doe and fawn stood watching the humans with utter trust.

Freda clapped her hands and cried out. Skafloc smiled. "I made it for you," he said, "because you are of summer and life and joy. Forget the winter's death and hardness, Freda. Here we have our own year."

They went down into the dell, casting off their cloak, and sat by the waterfall. Breezes ruffled their hair and berries clustered heavily around them. At Skafloc's command, the daisies she plucked wove themselves into a chain which he hung around Freda's neck.

She could not fear him or his arts. She lay back dreamily, eating an apple he had urged upon her—which had the taste of a noble wine, and seemed to do the same work— and listened to him:

> Laughter from your lips, dear,
> lures me like a war-cry.
> Bronze-red locks have bound me:
> bonds more strong than iron.

Never have I nodded
neck beneath a yoke,
but I wish now the welcome
warmth of your arms' prison.

Life was made for laughter,
love, and eager heartbeat.
Could I but caress you,
came I to my heaven.
Sorceress, you see me
seek your love with pleading:
how can Skafloc help it
when you have ensnared him?

"This is not meet—" she protested feebly, while smiles and sighs possessed her.

'Why, how can it but be meet? There is nothing else so right."

"You are a heathen, and I—"

"I told you not to speak of such things. Now you must pay the gild." And Skafloc kissed her, long and with all his skill, softly at first, wildly at last. She sought for a moment to fend him off, but she could not find the strength, for it only came back when she joined in the kiss.

"Was that so bad?" he laughed.

"No—" she whispered.

"Your grief is fresh, I know. Yet grief will fade, and those who loved you would not have it otherwise."

In truth, it had already gone. Tenderness remained, and a fleeting wistfulness: Could they but have met him!

"You must take thought for your morrow, Freda, and still more for the morrow of that blood which you alone now bear. I offer you the riches and wonders of Alfheim, aye, asking no dowry save your own dear self; and you and yours shall be warded with every strength that is mine; but first among my morning gifts to you will be my undying love."

It could not be compelled, but since it would have come of itself, elven arts had hastened the thawing of sorrow and the springing forth of love; for its blossoming, no other sunshine was needed than youth.

The day ended and night came to the vale of summer.

They lay by the waterfall and heard a nightingale. Freda was first to sleep.

Lying there with her in the crook of his arm, an arm of hers across his breast, listening to the soft breathing, himself breathing in the odours of her hair and her humanness, feeling her warmth, remembering how with tears and laughter she had wholly come to him, he suddenly knew something.

He had laid a snare for her, mostly in sport. Such mortal mays as he had spied now and again in his flittings about the land were seldom alone, and when they were, they had seemed to his elven mind too lumpish, in body and soul alike, to be worth his while. In Freda he found a human girl who could rouse lust in him, and he had wondered what it would be like to lie with her.

And the snare had caught him too.

He did not care. He lay drowsily back on the grass and smiled up at the Wain where it glittered in its endless wheeling around the North Star. The cool, cunning elf women had many powers; but, perhaps because they always kept their own hearts locked away, they had never drawn his out of him. Freda—

Leea was right. Like called to like.

XII

Several days later, Skafloc went out alone to hunt. He travelled on wizard skis which bore him like the wind, up hill and down dale, over frozen rivers and through snow-choked woods, well into the Scottish highlands by sunset. He had turned homeward, a roe deer lashed over his shoulders, when he saw from afar the glimmer of a camp-fire. Wondering who or what was camped in these bleak ranges, he went whispering over the snow with his spear at the ready.

Coming close through twilight, he descried one of mighty stature who squatted on the snow and roasted horseflesh over the blaze. Despite a chill wind, he wore only a wolfskin kilt, and the axe beside him flashed with unearthly brightness.

Skafloc sensed a Power, and when he saw that the other had but a single hand, his spine crawled. It was not thought good to meet Tyr of the Æsir alone at dusk.

But too late to flee. The god was already looking towards

him. Skafloc skied boldly into the circle of firelight and met Tyr's brooding dark eyes.

"Greeting, Skafloc," said the As. His voice was as of a slow storm through a brazen sky. He kept on turning the spit over the fire.

"Greeting, lord." Skafloc eased a little. The elves, without souls, worshipped no gods, but neither was there any ill will between them and the Æsir; indeed, some served in Asgard itself.

Tyr nodded curtly in sign for the man to unburden himself and hunker down. Stillness lasted for a long while, save for the low flames which sputtered and sang and wove highlights over Tyr's gaunt grim face.

He spoke at last: "I smelled war. The trolls mean to fare against Alfheim."

"So we have learned, lord," answered Skafloc. "The elves are prepared."

"The fight will be harder than you think. The trolls have allies this time," Tyr gazed sombrely into the flames. "More is at stake than elves or trolls know. The Norns spin many a thread to its end these days."

Again was silence, until Tyr said: "Aye, ravens hover low, and the gods stoop over the world, which trembles to the hoofbeats of Time. This I tell you, Skafloc: you will have sore need of the Æsir's naming-gift to you. The gods themselves are troubled. Therefore I, the war-wager, am on earth."

A wind shook his black locks. His eyes smouldered into the man's. "I will give you a warning," he said, "though I fear it helps naught against the will of the Norns. Who was your father, Skafloc?"

'I know not, lord, nor have I cared. But I can ask Imric—"

"Do not so. What you must ask Imric is that he say naught to anyone of what he knows, least of all yourself. For the day you learn who your father was will be a dark one, Skafloc, and what comes on you from that knowledge will also wreak ill on the world."

He jerked his head again, and Skafloc took a hasty departure, leaving the deer as a gift in return for the rede. But as he swept homeward with the noise of his passage loud in his ears, he wondered how good Tyr's warning had been—for the question of who he really was rose stark in his mind, and the night seemed full of demons.

Faster he fled and faster, heedless of how the wind cut at him, yet could not outrun the thing saddled on his back. Only Freda, he thought, clutching for breath, only Freda could banish the fear from him.

Ere dawn the walls and towers of Elfheugh were in sight, high athwart heaven. An elf guard blew on a horn to signal the gatekeepers. Through the opened way whizzed Skafloc, into the courtyard and on to the castle steps. Kicking off his skis, he ran into the keep.

Imric, returned early that evening, had been talking in private with Leea. "What if Skafloc be taken with a mortal maid?" He shrugged. "'Tis his own business, and a small matter indeed. Are you jealous?"

"Yes," his sister answered frankly. "However, 'tis more than that. See the girl for yourself. Try if you cannot sense that in some way she is meant as a weapon against us."

"Hm . . . so." The elf-earl tugged his chin and scowled. "Tell me what you know about her."

"Well, she hight Freda Ormsdaughter, from a broken family south in the Danelaw—"

"*Freda—Ormsdaughter—*" Imric stood aghast. "Why, that—means—"

Skafloc burst into the room. His haggardness shocked them. It was a little time until he could speak; then his tale flooded out of him.

"What did Tyr mean?" he cried at the end. "Who am I, Imric?"

"I see what he meant," answered the elf-earl harshly, "and therefore your birth is my secret alone, Skafloc. I will but say that you come of good stock, with naught shameful in its blood." And he put on his smoothest manner and spoke fair words which at length sent Skafloc and Leea away soothed.

But when they were gone, he paced the floor and muttered to himself. "Someone somehow has lured us onto a road that is tricky and beset." His teeth came together. "Best get rid of the girl—but no, Skafloc guards her with his whole might, and if I did contrive against her, he would soon know it and—The secret must be kept. Not that Skafloc would care; he thinks like an elf in that regard. But if he found out, the girl soon would; and 'tis one of the strongest laws laid on mankind that they have broken. She would be desperate enough to do anything. And we need Skafloc."

He turned plans over in his crafty brain. He thought of

luring Skafloc with other women. But no, his fosterling would recognize any potion for what it was; and over unforced love, the gods themselves had no might. If that love died of itself, the secret would no longer make any difference. But Imric dared not lay trust in so flimsy a chance. It followed that the truth about Skafloc's parentage must be buried, and soon.

The elf-earl cast back in his memory. As nearly as he could tell—it is not easy to keep thousands of years straight —only one besides himself knew the whole story.

He sent for Firespear, a trusty guardsman, still a youth of two centuries but cunning and sorcerous. "There was a witch who dwelt in a woodland south west of here, twenty-odd years ago," he said. "She may have died or moved away, but I want you to track her—and if she yet lives, slay her out of hand."

"Aye, lord," nodded Firespear. "If I may take a few huntsmen and hounds, we will start off at eventide."

Imric gave him directions. "Take what you will, and begone as swiftly as may be. Ask not for my reasons, nor talk about the matter afterwards."

Freda welcomed Skafloc back to their rooms with jubilations. Despite her wonder at the magnificence of Elfheugh, she had quailed, beneath an undaunted mien, when restlessness drove him outdoors from her. The castle dwellers, tall lithe elves and their women of immortal beauty, dwarfs and goblins and even more eldritch folk who toiled for them, the wyverns wherewith they went hawking, the lions and panthers they kept for pets, the proud quicksilver grace of the very horses and dogs, were alien to her. The elven touch was cool, the elven faces like statue faces yet at the same time inhumanly fluid, speech and garb and ways of a life that spanned centuries sundered them from her. The dim splendour of the castle which was also a barren tor, the sorceries adrift through its eternal warm twilight, the presences that haunted hills and woods and waters—oppressed her with strangeness.

But when Skafloc was by her side, Alfheim seemed to lie on the borders of Heaven. (God forgive her for thinking that, she whispered to herself, and for not fleeing this heathendom for the holy chill and darkness of a nunnery!) He was lively and merry and mischievous until she could not but laugh with him, his staves rushed out of him and every one to her praise, his arms and his lips awoke a craziness that did not stop before joy had for a moment dissolved the flesh itself and made them into One Who sings for ever. She had seen him fight, and knew there were few warriors in lands of men or Faerie who could stand before him, and of this she was proud; after all, she stemmed from warriors herself. (And she was not an unnatural daughter and sister, was she, because a spell she was helpless to withstand had so swiftly drawn the grief out of her and instead made her overflow with happiness? She had had no choice, Skafloc would not have waited for a year of mourning, and what better father could be gotten for the grandchildren of Orm and Ælfrida?) But with her he was always gentle.

She knew he loved her. He must, or why would he lie with her, spend well-nigh his whole time with her, who could have elf women? She did not know why—did not know how deeply her warmth had entered his soul which had never before felt the like. Skafloc had not been aware of his loneliness until he came on Freda. He knew that, unless he paid a certain price which he would not, he must sometime die, his life the barest flicker in the long elf memories. It was good to have one of his own sort by his side.

In their few days together they had done much, ridden the swift horses and sailed the slender boats and walked over many leagues of hill and woods. Freda was a skilled archer; Orm had wanted his womenfolk able to defend themselves. When she went among the trees with bow in hand and bronze hair shining, she seemed a young goddess of the hunt. They had watched the magicians and mummers, listened to the musicians and skalds, who beguiled the elves, though these were often too sly and subtle for human liking. They had guested Skafloc's friends, gnomes who dwelt under tree roots, slim white water-sprites, an old and sad-eyed faun, beasts of the wilderness. Though Freda could not converse, she was wide-eyed and a-smile at sight of them.

She had given scant thought to the future. Someday, of course, she must bring Skafloc to the lands of men and get him christened, a worthy deed for which her present sins would no doubt be forgiven her. Not now, though, not yet. Elfheugh was timeless, she had lost track of days and nights, and there was so much else to do.

She sped into his arms. What trouble still clung to him vanished at seeing her: young, slim, lithe and long-legged, more girl than woman and nonetheless his *woman*. He laid hands on her waist, flung her into the air, and caught her again, while they both laughed aloud.

"Set me down," she gasped. "Set me down so I can kiss you."

"Soon." Skafloc tossed her up again and made a sign. There she hung, weightless in midair, kicking out and choking between merriment and surprise. Skafloc pulled her to him and she hung above with her mouth on his.

"No sense craning my neck for this," decided Skafloc. He made himself weightless too and conjured forth a cloud, not wet but like white feathers, for them to rest on. A tree grew from its middle, heavy with different kinds of fruit, and rainbows arched through its leaves.

"Someday, madman, you will forget some part of your tricks and fall and break in little pieces," she said.

He held her close, looking into her grey eyes. Then he counted the freckles that dusted the bridge of her nose, and kissed her once for each of them. "I had best make you spotted like a leopard," he said.

"Do you need such an excuse?" she answered softly. "I have longed for you, my dearest. How went your hunt?"

He frowned as memory returned. "Well enough."

"You fret, darling. What's wrong? This whole night have horns blown and feet pattered and hoofs tramped. I see more armed men in the castle every day. What is it, Skafloc?"

"You know we are at war with the trolls," he said. "We are letting them come to us, for 'twould be hard to overrun their mountain fastnesses while they keep their full strength."

She shuddered in his arms. "The trolls—"

"No fear." Skafloc cast off his unease. "We will meet them at sea and break their power. Any who land we will let stay, in as much earth as they need to cover them. Then with its strength gone, it will be a romp to lay Trollheim under us. Oh, we will have lusty fighting, but Alfheim would have to work hard not to win."

"I fear for you, Skafloc."

Quoth he:

Fear of fairest
fay for chieftain
makes him merry—
means she loves him.

Girl, be gay now.
Gladly take I
gift you give me,
gold-bright woman.

Meanwhile he began undoing her girdle. Freda blushed. "Shameless are you," she told him, and fumbled with his garments.

Skafloc raised his brows. "Why," he asked, "what is there to be ashamed about?"

Firespear rode out shortly after sunset of the next night. A few sullen embers lay yet in the west. He and his dozen followers wore the green tunics of the chase, with cowled black cloaks flung above. Their spears and arrows were tipped with alloy of silver. About their curvetting horses bayed the elf-hounds, great savage beasts with coats red or ebon, furnace eyes and dagger fangs from which ran slaver, blood of Garm and Fenris and the Wild Hunt's dogs in them.

Forth they swept when Firespear's horn shouted. Drumroll of hoofs and belling of hounds rang between the hills. Like the wind they went, between ice-sheathed trees through a night that soon was pit-black. A glint of silver, jewelled hilts, bloody glare might be seen in a rush of shadows: no more; but the clamour of their passage rang from end to end of the woods. Hunters, charcoal burners, outlaws who heard that racket shuddered and signed themselves, whether with Cross or Hammer; and wild beasts slunk aside.

From afar the witch, squatting in the shelter she had built where her house formerly stood—for her greatest powers drew from things thereabouts and nowhere else—heard the troop coming. She crouched over her tiny fire and muttered, "The elves hunt tonight."

"Aye," squeaked her familiar. As the noise drew closer: "And I think they hunt us."

"Us?" The witch started. "Why say you that?"

"They are bound straight this way, and you are no friend to Skafloc, thus none to Imric." The rat chattered with fear and crawled into her bosom. "Now quickly, mother, quickly, summon aid or we are done."

The witch had no time for rites or offerings, but she howled the call which had been taught her, and a blackness deeper than the night arose beyond the fire.

She grovelled. Faint and cold, the little blue flames raced across him. "Help," she whimpered. "Help, the elves come."

The eyes watched her without anger or pity. The sound of the hunt grew louder. "Help!" she wailed.

He spoke, in a voice that blent with the wind but seemed to come from immeasurably far removed. "Why do you call on me?"

"They . . . they seek . . . my life."

"What of that? I heard you say once you did not care for life."

"My vengeance is not complete," she sobbed. "I cannot die now, without knowing whether my work and the price I paid are for naught. Master, help your servant!"

Nearer came the hunters. She felt the ground shiver beneath the galloping hoofs.

"You are not my servant, you are my slave," the voice rustled. "What is it to me whether your purpose is fulfilled? I am the lord of evil, which is futility.

"Did you think you ever summoned me and struck a bargain? No, you were led astray; that was another. Mortals never sell me their souls. They give them away."

And the Dark Lord was gone.

The witch shrieked and ran forth. Behind her the hounds, put off by the smell of him who had lately been here, barked and cast about. The witch turned herself into a rat and crawled down a hole beneath the Druid oak.

"She's near," called Firespear, "and—Ha! They have the scent!"

The pack closed in. Earth flew as they dug after their prey, ripping roots and yelping. The witch darted forth, changed into a crow, and winged aloft. Firespear's bow twanged. The crow sank to earth. It became a hag at whom the dogs rushed. The rat sprang from her bosom. A horse brought down its silver-shod foot to crush him.

The hounds tore the witch asunder. As they did she screamed at the elves: "All my curses! All woe do I wish on Alfheim! And tell Imric that Valgard the changeling lives and knows—"

There her words ended. "That was an easy hunt," said Firespear. "I was afraid we would need sorcery to track her wanderings through a score of years, maybe into foreign lands." He snuffed the wind. "As it is, we have the rest of the night for better game."

Imric rewarded his hunters well, but when they told him, in some puzzlement, what their quarry had said, he scowled.

XIII

Valgard found a high place at the troll court, grandson of Illrede and strong warrior with the freedom of iron as he was. But the lords looked askance at him—for he had elf blood too, and came from the lands of men; also, they were envious of a stranger who, after a tongue-spell had given him command of their speech, stepped at once into their ranks. Thus Valgard found no friends in Trollheim. Nor did he seek any, the looks and smells and ways of these folk not being to his liking.

They were, however, fearless and of terrible strength. Their warlocks had powers he doubted any human could ever wield. Their nation was strongest in Faerie by far except—maybe—for Alfheim. This suited Valgard well, for here was the means to his revenge and the gaining of his heritage.

Illrede told him what was planned. "Throughout the peace we built for war," said the king, "while the elves loafed and intrigued among themselves and took their pleasure. There are not quite so many of us as of them, but with those who march beside us this time we outnumber them by a good lot."

"Who are they?" asked Valgard.

"Most of the goblin tribes we have either overcome or made alliance with," said Illrede. "They have old grudges against both trolls and elves, but I have promised them loot and freedom for such slaves of their race as we have and a place just below us when we rule throughout Faerie. They are doughty fighters, and not few.

"Then we have companies from distant lands, demons of Baikal, Shen of Cathay, Oni of Cipangu, imps of Moorish deserts, adding up to a fair number. They have come for the looting and are not wholly to be relied on, but I will dispose them in battle according to what they can do. There are also stragglers who came alone or in little bands—were-wolves, vampires, ghouls, that sort. And we have plenty of dwarf thralls, some of whom will fight in exchange for freedom; and they can handle iron.

"Against this host the elves stand alone. They may be

able to scrape together a few odd goblins and dwarfs and whatnot else, but those scarcely count. The very best they can hope for is aid from the Sidhe. However, I have spied out that those mean to hold aloof unless their island is attacked, and we will be careful not to do that . . . in *this* war.

"True, the elf leaders are wily and learned in magic—but so are I and my chieftains." Illrede's laughter coughed forth. "Oh, we will break Alfheim like a dry stick across the knee!"

"Can you not call on the Jötuns for help?" asked Valgard, who was still learning the ins and outs of this world wherein he found himself. "They are akin to trolls, are they not?"

"Speak never of such!" rapped Illrede. "We dare no more call the ice giants to our help than the elves the Æsir." He shivered. "We do not wish to be more their pawns than we are already—the contending Powers beyond the moon. Even if they would answer, not we nor the elves would dare call—because if Æsir or Jötuns should move openly into Midgard, the other side would move against them, and then the last battle would be joined."

"How does this fit with what I was taught of . . . the new god?"

"Best not speak of mysteries we cannot understand." Illrede moved ponderously about the cave room where they were talking by smoky torchlight. "It is because of the gods, though, that no dweller in Faerie dares do much against men, particularly baptized men. A few sorceries, a horse borrowed overnight, a stolen babe or woman, little else and not often. For they are shy of us now, but if they came to fear us too much they would send to the gods, under whose ward they are, a call that must be heeded. Worst, they might call together upon the new white god, and that would be the end of Faerie."

Valgard winced. And that night he went to Asgerd's shallow grave and dug her up and took her aboard a small trollboat. South-west he sailed on such a witch-wind as Illrede had taught him how to raise, until he came to a hamlet on the Moray Firth in Scotland.

Beneath snowclouds and darkness he bore the wrapped shape to the church. Into its graveyard he crept, and in an offside corner dug a hole, and laid her in it, and covered it so that none could see he had been there.

"Now you are sleeping in holy ground, sister, as you would have wished," he whispered. "Wickedness have I wrought, but now mayhap you will pray for my soul—" And looking bewildered about him in the murk, with a fear gripping him who had never been afraid before: "Why am I here? What am I doing? She is not my sister. I am a thing made by witchcraft. I have no soul—"

He growled and loped back to his boat and sailed north-eastward as if devils were on his track.

Now came the time of the troll hosting. Illrede was too shrewd to gather his forces in one spot where elf scouts could see how large they were. Each part of his fleet sailed from its own harbour, with a wizard or other skilled one aboard a flagship to see that all came to the agreed meeting place at the same time. This would be somewhat north of the English elflands, so that the trolls could land on empty beaches rather than against strongholds. Illrede meant to break the elf sea power at that spot, and afterward move south by water and land alike until he had overrun the island. He would then leave part of his force there to root out any elves who had not died or yielded, while his main fleet went across the channel to Alfheim's remaining provinces. Some of his army would meanwhile have marched overland from Finnmark, Wendland, and the troll homes east of these. Thus the trolls would attack the Erlking from west and east—and, as soon as England was wholly conquered, north—and smash him.

"Swift are the elf warriors," said Illrede, "but I think the trolls will move faster for once."

"Give me in charge of England," begged Valgard, "and I will see that no male elf outlives my earldom."

"I have promised that to Grum," said Illrede; "but you, Valgard, shall sail with me, and in England I will make you second to Grum only."

Valgard said he was well content with this. His cold eyes measured the lord Grum, and he thought to himself that the troll might easily suffer a misfortune—and that would make him, Valgard, earl as the witch had said.

He boarded the flagship with Illrede and the royal guard. A big vessel it was, with high sides and a dwarf-made iron beak for ramming, dead black save for the horse skull which was its figurehead. The trolls aboard had arms and armour of alloy, though most carried also the stone-headed war tools which had weight to suit them. Illrede wore a golden coronet on his black helmet and furs over the dragon-skin coat on which even steel did not bite. The others were likewise richly clad. They were a boisterous, overweening crew. Valgard alone wore naught of ornament, and his face was set in bleak lines; yet his iron axe and the iron he wore made him an object of fear to the trolls.

There were many more ships in the royal part of the fleet, most of uncommon size, and the night rang with shouts and horn-blasts and tramping feet. Troll vessels of full length moved slower than elf, being broader and heavier and made with less skill, and morning found them still at sea. The trolls took shelter beneath awnings which shut off the hated sunlight, and let the ships ride, invisible to mortal eyes not given witch-sight.

The next night found the whole fleet assembling. Valgard was awed. It seemed to carpet the waters out to the horizon, and every vessel swarmed with men save those which bore the huge shaggy troll horses. Nevertheless, so well were the captains drilled in Illrede's plans that each went straight to its proper place.

Various were the ships and crews that sailed against Alfheim. The long, high, black troll craft formed the centre, a blunt wedge with Illrede's at the point. To starboard and larboard were the goblins, some manning troll-built vessels and some in their own slim red snake-prowed ships; merrier than the trolls were they, clad in fantastical garb over their silvery armour, and wielding for the most part light swords and spears and bows. Then the wings of the fleet spread outlandish pinions: great pike-bearing Shen and katana-wielding Oni, in painted junks; lithe imps in slave-rowed galleys, with engines of war mounted on the decks; barges of the wings demons from Baikal; iron-plated dwarfs; monsters of hill, woodland, marsh, who used naught but tooth and claw. All these were officered by trolls, and only the most reliable were in the first line, which was also anchored by more troll craft at the ends. A second wedge came behind the first, and beyond this were reserves that would go wherever they might be needed.

Horns hooted from troll ships, to be answered by goblin pipes, Shen gongs, imp drums. Clouds smoked low around masts, and the sea churned white from oarblades. Will-o'-the-wisps crawled over yards and tackle, casting faces into blue highlights. Winds sighed overhead, and harrying presences rode through the moon-flecked, snow-sullen clouds.

"Soon we join battle," said Illrede to Valgard. "Then you may find the revenge you seek."

The berserker answered not, only stared ahead into the darkness.

XIV

For more than a month after the elf raid on Trollheim, Imric worked hard. He could find out little about the enemy, for Illrede and his warlocks had screened their lands heavily with magic, but he knew that a force was being gathered from many nations and likeliest would strike first at England. Hence he strove to assemble the ships and men of his realm, and sent abroad for what help there might be.

Few came from outside. Each province of Alfheim was readying itself alone; the elves were too haughty to work well in concert. Moreover, it seemed that well-nigh all the mercenaries in Faerie had been hired years before by Illrede. Imric sent to the Sidhe of Ireland, promising rich booty in the conquest of Trollheim, and got back the cold word that enough wealth already gleamed in the streets of Tir-nan-Og and the caves of the leprechauns. Thus the elf-earl found himself standing nearly alone.

Nonetheless his strength was great, and as it swelled night by night in the hosting of the elves the stern joy among them grew likewise. Never, they thought, had so mighty a force come together in Alfheim. Though doubtless outnumbered, it must be immeasurably better man for man and ship for ship; and it would be fighting near home, in waters and on beaches that its people knew. Some of the younger warriors held that not only could England's elves beat off the troll fleet, they could unaided carry the war to Trollheim and break its will to theirs.

From Orkney and Shetland came Flam, son of that Flam who had fallen in Skafloc's foray and wild to avenge his father. He and his brothers were among the foremost skippers in Faerie, and their dragon fleet darkened the water as it swept southward. Shields blinked along the wales and wind hummed in the lines and the hiss of cloven sea at the bows might well have come from those serpent heads.

Out of the grey hills and moors of Pictland marched the wild chieftains with their flint-headed weapons and their leather breastplates. Shorter and heavier than true elves were they, dark of skin, with long black locks and beards blowing around their tattooed faces, for there was likewise blood of troll and goblin and still older folk in them, as well as Pictish women stolen in long-gone days. With them came certain of the lesser Sidhe who had entered with the Scots centuries ago, strong gnarly leprechauns leaping goat-like, tall beautiful warriors striding in shimmery mail with spears held high or riding in rumbling war-chariots that had sword blades on the hubs for mowing of men.

From the south, the hills and cave-riddled shores of Cornwall and Wales, came some of the most ancient elves in the island: mail-clad horsemen and charioteers whose banners told of forgotten glories; green-haired, white-skinned sea folk, who kept a grey veil of salt-smelling fog about them for the sake of dampness on land; a few rustic half-gods whom the Romans had brought and afterwards abandoned; shy, flitting forest elves, clan by clan.

The lands of Angle and Saxon did not hold so many since most of the beings who once dwelt there had fled or been exorcised; but such as still remained heeded the call. Nor were these elves, poor and backward though they often were, to be scorned in war, for no few among them could trace descent to Wayland or to Odin himself. They were the master smiths of the earldom, having some dwarf blood, and many chose to fight with their great hammers.

But the mightiest and proudest were those who dwelt around Elfheugh. Not alone in ancestry, but in beauty and wisdom and wealth, the lords whom Imric had gathered about him outshone all others. Fiery they were, going to battle as gaily clad as to a wedding and kissing their spears like brides; skilled they were, casting terrible spells for the undoing of their foes and the warding of their friends. The newcome elves stood in awe of them, though not thereby hindered in enjoying the food and drink they sent out to the camps or the women who followed in search of sport.

Freda was much taken with watching that host gather. The sight of those unhuman warriors gliding noiselessly through dusk and night, their visages half hidden to her eyes and thus made the more eerie, sent waves of shock and delight, fear and pride, through her. By holding high rank among them, Skafloc, her man, wielded more power than any mortal king.

But his lordship was over the soulless. And she remembered the bear strength of the trolls. What if he should fall before them?

The same thought came to him. "Maybe I ought to take you to what friends you have in the lands of men," he said slowly. "It may be, though I do not believe it, that the elves will lose. True it is that every omen we took was not good.. And if that should happen, this would be no place for you."

"No—no—" She regarded him briefly with frightened grey eyes, then hid her face on his breast. "I will not leave you. I cannot."

He ruffled her shining hair. "I would come back for you later," he said.

"No. . . . It might happen that someone there, somehow, talked me over or forced me to stay—I know not who that could be, save perhaps a priest, but I have heard of such things—" She recalled the lovely elf women and their way of looking at Skafloc. He felt her stiffen in his arms. Her voice came firm: "Anyhow, I will not leave you. I stay."

He hugged her in gladness.

Now word came that the trolls were putting out to sea. On the last night before their own sailing, the elves held feast in Elfheugh.

Vast was Imric's drinking hall. Freda, sitting by Skafloc near the earl's high seat, could not make out the further walls or get more than a glimpse of the vine-carved rafters. The cool blue twilight loved of the elves seemed to drift like smoke through the hall, though the air itself was pure and smelled of flowers. Light came from countless tapers in heavy bronze sconces. whose flames burned silvery and unwavering. It flashed back off shields hung on the walls and panels of intricately etched gold. All of precious metals and studded with gems were the trenchers and bowls and cups on the snowy tablecloths. And though she had grown used to delicate eating in Elfheugh, Freda's head swam at the many kinds of meat, fowl, fish, fruits, spices, confections, the ales and meads and wines, that came forth this evening.

Richly clad were the elves. Skafloc wore a tunic of white silk over linen breeches, a doublet whose colourfully embroidered pattern led the eye in a trackless maze, a goldworked belt with a jewelled dagger in an electrum sheath, shoes of unicorn leather, and a short ermine-trimmed cape whose scarlet was like a rush of blood from his shoulders. Freda had on a filmy dress of spider silk, across which played colours in a rainbow ripple; a necklace of diamonds fell over her firm small breasts, a heavy golden girdle was locked about her waist, golden rings weighted her bare arms, and she was shod in velvet. Both of them wore gemmed coronets, as befitting a lord of Alfheim and his lady of the hour. The great elves were no less splendid, and even the poorer chieftains from elsewhere shone with raw gold.

There was music, not alone the eldritch melodies that Imric favoured, but the harping of the Sidhe and the piping of the west country folk. There was talk, the quick cruel brilliant discourse of the elves, subtle mockery and thrust and parry with words, and sweet laughter went up and down the tables.

But when these had been cleared away and the jesters should have skipped forth, the cry went for a sword dance instead. Imric scowled, not liking to make omens plain to all, but since most of his guests wanted it, he could not well refuse.

The elves moved out on to the floor, men stripping off their more cumbersome garments and women everything; and thralls fetched for each man a sword. "What are they doing?" asked Freda.

" 'Tis the old war-dance," Skafloc told her. "I must be skald to it, I suppose, because no human could tread it unscathed even if he knew in full the measures. They dance to ninety and nine verses which the skald must make up as he goes alone, and if no one is hurt 'tis a great omen for victory; but if someone be slain it means defeat and ruin, and even a slash bodes ill. I like this not."

Soon the elf men stood in a wide double row, facing each other and crossing swords on high; and behind every man stood a woman, crouched and taut. The rows reached far into the dimness of the hall, an aisle with a roof of gleaming blades. Skafloc stood before the earl's seat.

"Hai, go!" shouted Imric so that it rang.

Skafloc chanted:

> Swiftly goes the sword-play,
> sweeping foemen backward
> to the beach where tumult
> talks with voice of metal:
> belling of the brazen
> beaks of cleaving axes,
> smoking blood, where sea kings
> sing the mass of lances.

As he called it out, the men danced forward, and a din of clashing swords lifted in time to the stave. The women likewise danced lithely ahead, and each man's left hand seized a woman's right and whirled her into the narrowing aisle where the words flashed and clanged.

Skafloc called:

Swiftly goes the sword-play,
stormlike in its madness:
shields are bloody shimmers,
shining moons of redness;
winds of arrows wailing,
wicked spearhead-lightning
lads will smite who lately
lay by lovely sweethearts.

Through and between the whirring, flickering blades wove the elf women in a measure swift and supple and tangled as the foamstreaks on a wave. The men danced to each other, beyond, and wheeled about, and everyone threw his sword in a glittering arc to the one across from him, just missing a lithe white body, and caught the weapon thrown at him.

Quoth Skafloc:

Swiftly goes the sword-play!
Swinging bloodied weapons,
shields and helms to shatter,
shout the men their war-cry.
While the angry, whining,
whirring blades are sparking,
howl the wolves their hunger,
hawks stoop low for feasting.

Round and about, swifter than mortal eye could follow, whirled the dance; and leaping and shrieking between the women went the swords. Now blades hummed low, and as two clashed points above the floor, an elf lady sprang over them; the keen edges came up just behind her. Now the dancing men each seized a partner and wove a glitter of metal about her spinning body. Now they fenced again in the dance, and the women sprang and capered between the fencers in those bare instants when the weapons were drawn back.

Skafloc's verses spilled out unbroken:

> Swiftly goes the sword-play!
> Song of metal raises
> din of blades for dancing
> (death for eager partner).
> Lur horns bray their laughter,
> lads, and call to hosting.
> Sweeter game was sleeping
> softly with your leman.

Bounding and dodging between the clamorous glaives, a flying white frenzy, Leea called out: "Oho, Skafloc, why does not that girl of yours who makes such a thing of caring for you come dance with us for luck?"

Skafloc did not break the flow:

> Swiftly goes the sword-play.
> Skald who lately chanted
> gangs unto the gameboard.
> Grim are stakes we play for.
> Mock not at the mortal
> may who is not dancing.
> Better luck she brings me
> by a kiss than magic.

But then a shudder went through the elves; for Leea, harking more to the words of Skafloc than to their beat, had danced into one of the blades. Red was the slash across her silken shoulders. She went on in the measures, her blood sprinkling the folk about her. Skafloc forced cheer into his tones:

> Swiftly goes the sword-play.
> Some must lost the gamble.
> Norns alone are knowing
> now who throws the dice best.
> Winner of the wicked
> weapon-game we know not,
> but our foes will bitter
> battle find in Alfheim.

However, other women, shaken by Leea's misfortune, were missing the hairsplitting rhythm and being slashed.

Imric called a halt ere someone should be slain and bring the very worst luck, and the feast broke up in ill-contented silence or furtive whisperings.

Skafloc went troubled with Freda to their rooms. There he left her for a while. He came back with a broad silver-chased girdle. On its inside was fastened a flat vial, also of silver.

He gave it to Freda. "Let this be my parting gift to you," he said quietly. "I got it of Imric, but I would that you wore it. For though I still think we shall win, I am not so sure after that cursed sword dance."

She took it, wordlessly. Skafloc said: "In the vial is a rare and potent drug. Should bad luck befall you and foes come nigh, drink it. You will be as one dead for several days, and belike any who see you will not think to do more than leave you or cast you outside; such is the way of trolls with a stranger's corpse. When you awaken you may have a chance to slip free."

"What use escaping, if you are dead?" asked Freda sorrowfully. "Better I should die too."

"Maybe. But the trolls would not kill you at once, and you Christians are forbidden self-slaughter, are you not?" Skafloc smiled wearily. " 'Tis not the most cheerful of farewell gifts, dearest one, but 'tis the best I have."

"No," she breathed. "I will take it, and thank you. But we have a better gift, one we can give to each other."

"Aye, so," he cried, and before long, both of them were again, for a while, merry.

XV

The elf and troll fleets met off the coast, well north of the earl's seat, shortly after dark of the next night. When Imric, standing by Skafloc in the prow of the flagship that led his wedge of vessels, saw the size of the enemy force, he drew a sharp, uneven breath.

"We English elves have most of the warcraft of Alfheim," he said, "yet they yonder have more than twice as much. Oh, if the other lords had but heeded me, when I told them Illrede had made truce only as another means of making war, and begged them to join me in crushing him for good!"

Skafloc knew somewhat of the rivalry and vanity, as well as the slothfulness and wishfulness, which had caused that inaction. Imric was not altogether without blame. However, too late now for such talk. "They cannot all be trolls," the human said, "and I look for small danger from goblins and trash like that."

"Mock not the goblins. They are good warriors when they have the weapons they need." Imric's taut countenance gleamed briefly out of darkness, caught in a fleeting moonbeam. A few snowflakes danced in that ray, borne on a raw wind. "Magic will avail either side little," he went on, "since the powers of both are in that regard more or less the same. Thus it turns on strength of hosts, and there we are weaker."

He shook his silvery-locked head, eyes glittering moon-blue. "I held, at the Erlking's last council, that it were best Alfheim drew together, letting the trolls have the outer provinces, even England, while we held fast and gathered ourselves for a counter-attack. But the other lords would have none of it. Now we shall see whose rede was best."

"Theirs was, lord," said Firespear boldly, "for we are going to butcher these swine. What—let them wallow in Elfheugh? The thought was unworthy of you." He hefted his pike and strained eagerly ahead.

Skafloc too, though he felt these were heavy odds, would have naught but battle. This would not be the first time valiant men had wrested victory from a powerful foe. He blazed with the wish to meet Valgard, Freda's mad brother who had wrought her so great ill, and cleave his brain.

And yet, thought Skafloc, if Valgard had not borne Freda off to Trollheim, he, Skafloc, would never have met her. So he owed the berserker something—a quick clean slaying, rather than a carving of the blood eagle on his back, ought to settle the debt .

War-horns blew their summons on both sides. Down came sails and masts, and the fleets rowed to battle with ships linked together by ropes. As they neared, the arrows began their flight, a moon-darkening storm that hissed over waves and struck home in wood or flesh. Three shafts rattled off Skafloc's mail; a fourth narrowly missed his arm and quivered in the ship's figurehead. With his night-seeing eyes he made out others aboard who were not so lucky, who sank wounded or slain under Trollheim's hail.

The moon showed ever less often through the hasty clouds, but will-o'-the-wisps danced amidst the spindrift and the waves surged with cold white glow. There was light enough to kill by.

Next spears, darts, and flung stones crossed between the ships. Skafloc cast a shaft which pinned a right hand to the mast of the troll flagship. Back came a rock which bounced with a clang off his helmet. He leaned on the rail, briefly dizzy, and the sea slapped salt water over his ringing head.

The horns yelled, almost mouth into mouth, and the lines shocked together.

Imric's ship pushed against Illrede's. The warriors in the bows smote back and forth. Skafloc's sword screamed past the axe of a troll and disabled an arm. He leaned into the line of shields at the enemy rail, his own moving just enough to catch the numbing thunder of blows, his steel blade working above its rim. On his left, Firespear thrust and hacked with his pike, yelling in battle madness, reckless of the shafts that reached for him. On his right, Angor of Pictland fought stolidly with his long axe. For a time the two sides traded blows, and whenever a man dropped from either line, another pressed into his place.

Then Skafloc buried his sword in the neck of a troll. As that one fell, Firespear jabbed into the breast of the one behind him. Skafloc leaped the rails, into that breach in the troll ranks, and cut down the man to his left. As the warrior to his right chopped at him, Angor's axe came down and the troll's head rolled into the sea.

"Forward!" roared Skafloc. The nearer elves swarmed after him. They stood back to back, hewing—hewing—at the trolls who snarled and grunted around them. And in this uproar, the other elves grappled fast and still more of them boarded the enemy.

Swords flew in a blur that spouted blood. The shock and crash of metal over-rode wind and sea. Above the struggle loomed Skafloc, eyes like blue hell-flames. He must needs stand a little ahead of the elves, lest his iron mail do them harm; but they covered his back, and meanwhile his shield stopped the trolls' clumsy thrusts and swipes from in front, his sword darted in and out like a viper. Erelong the enemy fell back from him and the bows were cleared.

"Now aft!" he yelled.

The elves advanced with blades over shields like heat-flicker over a mountain wall. Stubbornly did the trolls fight. Elves sank with crushed skulls, fell behind with splintered bones and gaping cuts. Nonetheless the trolls went back and back, none holding fast save their trampled dead.

"Valgard!" bawled Skafloc into the din. "Valgard, where are you?"

The changeling stood forth. Blood streamed from his temple. "A slingstone knocked me out," he said, "but now I am yare for battle."

Skafloc shouted and ran to meet him. A space had opened between the crews. The elves held the ship down to the mast partner, the trolls had crowded into the stern, and both sides were for the time being out of breath. But more elves kept boarding, and from their vessel, archers sent a steady rain of grey-feathered death.

Skafloc's sword and Valgard's axe met in a howl of steel and a shower of sparks. The madness did not come on the berserker; he fought with grim coolness, rock-steady on the rolling deck. Skafloc's sword caught his axe haft, but did not go far into the tough leather-wrapped wood. Instead, it was pushed aside. So was the shield behind—an opening through which Valgard chopped at once.

Lacking room or time for a full swing, his blow did not break mail-rings or bones. But Skafloc's shield-arm fell numbed to his side. Valgard hewed at the neck. Skafloc dropped to one knee, taking that dreadful smash on the helmet while he did. At the same time, he had been cutting at Valgard's leg.

Half senseless from the fury that dented his helmet and knocked him aside, he sank. Valgard stumbled with a ripped thigh. They rolled under the benches and the battle raged past them.

For Grum Troll-Earl had led a charge back from the stern. His huge stone-headed club crushed skulls right and left. Against him went Angor of Pictland, who struck out and hewed off the troll's right arm. Grum caught his falling club in his left hand and swung a blow that broke Angor's neck; but then the troll must crawl to shelter so that he might carve healing runes for his spouting wound.

Skafloc and Valgard came out again, found each other in the chaos, and took up their fight anew. Skafloc's left arm had gotten back its usefulness, while Valgard was still bleeding. Imric's fosterling smote with a force that bit through the berserker's mail, to be stopped by a rib. "That for Freda!" he shouted. "I'll have you done to her."

"Not so ill as I think you have," choked Valgard. Staggering and weakened, nonetheless he met Skafloc's next cut with his axe in midair. And the sword sprang in twain.

"Ha!" cried the berserker; but ere he could follow up his chance Firespear was at him like an angry cat, and others of Alfheim besides. The elves held the ship.

"You leave me no reason to stay here," said Valgard, "though I hope to see you again, brotherling." And he sprang overboard.

He had meant to get free of his byrnie before it dragged him too far under, but there was no need. Many ships had been wrecked by ramming or the sheer press of battle. The mast of one was floating by and he caught it with his left hand. His right still held the axe Brotherslayer and for a little he wondered if he should not let it go.

But no—accursed or not, it was a good weapon.

Others, who had had a moment to lighten their loads before fleeing the ship, also clung to the mast. "Kick out, brothers," shouted Valgard, "and we will reach a keel of our own—and win this battle yet."

Aboard the troll flagship, the elves yelled their glee. Skafloc asked: "Where is Illrede? He should have been aboard, yet I saw him not."

"Belike he is flying about, overseeing his fleet, even as Imric is doing in the form of a sea-mew," Firespear answered. "Let's chop a hole in this damned hulk and be back to the other."

There they found Imric waiting for them. "How goes the battle, foster father?" called Skafloc gaily.

The elf-earl's voice fell bleak on his ears: "Badly goes it, for however well the elves fight, the trolls throw two to one against them. And parts of the enemy are landing unopposed."

"Bad news in truth," cried Golric of Cornwall, "and we must fight like very demons or we are lost."

"I fear we are lost already," said Imric.

Skafloc could not at once grasp this. Looking around, he saw that the flagship drifted alone. Both fleets were breaking asunder as the linking ropes were cut by foemen; but the troll craft suffered less of this. And too often the trolls were laying one vessel on either side of an elf hull.

"To oars!" shouted Skafloc. "They need help. To oars!"

"Well spoke," fleered Imric.

The longship moved to the closest knot of battle. Arrows fell on it.

"Shoot back!" cried Skafloc. "In the name of hell, why don't you shoot back?"

"Our quivers are nigh empty, lord," said an elf.

Hunching low behind their shields, the elves rowed into the fight. Two of their fellow ships were at bay between three hireling craft and one troll dragon. As Imric's vessel neared, the bat-winged demons of Baikal descended on her.

The elves hewed manfully, but it was hard to fight enemies that struck from above with lances. They spent their last arrows, and still the swooping death smote.

Nonetheless they laid alongside a goblin ship, and it was from here that the arrows had come. Skafloc sprang across the rails and struck out with the elf sword he now carried. These small folk could not withstand close combat. One he chopped in two, a second he sent screaming with belly gashed open, the head of a third went bouncing from its shoulders. Firespear's pike transfixed two while he kicked in the breastbone of another. More elves boarded. The goblins fell back.

Skafloc reached their arrow chests and threw the heavy boxes across to his ship. Rather than lead a butchery into the stern, he blew retreat; the goblins here made no further difference to anyone but themselves. Elf bows twanged anew and the hovering demons toppled out of the sky.

The trolls closed in. Skafloc saw that the other two elf ships were rallying against the goblins. Oni, and imps. "If they can handle those, I suppose we can take care of the trolls," he said.

The green-skinned warriors grappled, boomed their cry, and came over the rail of the elf dragon. Skafloc ran to meet them, slipped on the bloody catwalk, and fell between the benches. A spear whizzed where his breast had been, with force to pierce ring-mail. Golric of Cornwall toppled, the point in his heart.

"Thanks," muttered Skafloc, rising. The trolls were on him. From above, their blows hailed on his shield and helm. He slashed at ankles, and a foeman went down. Before he could get his sword back into play, another troll was stooping over, thrusting for his face. He shoved up his iron-plated shield. The troll screamed and staggered back, endlessly screaming, half his own face seared away. Skafloc got back on to the catwalk and rejoined his elves.

Shock and thunder of blows sounded through ever more thickly drifting snow. The wind rose too, making the linked ships roll and pitch and bang hull against hull. Fighters lurched, fell off upper decks, catwalks, and benches, on to the lower deck, and rose to fight on. Erelong Skafloc's shield was beaten into uselessness. He cast it at the troll with whom he was trading blows, and thrust his edge-blunted sword into the heart.

Then he was seized from behind. He pushed his steel helmet backward. Naught happened save that the oak-branch arms tightened their grip. Twisting his head around, he saw that this troll was fully clad in leather, with hood and gloves. Skafloc used an elven wrestling break to get free, snapping his arms out between thumb and forefinger of the foeman. But at once he was caught in a bear hug. The ship rocked and cast them both down between the benches.

Skafloc could not squirm loose. He knew grimly that the creature could break his ribs like arrow shafts. He got his knees against the troll's belly, his hands around the thick throat, and braced himself.

Belike no other mortal man could have held his back arched against that frightful drag. Skafloc felt the strength drain from him like wine from an overturned cup. He poured all muscle and will and heart into his back and legs, and into the hands he clamped on the troll's windpipe. It seemed for ever that they rolled with the ship, and he knew he could not hold out much longer.

Then the troll let go and clawed at Skafloc's wrists, wild for air. The man rammed his enemy's head against the mast partner, once, twice, thrice, with a fury that sang in the wood and split the leather-clad skull.

Skafloc lay over the body, gasping, his heart nigh to bursting loose from his breast and a roar of blood in his ears. After a while he dimly saw Firespear bent over him and heard the guardsman's awed voice:

"Not elf nor human was yet known to have slain a troll in barehanded combat. Your deed is worthy of a Beowulf and will be unforgotten while the world stands. And now we have won."

He helped Skafloc up to the foredeck. Looking over the nearby waters, through the wind-slanted snowfall, the man saw that the outland mercenary ships had likewise been cleared.

But at what a cost—Not a score of elves on their three craft remained whole; most who lived were grievously hurt. The ships drifted shoreward, manned with corpses and a few warriors too weary to lift a sword.

And straining through the murk, Skafloc saw yet another

troll longship, fully crewed, bearing down on them.

"I fear we have lost," he groaned. "Naught is left but to save what we can."

The ships rolled helplessly toward tumbling surf. And on the strand waited a line of trolls, mounted on their great black horses.

A sea-mew dived out of the snow, shook himself and was Imric. "We have done well," said the elf-earl grimly. "Nigh half the troll fleet will not sail again. But that half is mostly their allies, and we—we are broken. Such of our craft as can still be worked are in full flight, while others like this await their doom." Sudden tears, perhaps the first in centuries, glimmered in his chill blank eyes. "England is lost. I fear me Alfheim is lost."

Firespear gripped the shaft of his pike. "We will go out fighting," he vowed; his voice was hollow with tiredness.

Skafloc shook his head, and as he thought of Freda waiting in Elfheugh a little strength flowed back into him. "We will go *on* fighting," he said. "First, though, we must save our lives."

" 'Tis a good trick if you can do it," said Firespear doubtfully.

Skafloc doffed his helmet. The locks beneath were matted with sweat. "We begin by taking off our armour," he said.

The elves could barely row enough to bring their three ships together within boathook reach. They gathered in one of these and raised mast and sail. Still their chances looked poor, for the approaching trolls were downwind, and both craft were quite near the lee shore.

Skafloc fought the steering oar, some of his folk poled out the sail, and they went quartering landward. The trolls dug in oars, seeking either to catch the elf vessel or drive it on to a skerry up ahead.

" 'Twill be a tight squeeze," said Imric.

"Tighter than they think!" Skafloc grinned without mirth and squinted through the driving snowflakes. He saw surf spume on the reef, heard it roar through the squealing of wind. Beyond were the shallows.

The trolls cut over the starboard quarter. Skafloc shouted a command to let the sail go, and put up his helm. The ship swung around and leaped before the wind. Too late, the trolls saw what he meant and tried to get out of the way. Skafloc rammed them amidships with a shock at which timbers groaned. The enemy vessel was pushed ahead of it, into the surf, on to the skerry—trapped and smashed!

Skafloc's elves worked the sail like madmen to his orders. Troll oars snapped as they slid past the other hull. The man had no hope of saving his own craft, but by using the foe's both as fender and as pivot, he could hit more easily, and at the far end of the reef where the sea was less angry. When his ship struck and hung fast, only a narrow spine of rock lay between it and the shallows.

"Save himself who can!" cried Skafloc. He leaped out on to the slippery stone and over into a neck-deep water. Seal-swift he darted for the beach. His comrades were with him, except those too badly hurt to move. They must stay in the breaking hull and drown in sight of land.

The rest waded ashore, and they were well past the troll line. Some of the riders saw them and galloped off to kill.

"Scatter!" shouted Skafloc. "Most can escape!"

Running into the snowstorm, he saw elves spitted on lances or trampled under hoofs. But the bulk of his little band were getting away. High swung the sea-mew.

And down on the bird stooped a mighty erne. Skafloc groaned. Crouched behind a rock, he saw the erne bear the mew to earth, and there they became Illrede and Imric.

Troll clubs thudded on to the elf-earl. He lay limp in a pool of his blood while they bound him.

If Imric was dead, Alfheim had lost one of its best leaders. If he lived—woe for him! Skafloc slithered off through the snow-covered ling. He scarcely felt weariness, or cold, or his stiffening wounds. The elves were beaten, and now he had but one goal: to reach Elfheugh and Freda ahead of the trolls.

XVI

Illrede's folk took sun-shelter and rested through a couple of days, for the struggle had worn them down too. Thereafter they set south, half by land and half by sea. The ships reached Elfheugh harbour the same night. Their crews went ashore, plundered what buildings they found in the open, and waited around the castle for their fellows.

The land troops, with Grum and Valgard at the head, went more slowly. Horsemen scoured the countryside, and whatever small bands of elf warriors sought to fight were slain—not without loss to the trolls. Outlying garths were looted and burned, their folk chained into long lines that stumbled neck linked to neck and wrists lashed together, with Imric in the lead. The trolls made merry with food and drink and women of Alfheim, and did not unduly hasten to reach Elfheugh.

But by their arts, or by the mere lack of word from their men, the castle dwellers knew at dawn of the battle night that Imric had lost. Later, looking down from their high parapets to the campfires that ringed them in, to the black ships drawn up on the strand or riding at anchor in the bay, they knew it had been no double loss but a clear victory for the invaders.

As Freda stood thus staring out of a window in her bed-chamber, she heard the faintest rustle of silken garments. She turned and saw Leea behind her. In the elf woman's hand gleamed a knife.

Pain and malice were on Leea's face, making it no longer the face of an idol carved in ivory by an ancient southland master. She said in human speech: "You weep dry tears for one whose love is raven food."

"I will weep when I know he is dead," answered Freda tonelessly. "But there was too much life in him for me to believe that he is now lying stark."

"Where then might he be, and what use is a skulking outcast?" Leea's pale full lips curved upward. "See you this dagger, Freda? The trolls are camped around Elfheugh, and your law forbids you to take your own life. But if you wish escape, I will gladly give you it."

"No. I will wait for Skafloc," said Freda. "And have we not spears and arrows and engines of war? Is there not ample meat and drink, and are the walls not high and the gates strong? Let such as had to remain in the castle hold it for those who went forth."

Leea's knife sank. She looked long at the slim grey-eyed girl. "Good is your spirit," she said at last, "and methinks I begin to see what Skafloc found in you. However, your rede is a mortal's—foolish and impatient. Can women hold a fort against storm when their men are fallen?"

"They can try—or fall like their men."

"Not so. They have other weapons." A cruel mirth flickered across Leea's countenance. "Women's weapons; but to use them we must open the gates. Would you avenge your lover?"

"Aye—with arrow and dagger, and poison if need be!"

"Then give the trolls your kisses: swift as arrows, sharp as knives, bitter and deadly as poison in the cup. Such is the way of the elf women."

"Sooner would I break the great law of Him above and be my own murderer than whore of my man's slayers!" flared the girl.

"Mortal chatter," scoffed Leea. She smiled her cat-smile. "I will find the caresses of trolls interesting, for a time. They are something new, at least, and hard it is to find anything fresh after many centuries. We open the gates of Elfheugh when our new earl arrives."

Freda sank on to the bed and buried her face in her hands. Leea said: "If you wish to follow out your human brainlessness, I will be quite glad to get rid of you. Tomorrow after daybreak, when the trolls sleep, I will let you from the castle with whatever you want to take. Thereafter you can do as you please—flee to lands of men, I suppose, and join your voice to the shrill whine of nuns whose Heavenly groom somehow never comes for them. I wish you joy of that!"

She departed.

For a time Freda lay on the bed, with darkness and hopelessness whelming her. Weep could she not, and the tears lay harsh in her throat. All was gone indeed, her kindred, her love—

No!

She sat up and clenched her fists. Skafloc was not dead. She would not believe that until she had kissed his bloodless lips—after which, if God was merciful, her heart would break and she would fall beside him. But if he lived . . . if he lay sorely wounded, mayhap, with foes ringing his lair and the need of her heavy on him—

She hastened to gather what she thought would be useful. Helm and byrnie of his, and the clothes that went therewith (unfilled by him, they seemed strangely empty, more so than any other man's dress laid aside), axe and sword and shield, spear and bows and many arrows. For herself she took also a light byrnie such as shield-mays among the elves were wont to use. It fitted well her slender form, and she could not but smile at the mirror as she set coif and gold-winged helmet over her ruddy locks. He liked to see her in that kind of dress, less boyish than playful.

The gear must needs be of elf metal, since the Faerie horses would not bear iron, but she supposed he could make good use of it.

Stockfish and other rations she added to her pile of goods, and furs and blankets and sewing kit and whatever else might be helpful. "I am becoming a housewife!" she said smiling again. The homely word gladdened her, like the sight of an old friend. Next she took certain things whose use she did not know but which Skafloc had set much store by: skins of wolf and otter and eagle, rune-carved wands of ash and beechwood, a strangely wrought ring.

When it was all packed together, she sought out Leea. The elf woman looked in astonishment at the Valkyrie figure before her. "What will you now?" she asked.

"I want four horses," answered Freda, "and help to load one of them with what I am taking. Then let me out of here."

" 'Tis still night, with trolls awake and prowling about. And elf horses cannot fare by day."

"No matter. They go more swiftly than any others, and speed is what I wish above aught else."

"Aye, you can reach a church ere dawn if you get past the foe," gibed Leea, "and the arms you bear may give you some protection along the way. But you cannot hope to keep Faerie gold long."

"I have no gold to speak of, nor do I go to any lands of men. It is the north gate I want you to open for me."

Leea's eyes widened, until she shrugged. " 'Tis foolishness. What good is Skafloc's clay? However, let it be as you will." Her mouth softened and she said, low, not altogether steadily: "Kiss him once for Leea, I pray you."

Freda said naught, but she knew that alive or dead Skafloc would not get that kiss.

The snow was flying thick when she left. Noiselessly the gate swung ajar, and the goblin guards, who had been promised freedom for their service, waved farewell. Freda rode out with her string of horses. She did not look back. Without Skafloc, Elfheugh's splendours were ash.

The wind whined around her and bit through layers of fur. She leaned down and whispered in her horse's ear: "Now quickly, quickly, best of steeds, quickly gallop! Swiftly north to Skafloc! Find him with your immortal wit and senses, and you shall sleep in golden stables and walk unsaddled through summer meadows for all your centuries."

There came a booming shout. Freda jerked erect in her seat. Terror poured through her. Nothing was more dreadful to her than the trolls, and they had seen——"Oh, swiftly, my horse!"

The wind of her gallop screamed about her, nigh ripping her from the saddle, forcing her to shield her eyes with an upraised arm. She could hardly see through the night and snow, even with her witch-sight, but she heard the roar of hoofs behind her.

Faster and faster, north, ever north, while the air hooted and bit, the pursuers yelped and the hoofbeats rolled. When she glanced back, she saw the trolls as a deeper shadow racing through the night. Could she but halt and command them home in the name of Jesus! But their earshot was less than their arrowshot.

The snow whirled thicker. Presently the trolls fell behind, though she knew they would track unwearyingly. And as she fled north she came nearer the south-ward-marching army of Trollheim.

Time brawled past like the wind. She caught a far-off glimpse of fire on a hilltop—belike some burning elf garth. The troops must be close, and they would have scouts widely across the land.

As if to answer her thought, a howl rose out of the murk to her right. She heard hoofs clatter. If they cut her off——

Athwart her path loomed a monstrous shape, a giant shaggy horse blacker than night with eyes like glowing coals, and on it a rider in black ring-mail, huge of thew and hideous of face—a troll! The elf horse veered aside, not fast enough. He reached out and caught the bridle and pulled the steed to a halt.

Freda screamed. Before she could cry on holiness, he had yanked her from the saddle, clutched her to him with one arm and clapped the other hand over her mouth. It was cold and smelled like a pit of snakes.

"Ho, ho, ho!" shouted the troll.

Out of the night, called through the windy dark by her far-sensed need, still gasping with the long run and the fear of coming too late, Skafloc sprang. One foot he set in the troll's stirrup, lifted himself up and drove dagger into throat.

And he caught Freda in his arms.

XVII

When the troll host reached Elfheugh, a horn sounded

from the watchtowers and the great brazen gates swung wide. Valgard reined in, narrowing his eyes. "A trick," he muttered.

"No, I think not," said Grum. "Few save women are left in the castle, and they expect us to spare them." He shook with laughter. "As we will! As we will!"

The hoofs of the huge-boned horses rang loud on the courtyard flagstones. Here it was warm and calm, in a cool half-light that rested blue on walls and sky-piercing turrets. Gardens breathed forth languorous odours; fountains splashed, and clear streamlets ran past little arbours meant for two alone.

The women of Elfheugh were gathered before the keep to meet the conquerors. Though he had seen elf-mays on the march south, and taken them, Valgard exclaimed under his breath at sight of these.

One stepped forth, thin robes clinging to every curve, and she outshone the rest as the moon the stars. She curtsied low before Grum, so that the cool mystery of her eyes was veiled by sweeping lashes. "Greeting, lord," she sang rather than spoke. "Elfheugh makes submission."

The earl puffed himself out. "Long has this castle stood," he said, "and no few assaults has it beaten off. Yet you were wisest, who chose to admit the might of Trollheim. Terrible are we to our foes, while our friends have good gifts of us." He smirked. "Erelong I will make you a gift. What is your name?"

"I hight Leea, lord, sister to Imric Elf-Earl."

"Call him not that, for now I, Grum, am earl in this island's Faerie realm, and Imric the least of my thralls. Bring in the prisoners!"

Slowly, heads bent and feet shuffling, the nobles of Alfheim were led forward. Bitter were their begrimed faces, and their shoulders were bowed by a weight more heavy than chains. Imric, hair stiff with his own crusted blood and blood in the prints of his bare feet, led the line. Naught did the elves say, nor even look at their women, as they were led down towards the dungeons. The commoner captives followed, a mile of misery.

Illrede arrived from the ships. "Elfheugh is ours," he said, "and we leave you, Grum, to hold it while we lay the rest of Alfheim under us. There are still English, Scottish, Welsh elfholds to be taken, and many elves skulking in the hills and woods, so you will have work enough."

He led the way into the keep. "We have a thing to do ere leaving," he said. "Imric took our daughter Gora, nine hundred years ago. Let her be brought forth to freedom."

As the king's men followed him, Leea plucked at Valgard's sleeve to draw him aside. Her gaze was intent. "I took you for Skafloc at first, a mortal who dwelt among us," she breathed. "Yet I can sense you are not human—"

"No." His lips twisted upward. "I am Valgard Berserk of Trollheim. In a way, though, Skafloc and I are brothers. For I am a changeling, born of the troll-woman Gora by Imric, and left in place of the baby who became Skafloc."

"Then—" Leea's fingers tightened on his arm. Her words hissed. "So you are the Valgard of whom Freda spoke? Her brother?"

"That one." His voice roughened. "Where is she?" He shook her. "And where is Skafloc?"

"I . . . do not know. . . . Freda has fled the castle, she said she was going to seek him. . . ."

"Then if she was not caught on the way, and I have heard nothing of such, she is with him. Ill is that!"

Leea smiled, with closed lips and hooded eyes. "At last I see what Tyr of the Æsir meant," she whispered to herself, "and why Imric kept the secret—" And to Valgard, boldly: "Why think you that is bad? You have slain all the seed of Orm but those two, and have been the means of bringing what is worse upon them. If you hated that house, as you must have done, what better revenge could you want?"

Valgard shook his head. "I had naught against Orm or his house," he muttered. And looking about him in sudden bewilderment, as if waking from an uneasy dream: "Though I must have hated them to have worked so much harm—on my own siblings—" He passed a hand over his eyes. "No, they are not my blood, are they . . . were they?"

He broke away from her and hastened after the king. Leea followed more slowly, still smiling.

Illrede sat in Imric's high seat. His gaze was fixed on the inner door, and he chuckled softly when he heard the tramp of his guardsmen. "They are bringing Gora," he murmured. "My little girl, who once laughed and played about my knees." He put a heavy hand on the changeling's shoulder. "Your mother, Valgard."

She shambled into the hall, gaunt, wrinkled, bent over from the centuries of crouching in darkness. Out of her skull-face the eyes stared, empty save where ghosts swam deep within them.

"Gora—" Illrede half rose and sank back again.

She blinked around, almost blind. "Who calls for Gora?" she mumbled. "Who calls for Gora calls for the dead. Gora is dead, lord, she died nine hundred years ago. They buried her under a castle; her white bones uphold its towers against the stars. Can you not let the poor dead troll-woman rest?"

Valgard shrank from her, lifting a hand as if to ward off the thing that stumbled over the floor towards him. Illrede reached out both arms. "Gora!" he cried. "Gora, know you not me, your father? Know you not your son?"

Her voice came windy and remote through the hall. "How can the dead know anyone? How can the dead give birth? The brain which gave birth to dreams is become the womb of maggots. Ants crawl within the hollowness where aforetime a heart beat. Oh, give me back my chain! Give me back the lover who held me down in the dark!" She whimpered. "Raise not the poor frightened dead, lord, and wake not the mad, for life and reason are monsters which live by devouring that which gives them birth."

She cocked her head, listening. "I hear hoofbeats," she said low. "I hear hoofs galloping out on the edge of the world. It is Time riding forth, and snow falls from his horse's mane and lightning crashes from its hoofs, and when Time has ridden by like a wind in the night there are only withered leaves left, blowing in the gale of his passage. He rides nearer, I hear worlds sunder before him—Give me back my death!" she shrieked. "Let me crawl back into my grave and hide from Time!"

She huddled sobbing on the floor. Illrede signed to his guards. "Take her out and kill her," he ordered. Turning to Grum: "Hang Imric by the thumbs over hot coals until we have conquered Alfheim and can give some thought to his reward." Rising, he shouted: "Ho, trollsmen, make ready to fare! We sail at once!"

Though the host had awaited a feast in Elfheugh, none who saw the king's face dared protest, and erelong most of the black ships were sweeping southward out of sight.

"So much the more for us," laughed Grum. He regarded how pale Valgard was and added: "Methinks you would do well to drink deep tonight."

"So I will," answered the berserker, "and ride to battle as soon as I can ready a host."

Now the troll chiefs gathered the women of the castle and took whom they wanted before turning the rest over to the men. Grum laid his remaining hand on Leea's waist. "You were wise to submit," he grinned; "therefore I cannot well let you fall in rank. Earl's lady shall you still be."

She followed him meekly, but as she went by Valgard she smiled sidelong at the changeling. The berserker's gaze could not but follow her. Never had he seen a woman like this; aye, with her he might forget the dark-haired witch who haunted his dreams.

The trolls gorged and guzzled for some days, then Valgard led men against another castle which held out yet, for a number of elves had managed to reach it. Though its size was not great, the walls were high and massive, and the defenders' arrows kept the trolls a good ways off.

Valgard waited through daylight. Near sunset he sneaked under cover of brush and rocky outcrop until he was almost under the walls without the drowsy light-bedazzled elves seeing him. At dusk the horns blew to battle and the trolls rushed forth. Valgard rose and with a mighty cast sent a grappling hook over a merlon. Up the rope tied to it he swarmed, to the very top, and winded his horn.

The elf sentries charged at him. Despite the iron he wore he had a desperate fight. But the trolls quickly found the rope and followed him. When they had cleared a space, others beneath could set up ladders. Soon the force was large enough to hew its way to the gates and open them for the rest.

There followed a wholesale slaughter of elves. More were taken captive and led in chains back to Elfheugh. Valgard plundered and burned through the countryside around, and returned with a huge booty.

Grum gave him sullen greeting, for he thought Valgard was getting too good a name among the trolls. "You could have stayed with the garrison you left," he said. "This place has scant room for both of us."

"Indeed," murmured Valgard, measuring the earl with his chill pale eyes.

However, Grum could do no less than hold feast for him and place him at the right of the high seat. The elf women served the trolls, and Leea came to Valgard with horn after horn of strong wine.

"To our hero, chief among warriors in lands of men or

Faerie," she drank. The silver light gleamed through her thin silks to her skin, and Valgard's head spun with more than the drink .

"You can give me better thanks than that," he cried, and pulled her on to his lap. Fiercely he kissed her, and she responded with the same eagerness.

Grum, who had slumped in his seat and drained his horns without a word, stirred in anger. "Back to your work, faithless bitch!" he snarled, and to Valgard: "Leave my woman be. You have your own."

"But I like this one better," said Valgard. "I will give you three others for her."

"Ha, I can take your three if I like—I, your earl. What I choose is mine. Leave her be."

"The loot should go to him who can best use it," taunted Leea, not moving from Valgard's lap. "And you have only one hand."

The troll sprang from his seat, blind with rage and clawing after his sword; for trolls ate with weapons on. "Help me!" cried Leea.

Valgard's axe seemed to leap of itself into his grasp. Ere Grum, awkward with his left hand, could draw blade, the changeling's weapon sank into his neck.

He fell at Valgard's feet with blood spurting and looked up into the twisted white face. "You are an evil man," said Grum, "but she is worse." And he died.

Uproar arose in the hall, metal flashed forth and the trolls surged against the high seat. Some cried for Valgard's death, others swore they would defend him. For a moment it was about to become a battle.

Then Valgard snatched the blood-smeared coronet, which had been Imric's, from Grum's head and set it on his own. He sprang on to the high seat and overrode the din with his shout for silence.

Slowly that stillness came, until naught but heavy breathing was heard. The bared weapons gleamed, the smell of fear was rank, and every eye rested on Valgard where he stood haughty in his strength.

He spoke, with iron in his tones: "This came somewhat sooner than I looked for, but it was bound to come. For what use to Trollheim was a cripple like Grum, unfit for battle, for anything save gobbling and bousing and sleeping with women that might have gone to better men? I, who come of blood as good as any in Trollheim, and who have shown I can win victory, am more fit to be your earl. Furthermore, I *am* now earl, by the will of my father King Illrede. Good will this be for all trolls, foremost those of England. I promise you victory, riches, high living and glory, if you hail me your earl."

He pulled the axe out of Grum and lifted it. "Whoever gainsays my right must do it on my body—now," he told them. "Whoever stands true will be repaid a thousandfold."

At this, the men who had followed him to the siege let forth a cheer. Others, who wished not to fight, joined them one by one, so it ended with Valgard's taking the high seat and the feast going on. Grum had not been very well liked, and what few kinfolk he had there were not close and were willing to take weregild.

Later, alone in his bedchamber with Leea, the changeling sat staring darkly at her. "This is the second time a woman has driven me to murder," he said. "Were I wise, I would chop your body in three."

"I cannot stop you, lord," she purred, and laid her white arms about his neck.

"You know I cannot do it," he said hoarsely. " 'Tis idle talk. My life is black enough without such peace as I can find in you."

Still later he asked her: "Were you thus with the elves—with Skafloc?"

She lifted her head over his so that the sweet-scented net of her hair covered both. "Let it suffice that I am thus with you, lord," she whispered, and kissed him.

Now Valgard ruled Elfheugh for some time. Through the early winter he was often afield, breaking down elf strongholds and hunting the fugitives with hounds and men. Few garths remained unburnt, and when elves sought to make a stand he led his troops roaring over them. Some of those men whom he took alive he threw into dungeons or put to slave work, but most he killed, and he divided their women among his trolls. He himself took none, having lust for none but Leea.

Word came from the south that Illrede's armies were driving the elves there before them. All Faerie parts of Valland and Flanders were held by the trolls. In the north, only the elves of Scania still were free; and they were hemmed in, and were being gnawed away as fast as their deep woodlands allowed. Erelong the trolls would be entering the middle lands where the Erlking lay.

Men had some glimpse of these doings—distant fires, galloping shadows, storm-winds bearing a brazen clangor. And the loosed magic wrought much havoc, murrains on the livestock and spoilt grain and bad luck in families. Sometimes a hunter would come on a trampled, bloody field and half-see ravens tearing at corpses which had not the look of men. Folk huddled in lonely houses, laid iron beneath the thresholds, and called on their various gods for help.

But as the weeks wore on, Valgard came to sit more and more in Elfheugh. For he had been to every castle and hill-town he could find, he had harried from Orkney to Cornwall, and such elves as had escaped him were well hidden—striking out of cover at his men, so that not a few trolls never came home; sneaking poison into food and water; hamstringing horses; corroding arms and armour; calling up blizzards as if the very land rose against the invader.

The trolls held England, no doubt of that, and daily their grip tightened. Yet never had Valgard longed for spring as now he did.

XVIII

Skafloc and Freda took shelter in a cave. It was a deep hole in a cliff that slanted back from the seashore, well north of the elf-hills. Behind it was a forest of ice-sheathed trees which grew thicker towards the south and faded into moor and highland toward the north. Dark and drear was that land, unpeopled by men or Faerie folk, and thus about as safe as any place from which to carry on the war.

They could use little magic, for fear of being sensed by the trolls, but Skafloc did a good deal of hunting in guise of the wolf or otter or eagle whose skins Freda had brought, and he conjured ale from seawater. It was hard work merely to keep alive in that wintery world—the hardest winter that England remembered since almost the time of the Great Ice—and he spent most of his days ranging for game.

Dank and chill was the cave. Winds whittered in its mouth and surf pounded on the rocks at its foot. But when Skafloc came back from his first long hunt, he thought for a moment he had found the wrong place.

A fire blazed cheerily on a hearthstone, with smoke guided out a rude pipe of wicker and green hides. Other skins made a warm covering on floor and walls, and one hung in the cave mouth against the wind. The horses were tethered in the rear, chewing hay that Skafloc had magicked from kelp, and the spare weapons were polished and stacked in a row as if this were a feasting hall. And behind each weapon was a little spray of red winter berries.

Crouched over the fire and turning meat on a spit was Freda. Skafloc stopped in midstride. His heart stumbled at sight of her. She wore only a brief tunic, and her slim long-legged body, with its gentle curves of thigh and waist and breast, seemed poised in the gloom like a bird ready for flight.

She saw him come in, and from under tousled ruddy hair, in the flushed and smoke-smudged face, her great grey eyes kindled with gladness. Wordlessly she sped to him, with her dear coltish gait, and they held each other close for a while.

He asked wonderingly: "How did you ever do this, my sweet?"

She laughed softly. "I am no bear, or man, to make a heap of leaves and call that home for the winter. Some of these skins and so on we had, the rest I got for myself. Oh, I am a good housewife." Pressing against him, shivering: "You were so long away, and time was so empty. I had to pass the days, and make myself weary enough to sleep at night."

His own hands shook as he fondled her. "This is no stead for you. Hard and dangerous is the outlaw life. I should take you to a human garth, to await our victory or forget our defeat."

"No—no, never shall you do that!" She grasped his ears and pulled till his mouth lay on hers. Presently, half laughing and half sobbing: "I have said I will not leave you. No, Skafloc, 'twill be harder than that to get rid of me."

"Truth to tell," he admitted after a while, "I do not know what I would do without you. Naught would seem worth the trouble any more."

"Then do not leave me, ever again."

"I must hunt, dearest one."

"I will hunt with you." She waved at the hides and the roasting meat. "I am not unskilled at that."

"Nor at other things," he laughed. Turned grim again: "It is not game alone I will be stalking, Freda, but also trolls."

"There too will I be." The girl's countenance grew hard

as his own. "Think you I have no vengeance to take?"

His head lifted in pride, until he bent to kiss her anew like an osprey stooping on its catch. "Then so be it! And Orm the warrior could be glad of such a daughter."

Her fingers traced the lines of his cheekbone and jaw. "Know you not who your father was?" she asked.

"No." He grew uneasy, remembering Tyr's words. "I never did."

"No matter," she smiled, "save that he too could be proud. I think Orm the Strong would have given all his wealth for a son like you—not that Ketil and Asmund were weaklings. And failing that, he must be glad indeed to see you joined with his daughter."

As the winter deepened, life grew yet harder. Hunger was often a guest in the cave, and chill crept in past the hide door and the fire until only huddled together in bearskins could Skafloc and Freda find warmth. For days on end they would be afield, riding the swift elf horses which sank not into the snow, seeking game in a vast white emptiness.

Now and again they would come on the blackened ruins of an elf garth. At such times Skafloc grew white about the nostrils and said nothing for many hours. Once in a while a living elf would appear, gaunt and ragged, but the man did not try to build up a band. It would only draw the enemy's heed without being able to stand before him. Could help be gotten from outside, then there might be sense in leagues like that.

Always he was on the lookout for trolls. If he found their tracks, he and the girl would be off at a wild gallop. At a large group they would shoot arrows from afar, then wheel and race away; or Skafloc might wait for daylight, then creep into whatever the shelter was wherein the trolls slept and cut throats. Were there no more than two or three, he would be on them with a sword whose whine, together with Freda's arrow-buzz, was the last sound they heard.

Relentless was that hunt, on both sides. Often they crouched in cave or beneath windfall while troll pursuit went before their eyes, and naught but a thin screen of wizardry wrought by the rune staves, hardly hiding them from a straight-on glance, covered their spoor. Arrows and spears and slung stones hissed after them when they fled from shooting down two or three of a company. From their home cave they saw troll longships row past, near enough for them to count the rivets in the warriors' shields.

And it was cold, cold.

Yet in that life they truly found each other. They learned that their bodies were the least of what there was to love. Skafloc wondered how he could have had the heart to wage his fight without Freda. Her arrows had brought down trolls, and her daring schemes of ambush still more—but the kisses she gave him in their dear moments of peace were what drove him to his own deeds, and the help and comfort she gave every hour were what upheld his strength. And to her, he was the greatest and bravest and kindest of men, her sword and shield at once, lover and oath-brother.

She even owned to herself, feeling a little guilty that she did not feel very guilty, that she did not much miss her Faith. Skafloc had explained that its words and signs would upset the magic he needed. For her part, she decided it would be blasphemous to use them for mere advantage in a war between two soulless tribes; better, even safer maybe, to leave prayers unspoken. As for that war, since it was Skafloc's it was hers. Someday after it was won she would get him to listen to a priest, and surely God would not withhold belief from a man like this.

Harsh was the outlaw life, but she felt her body respond, in keenness of sense and tautness of sinew and endurance of spirit. The wind flogged the blood in her veins till it tingled; the stars lent their brightness to her eyes. When life balanced on a sword-edge, she learned to taste each moment of it with a fullness she had not dreamed before.

Strange, she thought, how even when hungry and cold and afraid they had no hard words between them. They thought and acted like one, as if they had come from the same mould. Their differences were merely those in which each filled the need of the other.

"I bragged once to Imric that I had never known fear, or defeat, or love-sickness," said Skafloc. He lay in the cave with his head on her lap, letting her comb his wind-tangled hair. "He said those were the three ends and beginnings of human life. At that time I understood him not. Now I see he was wise."

"How should he know?" she asked.

"I cannot say, for elves know defeat only sometimes, fear seldom, and love never. But since meeting you, dear, I have found all three in myself. I was becoming more elf than man. You are making me human again, and elfhood fades within me."

"And somewhat of elf has entered my blood. I fear that less and less do I think of what is right and holy, more and more of what is useful and pleasant. My sins grow heavy—"

Skafloc hauled her face down to his. "In that you do well. This muttering of duty and law and sin brings no good."

"You speak profanely—" she began. He stopped her words with a kiss. She sought to pull free, and it ended in a laughing, tumbling wrestling match. By the time they were done, she had forgotten her forebodings.

But after the trolls finished wasting the elf lands, they withdrew into their strongholds, rarely venturing out except in troops too big to attack. Skafloc, who by killing a number of deer had laid in ample frozen meat, grew moody in idleness. His banter dropped off and he spent days at a time hunched surly in the cave.

Freda sought to cheer him. "Now are we in less danger," she said.

"What good is that, when we cannot fight?" he answered. "We only wait for the end. Alfheim is dying. Soon every realm in Faerie will belong to the trolls. And I—I sit here!"

Another day he went out and saw a raven beating upwind under the lowering sky. The sea dashed on rocks at his feet, rattled and roared back for a new leap, and spindrift froze where it struck.

"What news?" called Skafloc in the raven tongue. It was not in such words that he spoke or was spoken to, for beasts and birds have different sorts of language from men, but the meaning is near enough.

"I come from south beyond the channel to fetch my kindred," replied the raven. "Valland and Wendland have fallen to the trolls, Scania totters, and the Erlking's armies go back and back towards his middle domains. Good is the feasting, but ravens had best hurry thither, for the war cannot last much longer."

At this such anger blazed up in Skafloc that he put an arrow to his bow and shot the bird. But when it lay dead at his feet the wrath drained from him, leaving an emptiness which sorrow rose slowly to fill.

"It was wicked to slay you, brother," he said low, "who have done no harm, who rather do good by clearing the stinking clutter of the past from this world. Friendly you were to me, and defenseless, yet I slew you and let my foes sit in peace."

He turned back into the cave, and of a sudden he was weeping. The sobs nigh shook his ribs apart. Freda held him, murmuring to him as to a child, and he wept himself out on her breast.

That night he could not sleep. "Alfheim is falling," he mumbled. "Before the snows melt, Alfheim will be a memory. Naught is left but for me to ride against the trolls and take as many as may be down hell-road with me."

"Say not that," she answered. "It would be a stupid betrayal of your trust—and of me too. Better and braver to live, fighting."

"Fighting with what?" he asked bitterly. "The elf ships are sunken or scattered, the warriors dead or in chains or hunted like us. Wind, snow, and wolves dwell in the proud castles, and the foe sits in the high seat of our olden lords. Alone are the elves, naked, starving, weaponless——"

She kissed him. As it were a lightning bolt, he seemed to see before his eyes the gleam of a sword lifted high across darkness.

For a long moment she felt him stiff as an iron bar but trembling as if that bar were hammerstruck; and then he breathed into the gloom: "The sword—the naming-gift of the Æsir—aye, *the sword*—"

A formless fear sprang high in her. "What do you mean? What sword is this?"

So as they lay in the dark, close together against the frost, he whispered it to her, soft in her ears as if afraid the night would listen. He told how Skirnir brought the broken glaive, how Imric hid it in the wall of Elfheugh's dungeons, and how Tyr had warned that the time was nigh when he would have need of it.

In the end he felt her shiver in his clutch, she who had hunted armed trolls. Her voice came small and unsteady: "I like it not, Skafloc. It is no good thing."

"Not good?" he cried. "Why, it is the one last great hope we have left. Odin, who reads the morrow, must have foreseen this day of Alfheim's undoing—must have given us the sword against it. Weaponless? Ha, we will show them otherwise!"

"It is wrong to deal with heathen things, most of all when the heathen gods offer them," she pleaded. "Evil must come of it. Oh, my beloved, forget the sword!"

"True, the gods doubtless have their own ends," he said "but those need not be at odds with ours. I think Faerie is a chessboard on which Æsir and Jötuns move elves and trolls, in some game beyond our understanding. Yet the wise chessplayer takes care of his pieces."

"But the sword is buried in Elfheugh."

"I will get in somehow. I have an idea already."

"The sword is broken. How shall you—we—find that giant who it is said can mend it? How make him forge it anew to be used against his kin the trolls?"

"There will be a way." Skafloc's tone rang like metal. "Even now I know one means to find out how, though it is dangerous. We may well fail, aye, but the gods' gift is our last chance."

"The gods' gift." She began to weep in her turn. "I tell you, naught but harm can come of this. I feel it in me, cold and heavy. If you embark on this search, Skafloc, our days together are numbered."

"Would you leave me on that account?" he asked, aghast.

'No—no, my darling—" She clung to him, blind with darkness and tears. "It is but a whisper in my soul—yet I know—"

He drew her closer still. Wildly he kissed her, until her head swam, and he laughed and was joyous; finally she could do no else than drive the fears from her awareness, for they were unworthy of Skafloc's bride, and be glad with him.

But there was a yearning in her love which had not been there before. In her inmost deeps, she felt that they would not have many more times like this.

XIX

A few hours before the next night ended, after a blinding elf-gallop from the cave, they reined in their horses. Skafloc could not wait, when Alfheim was dying. The half moon rode in a cloudy sky, its wan light filtering through icicled trees to sheen on the snow. Breath smoked upwards in the still, cold air, to glimmer like ghosts that fled the lips of dying men.

"We dare go no nearer Elfheugh together." Skafloc's whisper sounded unnaturally loud in that quiet, in the shadowiness of that thicket which hid them. "But I can make it alone, on wolf foot, ere dawn."

"What is your haste?" Freda clung to his arm and he tasted salt on her cheek. "Why not, at least, go by day, when *they* will be asleep?"

"The skinturning cannot be done in sunlight," he told her. "And once inside the castle walls, day or night are the same; most of the trolls are as likely to be sleeping as wakeful at any hour. When I am in, there are those who can help me. I think chiefly of Leea."

"Leea—" Freda bit her lip. "I like it not, this whole crazy doing. Have we no other way at all?"

"None that come to my mind. You, my sweet, have the hardest task—that I admit—waiting here, alone until I return." He looked at her shadowed face as if to learn every line of it. "Remember, now, make a tent of those hides we brought, before sunrise, to shelter the horses from it. And remember I will have to come back in man shape, with the burden I shall be carrying. Thus I can go by day, safe till dusk, but slower, so I will not get here until sometime tomorrow night. Be not reckless, princess. If trolls come near, or if I am not back by the third evening, be off. Fly to the world of men and sunlight!"

"I can endure waiting," she said tonelessly, "but to leave this place, not knowing whether you lived or—" she choked "—or died, that may be past my strength."

Skafloc swung from his saddle into the snow, which crunched underfoot. Quickly he stripped himself naked. Shivering, he fastened the otter skin about his loins and the eagle skin over his shoulders, and flung the wolf skin cloaklike over both.

Freda dismounted too. Hungrily, they kissed. "Farewell, dearest one," he said. "Until I bring the sword, farewell."

He turned away, not daring to linger by the quietly crying girl, and drew the grey pelt tighter about him. He dropped on all fours and said the needful words. Then he felt his body shift and recast itself, felt his senses blurred with change. And Freda saw him alter, swiftly as if he melted, until a great wolf stood beside her with eyes glowing green in the dark.

Briefly the cold nose nuzzled her palm, and she rumpled the rough coat. He padded away.

Over the snow he went, weaving between trees and among bushes, loping faster and more tireless than a man. It was strange, being a wolf. The interplay of bone, muscle, and sinew was something else from what it had been. The air ruffled his fur. His sight was dim, flat, and colourless. But he heard every faintest sound, every sigh and whisper, the night's huge stillness had turned murmurous—many of those tones too high for men ever to hear. And he smelled the air as if it were a living thing, uncounted subtle odours, hints and traces swirling in his nostrils. And there were sensations for which men had no words.

It was like being in a new world, a world which in every way *felt* different. And he himself was changed, not alone in body but in nerve and brain. His mind moved in wolfish tracks, narrower though somehow keener. He was not able in beast shape to think all the thoughts he did as a man, nor, on becoming man again, to remember all he had sensed and thought as a beast.

On and on! The night and the miles fled beneath his feet. The woods stirred with their secret life. He caught the scent of hare—frightened hare, crouched nearby with big eyes upon him—and his wolf mouth droled in greed. But his man soul drove the gaunt grey frame ahead. An owl hooted. Trees and hills and ice-scabbarded rivers went by in a blur, the moon trudged across heaven, and still he ran.

And at last, looming against silver-tinged clouds but its towertops crusted with frosty winter stars, he saw Elfheugh. Elfheugh, Elfheugh, the lovely and fallen, now a menace bulking black across the sky!

He flattened himself on his hairy belly and slid up the hill towards those walls. Every wolf-sense reached out, searching around him . . . were enemies nigh?

The snaky troll smell came to him. He lowered his tail and bared his fangs. The castle reeked of troll—and of worse, fear and pain and throttled wrath.

With his dim wolf-eyes he could not well see the top of the wall under which he crouched. He heard the guardsmen pace above him, and winded them, and trembled with the longing to rip out their throats.

Easy, easy, he told himself. There they went, they were past him, now to turn his skin again.

Already beast, he needed but to will the change. He writhed, felt the shifting and shrinking, and his brain swam. Then he beat the broad wings of the eagle and rose heavenward.

His sight was sharp now, inhumanly so; and the glory of flight, of wind and skyey endlessness, sang through every feather of him. Yet the austere eagle brain had will to refuse that magnificent drunkenness. His eyes were not an owl's, and aloft he was a target for troll arrows.

Over the wall he went and soared across the courtyard, braking himself with the air awhistle in his pinions. He landed by the keep, in the shadow of a thickly ivied tower, and again he shuddered with change. There, otter, he waited a while.

He could not smell in this shape quite so well as a wolf, though better than a man, but his eye saw further and his ears were as good. Also, his body had a wiry alertness wherein every hair and whisker tip tingled with sensations indescribable to man; and his swiftness and suppleness, the luster of his pelt, were a joy to the vain, cocky, frolicsome otter brain.

Tense and still he lay, straining every sense. He heard startled halloos from the battlements. Someone must have had a glimpse of the eagle and he had best not dawdle here.

He slipped lithe along the wall, keeping to the shadows. An otter was too big to be safe—better had he been weasel or rat—but was the best he could do. Glad he was that Freda had brought those three magic skins. A tenderness welled up in him, but he could not stop to think about her, not yet.

A door stood ajar, and through this he sneaked. It was in the back of the building. However, he knew each corner and cranny of that labyrinth. His whiskers twitched as he snuffed the air. Though the place stank of troll, it was also heavy with the smell of sleep. In that much he was lucky. He could make out some few who moved around, but they would be easy to avoid.

He padded by the feasting hall. Trolls sprawled throughout, snoring drunkenly. The tapestries hung in rags, the furnishings were scarred and stained, and the ornaments of gold and silver and gems, the work of centuries, had been stolen. It would have been better, thought Skafloc, to be overrun by goblins. They were at least a mannered people. These filthy swine—

Up the stairs towards Imric's chambers he wound. Whoever was now earl would most likely sleep there . . . and have Leea beside him.

The otter flattened against the wall. His soundless snarl showed needle teeth. His yellow eyes blazed. Around the curve he smelled troll. The earl had posted a guard and—

Like a grey thunderbolt the wolf was on the troll. Drowsy,

the warrior could not know what struck until fangs closed in his throat. He fell in a clatter of mail, clawing at the beast on his breast, and thus he died.

Skafloc crouched. Blood dripped from his jaws. It had a sour taste. That had been quite a racket... no, no sound of alarm or awareness... the castle was so big, after all— He would have to risk the body being found ere he was away. Indeed, it almost surely would be come upon—no, wait—

Quickly, as a man, Skafloc used the dead troll's sword to hack that throat until it could not be seen that teeth rather than blade had torn out life. They might think the guard had been slain in some drunken quarrel. They had better! The thought was grim in him while he wiped and spat the blood from his mouth.

Otter again, he raced onward. At the head of the stairs, the door to Imric's rooms stood closed, but he knew the secret hiss and whistle that would compel the lock. Softly he gave them, nosed the door open a crack, and entered.

Two slept in Imric's bed. If the earl awoke, that would be the end of Skafloc's quest. He crawled on his lissome otter stomach towards the bed, and every movement seemed doomsday loud.

Reaching there, he braced himself on his hind legs. Leea's goddess face lay on one pillow in a cloud of silvery-gold hair. Beyond her was a tawny-maned head with a countenance harsh even in slumber—but in every blunt, sinewy line it was his own.

So Valgard the evil-worker was the new earl. Barely could Skafloc hold himself from sinking wolf teeth in that throat, tearing with eagle beak at the eyes, nuzzling with otter tongue among the ripped-out guts.

But those were beast wishes. Fulfilling them would too likely make a noise and thus cost him the sword.

He touched the smoothness of Leea's cheek with his nose. Her long lashes fluttered, and recognition flared in her eyes.

Very slowly she sat up. Valgard stirred and moaned in his sleep. She froze. The berserker mumbled to himself. Skafloc caught fragments: "—changeling—the axe—O Mother, Mother!—"

Leea slid one leg to the floor. Poised on that small foot, she eased her whole body out. Its whiteness gleamed through the swirling veil of her hair. Like a shadow she slipped out of the room, through another, and into a third. Skafloc padded after. Soundlessly, she had closed every door between.

"Now we can talk," she breathed.

He stood forth, man once more, and she fell into his arms with a half laugh, half sob. She kissed him until, no matter Freda, he was hotly aware of how lovely a woman he held.

She saw it, and tried to draw him towards a couch. "Skafloc," she whispered. "My darling."

He mastered himself. "I have no time," he said roughly. "I am come for the broken sword which was the Æsir's naming-gift to me."

"You are tired." Her hands traced the haggardness of his face. "You have been cold and hungry and in peril of life. Let me rest you, comfort you. I have a secret room——"

"No time, no time," he growled. "Freda waits for me in the very heart of the troll holdings. Lead me to the sword."

"Freda." Leea went a shade more pale. "So the mortal girl is still with you."

"Aye, and a doughty warrior for Alfheim has she been."

"I have not done too badly myself," Leea said with an odd pairing of her old malicious humor and a new wistfulness. "Already Valgard has slain Grum Troll-Earl for my sake. He is strong, but I am bending him." She swayed closer. "He is better than a troll, he is almost you——but he is not you, Skafloc, and I weary of pretending."

"Oh, hurry!" He shook her. "If I am caught it could be the end of Alfheim, and every minute strengthens the chance."

She stood quiet for a space. Finally she looked away, out the broad glass window, to a world where clouds had engulfed the moon, a land silent and frozen in the dark before dawn. "Indeed," she said. "You are right, of course. And what is better or more natural than that you should hasten back to your love——to Freda?"

She swung on him, shaken with noiseless mirth. "Do you want to know who your father was, Skafloc? Shall I tell you who you really are?"

He clamped a hand over her mouth. The old fear choked him. "No! You have heard what Tyr warned!"

"Seal my lips," she said, "with a kiss."

"I cannot wait——" He obeyed her. "Now can we go?"

"Cold was that kiss," she murmured desolately. "Cold as duty ever was. Well, let us be on our way. But you are naked and unarmed. Since you cannot carry the iron sword away as a were-beast, you had best have some clothes." She opened a chest. "Here are tunic, breeches, shoon, mantle, whatever else you like."

He tumbled into the garments with feverish haste. Richly fur-trimmed, they must have been made over for Valgard from Imric's, since they fitted him well. At his belt he hung a sax. Leea threw a flame-red cloak over her own nakedness. Then she led the way out, to another stair.

Down they wound and down. The well was chill and silent, but this silence was stretched near the breaking point. Once they passed a troll on watch. Skafloc's hackles rose, and he reached for the sax at his belt. But the guard only bowed his head, taking the man for the changeling. In his outlaw life, Skafloc had let grow a full though close-cropped beard like Valgard's.

Presently the dungeons were reached, where only widely spaced torches lit the dank gloom. Skafloc's steps made slithery sounds down corridors whose shadows looked wellnigh solid. Leea flitted ahead, wordless.

They came at last to a place where the stone showed a lighter splash of cement in which were scratched runes. Nearby was a closed door. Leea pointed to it. "In yonder cell Imric kept the changeling-mother," she said. "Now he is in there himself, hung by his thumbs over an undying fire. It is often Valgard's pleasure when drunk to lash him senseless."

Skafloc's knuckles stood white on his sword haft. And yet, he could not help thinking at the back of his mind, was this worse than what Imric had done to the troll-woman, and to how many others? Was Freda—was the White Christ of whom she had told a little—not right in saying that wrongs only led to more wrongs and thus at last to Ragnarök; that the time was overpast when pride and vengefulness give way to love and forgiveness, which were not unmanly but in truth the hardest things a man could undertake?

Yet Imric had fostered him, and Alfheim was his land, and what *was* the reason he must not know of his human birth—? He dug the tip of the sax fiercely into the wall.

A noise drifted faintly down, shouting of voice and clatter of feet. "An alarm," breathed Leea.

"Belike they found the guard I had to kill." Skafloc dug harder. The cement scraped slowly from the stone.

"Were you seen entering?" she demanded.

"I may have been glimpsed in eagle shape." Skafloc's tool snapped. He cursed and dug on with the broken blade.

"Valgard is shrewd enough, if he hears about that eagle, to think this may be no ordinary killing. If he sends men to ransack the castle, and they find us—Hurry!"

The racket above beat on their ears, less loud than the scrape of metal on stone or an ages-old dripping of water.

Skafloc got the blade into a crack and heaved. Once—twice—thrice, and the stone crashed out!

He reached into the niche beyond. His hands shook as he brought forth the sword.

Earth clung damp to the halves of the broad blade. It had been two-edged, and so huge and heavy that only the strongest of men could readily wield it. However long buried, it had not rusted, nor had the edges lost their razor sharpness. Guard, haft, and pommel shone golden, with a coiling dragon shape engraved so that they made its tail, body, and head; the bright rivets were like a hoard on which it lay. Runes that Skafloc could not read went down the dark blade. He had the feeling that the mightiest of these were hidden on the tang.

"The weapon of the gods." He held it with awe. "The hope of Alfheim—"

"Hope?" Leea stepped back, hands raised as if to fend something off. "I wonder! Now that we have the thing, I wonder."

"What mean you?"

"Can you not sense it? The power and hunger locked in that steel, held by those unknown runes. The sword may be *from* the gods, but it is not *of* them. There is a curse on it, Skafloc. It will bring the bane of all within its reach." She shivered with a cold not that of the dungeon. "I think . . . Skafloc, I think it were best if you walled that sword up again."

"What other hope have we?" He wrapped the pieces in his cloak and took the bundle under one arm. "Let us away."

Unwillingly, Leea led him to a stair. "This will be tricky," she said. "We can scarce avoid being seen. Let me speak for both of us."

"No, that would be dangerous for you afterwards, unless you go off with me."

She swung around, her face alight. "You care about me?"

"Why, of course, as about the whole of Alfheim."

"And . . . Freda?"

"For her I care more than for the whole rest of the world, gods and men and Faerie together. I love her."

Leea turned forward again. Her voice fell colourless: "I will be able to save myself. I can always tell Valgard you forced or tricked me."

They came out on the first floor. It was a bustle of scuttling guards, uproar and confusion. "Hold!" bawled a troll when he saw them.

Leea's countenance flared like fire-gleam off ice. "Would you halt the earl?" she asked.

"Pardon—your pardon, lord," stammered the troll. " 'Twas only that—I saw you but a moment ago, lord—"

They went out into the courtyard. Every nerve in Skafloc shrieked that he should run, every muscle was knotted in expectancy of the cry that would mean he was found out. Run, run! He shook with the task of walking slowly.

Few trolls were outside. The first white streaks of the hated dawn were in the east. It was very cold.

Leea stopped at the west gate and signed that it should be opened. She looked into Skafloc's eyes with a withdrawn blind gaze.

"From here you must make your own way," she said softly. "Know you what to do?"

"Somehow," he answered, "I must find the giant Bolverk and make him bring it forth anew for me."

"Bolverk—evil-worker—his very name is a warning. I have begun to guess what sword this is and why no dwarf would dare reforge it." Leea shook her head. "I know that stubborn set to your jaw, Skafloc. Not all the hosts of hell shall stop you—only death, or the loss of your will to fight. But what of your dear Freda on this quest?" She sneered the last words.

"She will come along, though I will try to persuade her to shelter." Skafloc smiled in pride and love. The dim dawnlight touched his hair with frosty gold. "We are not to be parted."

"No-o-o. However, as to finding the giant, who can tell you the way?"

Skafloc's face bleakened. "It is not a good thing to do," he said, "but I can raise a dead man. The dead know many things, and Imric taught me the charms to wring speech from them."

"Yet it is a desperate deed, for the dead hate that breaking of their timeless sleep, and wreak vengeance for it. Can you stand against a ghost?"

"I must try. I think my magic will be too strong for it to strike at me."

"Perhaps not at you, but—" Leea paused before going on slyly: "That would not be as terrible a revenge anyway as what it could work through—say—Freda."

She watched the blood drain from his cheeks and lips. Her own went whiter. "Do you care for the girl that much?" she whispered.

"Aye. More," he said thickly. "You are right, Leea. I cannot risk it. Better Alfheim should fall than—than—"

"No, wait! I was going to give you a plan. But I would ask you one thing first."

"Hurry, Leea, hurry!"

"Only one thing. If Freda should leave you—no, no, do not stop to tell me she won't, I merely ask—if she should, what would you do?"

"I know not. I cannot dream of that."

"Perhaps—win the war and come back here? Become elf again?"

"Belike. I know not. Hurry, Leea!"

She smiled her cat-smile. Her eyes rested dreamy upon him. "I was simply going to say this," she told him, "that instead of raising just any dead man, call on those who would be glad to help you and whose own revenge you would be working. Has not Freda a whole family, slain by Valgard? Raise *them*, Skafloc!"

For a moment he stood moveless. Then he dropped the sword-bundle, swept Leea into his arms, and kissed her with numbing power. Grabbing anew the burden, he sprang through the gate and rushed into the forest.

Leea stared after him, fingers on her tingling lips. If she was right about what sword that was, the same thing was about to happen that had happened aforetime. She began to laugh.

Valgard learned that his likeness had been seen within the castle. His leman, looking dazed and atremble, said forlornly that something had cast a spell on her while she slept, so that she remembered naught. But there were tracks in the snow, and the troll hounds could follow dimmer trails than this.

At sunset, the earl led his warriors on horseback in pursuit.

Freda stood in her thicket, staring through the bare moon-ghostly woods towards Elfheugh.

She was cold on this second night of her waiting, so cold that it had long since passed feeling and become like a part of herself. She had huddled in the shelter among the horses, but they were cool and elfly, not the warm sweet-smelling beasts of home. Strangely, it was the thought of Orm's horses that brought her loneliness back to her. She felt as if she were the last living creature in a world of nothing but moonlight and snow.

She dared not weep. Skafloc, Skafloc! Lived he yet?

A rising wind blew clouds ever thicker across the sky, so that the moon seemed to flee great black dragons which swallowed it and spewed it briefly back out. The wind wailed and roared around her, whipping her garb, sinking teeth into her flesh. Hoo, hoo, it sang, blowing a sudden sheet of snowdrift before it, white under the moon, hoo, halloo, hunting you!

Hoo, hoo! echoed the troll horns. Freda stiffened. Fear went through her like a dagger. *They* hunted—and what game could it be save—

Soon she heard the baying of their hounds, nearer, nearer, the huge black dogs with red coals for eyes. O Skafloc! Freda stumbled forward, scarce hearing her own sobs. Skafloc!

Fresh darkness closed on her. She crashed into a bole. Wildly she beat at it, get out of the way, you thing, step aside, Skafloc needs me—Oh!

In the returned moonlight she saw a stranger. Tall he was, with a cloak tossing like wings around him. Old he was, his long hair and beard blowing wolf-grey in that hurried light; but the spear he carried could have been wielded by no mortal man. Though a wide-brimmed hat threw his face into shadow, she saw the gleam of a single eye.

She trod backward, gasping, seeking to call upon Heaven. The voice stopped her, deep, slow, a part of the wind yet somehow moving steady as a glacier: "I bring help, not harm. Would you have your man back?"

She sank dumbly to her knees. For a moment, in the blurry, wavering moonlight, she saw past drifting snow, past frozen miles, to the hill up which Skafloc fled. Weaponless he was, spent and reeling, and the hounds were on his heels. Their barking filled the sky.

The vision faded. She looked to the night shape that stood over her. "You are Odin," she whispered, "and it is not for me to have dealings with you."

"Nonetheless I can save your lover—and I alone would, for he is heathen." The god's one eye held her as if she were speared. "Will you pay my price?"

"What do you want?" she gasped.

"Hurry, the hounds are about to rend him!"

"I will give it to you—I will give it—"

He nodded. "Then swear by your own soul and everything which is holy to you, that when I come for it you will give me what is behind your girdle."

"I swear!" she cried. Tears blinded her, the weeping of one set free. Odin could not be relentless as they said, not when he asked for such a mere token, the drug Skafloc had given her. "I swear it, lord, and may earth and Heaven alike forsake me if I do not keep my oath."

"That is well," he said. "Now the trolls are off on a false spoor, and Skafloc is here. Woman, remember your word!"

Darkness came back as a cloud bedecked the moon. When it had blown past, the Wanderer was gone.

Freda hardly knew that. She was clinging to her Skafloc. And he, bewildered at being snatched somehow from the jaws of the troll hounds to safety and his darling, was not too mazed to answer her kisses.

XX

They spent no more than two days resting in the cave before Skafloc busked himself to go.

Freda did not weep, but she felt the unshed tears thick in her throat. "You think this is dawn for us," she said once, the second day. "I tell you it is night."

He looked at her, puzzled. "What mean you?"

"The sword is full of wickedness. The deed we go to do is wrong. No good can come of it."

He laid his hands on her shoulders. "I understand you do not like making your kin travel the troublous road," he said. "Nor do I. Yet who else among the dead will help and not harm us? Stay here, Freda, if you cannot bear it."

"No—no, I will be at your side even at the mouth of the

grave. It is not that I fear my folk. Living or dead, there is love between us; and the love is yours too, now." Freda lowered her glance and bit her lip to halt its trembling. "Had you or I thought of this, I would have less foreboding. But Leea meant no boon in her rede."

"Why should she wish ill on us?"

Freda shook her head and would not answer. Skafloc said slowly: "I must own that I like not altogether your meeting with Odin. It is not his way to set a low price, but what he really is after I cannot guess."

"And the sword—Skafloc, if that broken sword is made whole once more, a dreadful power will be loose in the world. It will work unending woe."

"For the trolls." Skafloc straightened until his fair locks touched the smoky cave roof. His eyes flashed lightning-blue in the gloom. "There is no other road than the one we take, hard though it be. And no man outlives his weird. Best to meet it bravely face to face."

"And we side by side." Freda bowed her shining bronze head on his breast, and now the tears flowed heavily. "One thing do I ask, my dearest of all."

"What is that?"

"Ride not out this eventide. Wait one day more, only one, and then we will go." Her fingers dug into the muscles of his arms. "No longer than that, Skafloc."

He nodded unwillingly. "Why?"

She would not say, and in their love that followed he forgot the question. But Freda remembered. Even when she held him most closely and felt his heartbeat against hers, she remembered, and it gave a terrible yearning to her kisses.

In some blind way, she knew this was their last night.

The sun rose, glimmered wanly at noon, and sank behind heavy storm-clouds scudding in from the sea. A wolf-toothed wind howled over the breakers that dashed themselves to noisy death on the strand rocks. Soon after darkfall there came for a while the far-off sound of hoofs at gallop through the sky, outrunning the wind, and a baying and yelping. Skafloc himself shivered. The Wild Hunt was out.

They mounted their elf horses, leading the other two with their goods, for they did not expect to return. Lashed across his back, Skafloc had the broken sword wrapped in a wolf skin. His elven blade was sheathed at his side, his left hand carried a spear, and both riders wore helm and byrnie under their furs.

Freda looked back at the cave mouth as they trotted off. Cold and murky it was, but they had been happy there. She pulled her eyes away and held them steadfastly forward of her.

"Ride!" shouted Skafloc, and they broke into full elf-gallop.

The wind skirled and bit at them. Sleet and spindrift blew off the waters in stinging sheets, white under the flying fitful moon. The sea bellowed inward from a wild horizon, bursting on skerries and strand. When the breakers foamed back, the rattle of stones was like some ice-bound monster stirring and groaning. The night was gale and sleet and surging waves, a racket that rang to the riven driven clouds. The moon climbed higher, keeping pace with their surge and clatter of gallop along the cliffs.

Now swiftly, swiftly, best of horses, swiftly southward by the sea, spurn ice beneath your hoofs, strike sparks from rocks, gallop, gallop! Ride with the air loud in your ears and bleak in your lungs, ride through a moon-white curtain of hissing sleet, through darkness and the foeman's land. Swiftly, ride swiftly, south to greet a dead man in his howe!

A troll horn screamed when they raced past Elfheugh harbour. Witchsight or no, they could not make out the castle, but they heard hoofbeats behind them. That thunder soon dwindled; the trolls rode not so fast, nor would they follow where their quarry went tonight.

Swiftly, swiftly, through woods where the wind skirls in icy branches, dodging between trees that claw with naked twigs—past frozen bog, over darkling hillcrest, down into the low country and across bare fields—gallop, gallop!

Freda began to know the way. The wind still drove sleet before it in these parts, but the clouds were thinning and the crooked moon cast glitter on ploughlands and paddocks locked in snow. She had been here before. She remembered this river and that darkened croft, here she had gone hunting with Ketil, there she and Asmund had fished throughout one lazy summer day, in yonder meadow had Asgerd woven chains of daisies for them—how long ago?

The tears froze on her cheeks. She felt Skafloc reach out to touch her arm, and she smiled back into his shadowy face. Her heart could scarce endure this return, but he was with her, and when they were together there was nothing they could not stand.

And now they were reining in.

Slowly on their panting, shaking horses, not saying a word but riding hand in hand, they came into what had been the garth of Orm. They saw great snowdrifts, white in the moonlight, out of which stuck charred ends of timbers. And high at the head of the bay bulked the howe.

A fire wavered over it, roaring and blazing in blue-tinged white—heatless, cheerless, leaping far aloft into the dark. Freda crossed herself, shuddering. Thus had the grave-fires of the old heathen heroes burned after sunset. Belike her unholy errand had kindled this one; it could not be Christian ground wherein Orm lay. But however far into the nameless lands of death he had wandered, he was still her father.

She could not fear the man who had ridden her on his knee and sung songs for her till the hall rang. Nonetheless she was racked with trembling.

Skafloc dismounted. He felt his own clothes drenched with sweat. Never before had he used the spells he must make tonight.

He went forward—and stopped, breath hissing between his teeth as he snatched for his sword. Black in the light of moon and fire, a shape sat moveless as if graven atop the barrow, under the howling flames. If he must fight a drow—

Freda whimpered, the voice of a lost child: "Mother."

Skafloc took her hand. Together they climbed the barrow.

The woman who sat there, heedless of the fire, might almost have been Freda, thought Skafloc bewilderedly. She had the same pert features, the same wide-set grey eyes, the same red-sparked brown hair. But no, no . . . she was older, she was hollowed out by sorrow, her cheeks were sunken, her eyes stared emptily out to sea, her hair streamed unkempt in the gale. She wore a thick fur cloak, with rags beneath, over her gaunt frame.

When Skafloc and Freda came into the light, she slowly turned her head. Her glance sought him.

"Welcome back, Valgard," she said dully. "Here I am. You can do me no more harm. You can only give me death, which is my fondest wish."

"Mother." Freda sank to her knees before the woman.

Ælfrida stared at her. "I do not understand," she said after a time. "It seems to be my little Freda—but you are dead. Valgard took you away, and you cannot have lived long." She shook her head, smiled, and held out her arms. "It was good of you to leave your quiet grave and come to me. I have been so lonely. Come, my little dead girl, come lie on my breast and I will sing you to sleep as I did when you were but a baby."

"I live, Mother, I live—and you live—" Freda strangled on her tears and must cough. "See, feel, I am warm, I am alive. And this is not Valgard, it is Skafloc who saved me from him. It is Skafloc, my lord, a new son for you—"

Ælfrida climbed to her feet. Heavily she leaned on her daughter's arm. "I have waited," she said. "I have waited here, and they thought I was mad. They bring me food and other needs, but do not linger, because they fear the mad-woman who will not leave her dead." She laughed, softly, softly. "Why, what is crazy about that? The mad are those who leave their beloved ones."

She scanned the man's face. "You are like to Valgard," she said in the same quiet way. "You have the height of Orm, and your looks are half his and half mine. But your eyes are kinder than Valgard's." Again she uttered her tender laugh. "Why, now let them say I am mad! I waited, that is all, I waited, and now out of night and death two of my children have returned to me."

"We may bring home more ere dawn," said Skafloc. He and Freda led her down the mound.

"Mother lived," whispered the girl. "I thought her dead too, but she lived, and sat forsaken in the winter—What have I done?"

She wept, and Ælfrida comforted her.

Skafloc dared not wait. He staked out the howe with his rune wands, one at each corner. He put on his left thumb the bronze ring whose stone was flint. He stood on the west side of the grave with his arms raised. On the east side roiled the sea, and the moon fled through ragged clouds. Sleet blew in on the wind.

Skafloc spoke the spell. It wrenched his body and seared his throat. Shaken with the might that surged up in him, he made the signs with his lifted hands.

The fire roared taller. The wind shrieked like a lynx and clouds swallowed the moon. Skafloc cried out:

Waken, chieftains,
fallen warriors!

Skafloc calls you,
sings you wakeful.
I conjure you,
come on hell-road.
Rune-bound dead men,
rise and answer!

The barrow groaned. Higher and ever higher raged the icy flame above it. Skafloc chanted:

Grave shall open.
Gang forth, deathlings!
Fallen heroes,
fare to earth now.
Stand forth, bearing
swords all rusty,
broken shields,
and bloody lances.

Then the howe opened with leaping fires, and Orm and his sons stood in its mouth. The chieftain called:

Who dares burst
the mound, and bid me
rise from death
by runes·and song-spells?
Flee the dead man's
fury, stranger!
Let the deathling
lie in darkness.

Orm stood leaning on his spear. Earth still clung to him, and he was bloodless and covered with rime. His eyes glared unblinking in the flames that roared and whirled around him. On his right stood Ketil, stiff and pale, the gash in his skull black against his hair. On his left was Asmund, wrapped in shadow, arms folded over the spear wound in his breast. Dimly behind them, Skafloc could see the buried ship and the crew stirring awake within it.

He bit back the fear that came out of the grave-mouth and said:

Terror shall not
turn my purpose.

Runes shall bind you.
Rise and answer!
In your ribs
may rats build nests,
if you keep hold
on what I call for!

Orm's voice rolled far and windy and strange:

Deep is dreamless
death-sleep, warlock.
Wakened dead
are wild with anger.
Ghosts will take
a gruesome vengeance
when their bones
are hailed from barrow.

Freda stood forth. "Father!" she cried. "Father, know you not your daughter?"

Orm's dry eyes flamed on her, and the wrath faded in them. He bowed his head and stood in the whirling, hissing fire. Quoth Ketil:

Gladly see we
gold-decked woman.
Sun-bright maiden,
sister, welcome!
Ashy, frozen
are our hollow
breasts with grave-cold.
But you warm us.

Ælfrida came slowly up to Orm. They looked at each other, there in the restless heatless firelight. She took his hands; they were cold as the earth in which they had lain. Quoth he:

Dreamless was not
death, but frightful!
Tears of yours, dear,
tore my heart out.
Vipers dripped
their venom on me

when in death
I heard you weeping.

This I bid
you do, beloved:
live in gladness,
laughing, singing.
Death is then
the dearest slumber,
wrapped in peace,
with roses round me.

"That I have not strength to do, Orm," she said. She touched his face. "There is frost in your hair. There is mould in your mouth. You are cold, Orm."

"I am dead. The grave lies between us."

"Then let it be so no longer. Take me with you, Orm!"

His lips touched hers.

Skafloc said to Ketil:

Speak forth, deathling.
Say me whither
Bolverk giant
bides, the swordsmith.
Tell me further,
truly, warrior,
what will make
him hammer for me.

Quoth Ketil:

Ill your searching
is, you warlock!
Worst of evil
will it fetch you.
Seek not Bolverk.
Sorrow brings he.
Leave us now,
while life is left you.

Skafloc shook his head. Then Ketil leaned on his sword and chanted:

North in Jötunheim,
nigh to Utgard,

> dwells the giant,
> deep in mountain.
> Sidhe will give
> a ship to find him.
> Tell him Loki
> talks of sword-play.

Now Asmund spoke from where he stood with his face in shadow, and sorrow was in his voice:

> Bitter, cruel —
> brother, sister —
> fate the Norns
> made fall upon you.
> Wakened dead men
> wish you had not
> wrought the spell
> that wrings the truth out.

Horror came on Freda. She could not speak, she crept close to Skafloc and they stood facing the sad wise eyes of Asmund. He said slowly while the fires flamed white around his dark shape:

> Law of men
> is laid on deathlings.
> Hard it is
> to hold unto it.
> But the words
> must bitter leave me:
> Skafloc, Freda
> is your sister.

> Welcome, brother,
> valiant warrior.
> All unwitting
> are you, sister.
> But your love
> has broken kinship.
> Farewell, children,
> fey and luckless!

The howe closed with a shattering groan. The flames sank and the moon gleamed wanly forth.

Freda moved away as if Skafloc were become a troll. Like a blind man, he stumbled towards her. A dry little sob rattled in her throat. She turned and fled from him.

"Mother," she whispered. "Mother."

But the howe was bare under the moon. Nor did men ever see Ælfrida again.

Daybreak stole over the sea. The sky was low and heavy, clouds hanging as if frozen above an empty white land. A few snowflakes drifted down.

Freda sat on the barrow and stared before her. She was not weeping. She wondered if she could.

Skafloc returned from sheltering the horses in a thicket. He lowered himself down beside her. His face and voice were dull as the dawn: "I love you, Freda."

She said no word. After a while he went on: "I cannot do other than love you. What matters the chance which made us of the same blood? It means naught. I know of folk, human folk, who commonly made such marriages. Freda, come with me, forget the cursed law——"

"It is God's law," she said with no more tone than he. "I cannot knowingly break it. My sins are too thick already."

"I say that a god who would come between two who have been to each other what we have been, is not one I would heed. If he dared come near me, I would send him home howling."

"Aye—a heathen you are!" she flared. "Fosterling of soulless elves, for whom you would rouse the very dead to new anguish." A faint colour tinged her. "Well, go back to your elves! Go back to Leea!"

He stood up when she did. He tried to take her hands, but she wrenched them free. His wide shoulders sagged.

"No hope?" he asked.

"None." She started off. "I will seek a neighbour garth. It may be I can atone for what I did." Suddenly she swung around to face him. "Come with me, Skafloc! Come, forget your heathendom, be christened and make your peace with God."

He shook his head. "Not with that god."

"But . . . I love you, Skafloc, I love you too much to wish your soul anywhere than in Heaven."

"If you love me," he said mutedly, "stay with me. I will lay no hand on you save as—as a brother. But stay with me."

"No," she said. "Goodbye."

She ran.

He followed. The snow crunched beneath their feet. When he passed and stopped in front of her, making her stop too, she saw that his lips were drawn back as if a knife were being turned within him.

"Will you not even kiss me farewell, Freda?" he asked.

"No." He could barely hear her, and she looked away from him. "I dare not."

Anew she fled.

He stood watching her go. The light struck coppery sparks from her hair, the only colour in this grey and white world. She rounded a clump of trees and was lost to sight. He walked slowly the other way, out of the empty garth.

XXI

Within the next few days, that long cruel winter began to die. And one evening at sunset Gulban Glas Mac Grici stood atop a hill and on the south wind caught the first supernaturally faint breath of spring.

He leaned on his spear and gazed across the twilit snow that sloped down to the sea. An ember of sunset smouldered in the west. Darkness and stars rose out of the east, and thence too he saw a fisher boat coming. It was a plain mortal craft, bought or stolen from some Englishman, and he at the steering oar was flesh-and-blood human. Yet a strangeness brooded over him, and his sea-stained garments were of elven cut.

As he grounded his keel and sprang ashore, Gulban recognized him. The Irish Sidhe held mostly aloof from the rest of Faerie, but they had had traffic with Alfheim in past years and Gulban remembered the merry youth Skafloc who had been with Imric. But he had become lean and grim, more even than the fortunes of his people might warrant.

Skafloc walked up the hill toward the tall warrior-chief etched black against a sky of red and greenish-blue. Nearing, he saw it was Gulban Glas, one of the five guardians of Ulster, and hailed him.

The chief returned grave greetings, bending his golden-helmed head till the long black locks covered his cheekbones. He could not keep from shrinking a little away as he sensed the wickedness asleep in a wolfskin bundle on Skafloc's back.

"I was told to await you," he said.

Skafloc regarded him with weary surprise. "Have the Sidhe that many ears?" he asked.

"No," said Gulban, "but they can tell when something of portent is nigh—and what could it concern this time save the war between elves and trolls? So we looked for an elf to come with strange tidings, and I suppose you are that one."

"Elf—yes!" Skafloc spat. The lines were deep in his face and his eyes were bloodshot; nor was his carelessness about the state of his garb usual in Alfheim, however desperate the times.

"Come," said Gulban. "Lugh of the Long Hand must think this a great matter, for he has called all the Tuatha De Danaan to council in the cave of Cruachan, and the lords of other people of the Sidhe as well. But you are tired and hungry. First must you come to my house."

"No," said the man with a bluntness equally strange to elves. "This cannot wait, nor do I want more rest and food than I need to keep going. Take me to the council."

The chieftain shrugged and turned away, his night-blue mantle swirling about him. He whistled, and two of the lovely light-footed horses of the Sidhe came galloping up. They snorted and shied from Skafloc.

"They like not your burden," said Gulban.

"Nor do I," answered Skafloc shortly. He caught a silky mane and swung into the saddle. "Now swiftly!"

Away they went, almost as fast as elf steeds, soaring over hills and dales, fields and forests, loughs and frozen rivers. In the dusk Skafloc saw some other of the Sidhe glimpsewise: a flashing-mailed horseman with a spear of bright terror, a gnarly leprechaun at the door of his burrow, a strangely beak-like face on a gaunt cloak-wrapped man who had grey feathers for hair, a flitting shadow and a faint skirl of pipes in secret groves. The wintry air had a little mist in it, aglimmer above crusted snow. Night gathered softly. Stars blinked forth, bright as Freda's eyes—No! Skafloc hauled his mind from such thoughts.

Erelong the riders were at the Cave of Cruachan. Four watchmen outside touched swords to brows in salutation. They took the curvetting horses, and Gulban led Skafloc inside.

Sea-green light filled the vast and rugged vaulting of the cave. Flashing stalactites hung from the roof, and shields on the walls gave back the clear glow of tapers. Though there was no fire, it was warm here, with a ghost of Ireland's peatsmoke odour. Rushes had been spread. The soft rustle of them beneath his feet was all the sound Skafloc heard as he walked to the council table.

At its foot were the leaders of the people of Lupra, small and strong and roughly clad: Udan Mac Audain, king of the leprechauns, and Beg Mac Beg his tanist; Glomhar O'Glomrach, mighty of girth and muscled arm; the chiefs Conan Mac Rihid, Gaerku Mac Gaird, Mether Mac Mintan, and Esirt Mac Beg, clad in hides and raw gold. With such folk a mortal could feel at home.

But at the head of the table were the Tuatha De Danaan, the Children of the earth-mother Dana, come from Tir-nan-Og the Golden to hold council in the Cave of Cruachan. Silent and awesome they sat, beautiful and splendid to look upon, and the very air seemed full of the power that was in them. For they had been gods in Ireland ere Patrick brought the White Christ hither, and though they had had to flee the Cross, still they wielded great powers and lived in a splendour like that of old.

Lugh of the Long Hand sat in the throne at the very head, and on his right he had the warrior Angus Og and on his left the sea king Mananaan Mac Lir. Others of the Tuatha De Danaan were there, Eochy Mac Elathan the Dagda Mor, Dove Berg the Fiery, Cas Corrach, Coll the Sun, Cecht the Plow, Mac Greina the Hazel, and many more, high in fame; and with the lords were their wives and children, and harpers and warriors who followed them. Glorious it was to see that assemblage, albeit a terrible glory.

Save to Skafloc, who no longer cared about majesty or wonder or danger. He strode towards them, head held stiff, and his eyes met squarely the dark brilliance of Lugh's while he gave greeting.

The deep voice of him of the Long Hand rolled from the stern countenance: "Be welcome, Skafloc of Alfheim, and drink with chiefs of the Sidhe."

He signed that the man should sit in an empty seat near his own left, with none save Mananaan and his wife Fand in between. The cupbearers brought golden bowls of wine from Tir-nan-Og, and the harps of the bards rippled a luring melody as they drank.

Strong and sweet was that wine; it entered Skafloc like a flame to burn out the weariness in him. But that made the bleakness stand forth the sharper.

Angus Og, the fair-locked warrior, asked: "How goes it in Alfheim?"

"You know how badly it goes," snapped Skafloc. "The elves fight alone and fall—even as one by one all the divided people of Faerie will fall and be swallowed by Trollheim."

Lugh's words came steady and implacable: "The Children of Dana have no fear of trolls. We who overcame the Fomorians, and who even when defeated by the Miletians became their gods, what have we to dread? Glad would we have been to fare in aid of Alfheim—"

"Glad indeed!" Dove Berg smote the table with his fist. His hair was torch-red in the green twilight of the cave, and his shout woke echoes between its walls. "There has not been so grand a fight, so much glory to be won, in over a hundred years! Why could we not go?"

"Well you know the answer," said Eochy Mac Elathan, the Father of Stars. He sat wrapped in a cloak like blue dusk, and bright points of light winked and glittered in it and in his hair and deep within his eyes. When he spread his hands, a little shower of such glints was strewn to dance on the air. "This is more than a simple hosting in Faerie. This is a game in the long strife between the gods of the North and their foes from the Undying Ice; and hard it is to know which side is the more to be wary of. We will not risk our freedom to become pieces on the chessboard of the world."

Skafloc gripped the arms of his chair till his knuckles stood white. His voice wavered a bit: "I come not for help in war, however sorely 'tis needed. I want the loan of a ship."

"And may we ask why?" Coll spoke. Bright was his face, and flames wavered over his gleaming hauberk and the sun-rayed golden brooch at his throat.

Skafloc told quickly of the Æsir's gift to him, and finished: "I made shift to steal the sword from Elfheugh, and by magic found out that I could get a vessel from the Sidhe which would bear me to Jötunheim. So I came hither to ask for it." He bent his neck. "Aye, as a beggar I come. But if we win, you shall not find the elves are niggardly."

"I would fain see this glaive," said Mananaan Mac Lir. Tall and strong and lithe he was, white of skin and silvery-gold of hair, the faintest greenish tinge in both. His eyes were slumbrous, a shifting green and grey and blue, his voice soft though it could rise to a roar. Richly clad he was; and his knife bore gold, silver, crusted jewels on hilt and sheath; but over his shoulders he wore a great leather cloak that had seen use in many weathers.

Skafloc unwrapped the broken sword, and the Sidhe, who could handle iron as well as endure daylight, crowded around it. They recoiled at once, feeling what venom was locked in that blade. A murmuring rose among them.

Lugh lifted his crowned head and looked hard at Skafloc. "You deal in evil things," he said. "A demon sleeps in this sword."

"What would you await?" shrugged Skafloc. "It carries victory."

"Aye, but it also carries death. It will be your bane if you wield it."

"And what of that?" Skafloc gathered his bundle together. The steel rang, loud in the silence that had fallen, as the two pieces clashed together; and something in that harsh belling sent chills through those who heard.

"I ask for a ship," went on Skafloc. "I ask in the name of what friendship there has been between Sidhe and elves, in the name of your honour as warriors, and in the name of your mercy as children of the earth-mother Dana. Will you lend it to me?"

More silence followed. At last Lugh said: "It goes hard not to help you—"

"And why not help?" cried Dove Berg. His knife gleamed forth, he tossed it on high and let it twirl back, rippling with light, to his hand. "Why not raise the hosts of the Sidhe and fare against barbarous Trollheim? How drab and poor will Faerie be if the elves are crushed!"

"And how soon would the trolls fall on us?" added Conan.

"Be still, my lords," commanded Lugh. "What we as a whole do must be thought on." He straightened to his full towering height. "However," he said, "you are our guest, Skafloc Elven-Fosterling. You have sat at our board and drunk our wine; and we remember how we were erstwhile guested in Alfheim. At the very least, we cannot refuse so small a boon as the loan of a ship. Also, I am Lugh of the

Long Hand, and the Tuatha De Danaan do what they will without asking Æsir Jötuns."

At this a shout lifted, weapons blazed forth, swords dinned on shields, and the bards swept out war-chants on their wild strings. Cool and quiet in the tumult, Mananaan Mac Lir said to Skafloc:

"I will offer you a craft. She is only a boat in size, but nonetheless the foremost of my fleet. And since she is tricky to handle, and the journey will be of interest, I will come along myself."

At this, Skafloc was glad. A large crew would be no better than a small one—worse, maybe, because of the heed it might draw—and the sea king ought to make the best of shipmates. "I could thank you in words," he said, "but would liefer do it in oaths of brotherhood. To-morrow—"

"Not so swiftly, hot-head," smiled Mananaan. His sleepy-seeming eyes dwelt on Skafloc with more care than showed. "We will rest and hold feast for a while. I see you need some mirth, and besides, a voyage to Giant Land is not to be undertaken without a good deal of making ready."

Skafloc could say naught against that. Inwardly he raged. He would have no joy of those days. Wine merely brought forth memory—

He felt a light touch on his arm, and faced about to Fand, the wife of Mananaan.

Stately and beautiful were the women of the Tuatha De Danaan, for they were goddesses born. There were no words to tell of their radiance. And in that company Fand stood out.

Her silken hair, golden as sunlight at summer evening, fell in waves from her coronet to her feet. Her robe shimmered with rainbow hues, her round white arms flashed with jewelled rings, yet she herself outshone any attire.

Her wise violet eyes looked through Skafloc's, into him. Her low voice was music. "Would you have trekked to Jötunheim alone?"

"Of course, my lady," said Skafloc.

"No living human has gone there and returned, save Thjalfi and Roskva, and they went in company with Thor. You are either very brave or very reckless."

"What difference? If I die in Jötunheim, it is the same as anywhere else."

"And if you live—" She seemed more in pain than afraid.

"If you live, will you indeed bring back the sword and unleash it ... knowing that in the end it must turn on you?"

He nodded indifferently.

"I think you look on death as your friend," she murmured. "That is a strange friend for a young man to have."

"The only faithful friend in this world," he said. "Death is always sure to be at your side."

"I think you are fey, Skafloc Elven-Fosterling, and that is a sorrow to me. Not since Cu Chulain—" for a moment her eyes blurred "—not since him has such a man as you might become lived among mortals. Also, it grieves me to see the merry mad boy I remember grown so dark and inward. A worm gnaws in your breast, and the hurt drives you to seek death."

He answered naught, folded his arms and looked beyond her.

"Yet grief dies too," she said. "You can outlive it. And I will seek by my arts to shield you, Skafloc."

"That is fine!" he growled, unable to stand more. "You magicking for my body and *she* praying for my soul!"

He swung away towards the winecups. Fand sighed.

"You sail with sorrow, Mananaan," she told her husband.

The sea king shrugged. "Let him mope as he wishes. I will enjoy the trip anyway."

XXII

Three days later, Skafloc stood on a shore and watched Mananaan's boat sculled forth by a leprechaun from the grotto where she was berthed. She was a small slender craft, her silvery hull seeming too frail for deep water. The mast was inlaid with ivory, the sail and tackle interwoven with dyed silk. A gallant golden image of Fand as a dancer stood on prow for figurehead.

The lady herself saw them off. Otherwise the Tuatha had said their farewells and no one was about in the cool grey mists of morning. The fog glittered like dewdrops in her braided hair, and her eyes were a brighter and deeper violet than before, as she bade Mananaan goodspeed.

"Luck be with you in your faring," she said to him, "and may you soon return to the green hills of Erin and the golden streets of the Land of Youth. My look shall be bent seaward by day and my listening to the waves by night, for news of Mananaan's homecoming."

Skafloc stood apart. He thought about how he might have been seen off by Freda. Quoth he to himself:

> Luckless is the lad
> who leaves without his dearest
> sweetheart there and speaking
> softly, in the morning.
> Colder than her kisses
> comes the blowing spindrift.
> Heavy is my heart—
> but how could I forget her?

"Let us away," said Mananaan. He and Skafloc stepped into the boat from the small dock and raised the glowing sail. The man took the steering oar while the godling struck a chord on his harp and sang:

> Wind, I call you, old, unresting,
> from the deeps of sea and sky.
> Blow me outward on my questing,
> answer me with eager cry.
> From the hills of home behind you,
> out through shifting leagues of sea,
> blow, wind, blow! My song shall bind you.
> South wind, sea wind, come to me.
> *Come to set my vessel free.*

At his music, a strong breeze sprang up and the boat surged forth into waves cold and green that threw salt spray onto the lips. Swift as elf craft were those of Mananaan, and erelong the grey land was not to be told from grey clouds on the world's rim.

"Meseems that finding Jötunheim will mean more than just sailing north," said Skafloc.

"True," replied Mananaan. "It will need certain spells. Still more will it need stout hearts and arms."

He squinted ahead. The wind tossed his hair about the countenance that was at once majestic and merry, keen and cool. "The first phantom breath of spring goes over the lands of men," he said. "This has been the worst winter in centuries, and I think the reason is that Jötun powers were abroad. We sail into the everlasting ice of their home."

His gaze swung back to Skafloc. "It is past time that I should voyage to the edge of creation. Am I not a king of the Ocean Sea? Yet I should not have waited so long, but gone when the Tuatha De Danaan were gods and had their full might." He shook his head. "Even the Æsir, who are still gods, came not unscathed back from their few ventures into Jötunheim. As for us two—I know not. I know not."

Then boldly: "But I sail where I will! There shall be no water in the Nine Worlds unploughed by the keels of Mananaan Mac Lir."

Skafloc made no answer, wrapped as he was in himself. The boat handled like a live thing. Wind harped in the rigging and spray sheeted in a rainbowed veil about the beautiful image of Fand. The air was chill but the sun had come blindingly forth, drunk up the mists and scattered diamond dust on the waves. Those romped and shouted, under a blueness filled with scudding white clouds. The rudder sent a thrum into Skafloc's arm. He could not but feel the freshness of this morning. Quoth he, low:

> Clear the day is, coldly
> calling with a wind-voice
> to the sea, where tumbles
> titan play of billows.
> Stood you by my side now,
> sweetheart, on the deck-planks,
> life were full of laughter.
> (Long you for me, Freda?)

Mananaan regarded him closely. "This quest will need all that a man has to give," he said. "Leave nothing back on shore."

Skafloc flushed in anger. "I bade no one come who feared death," he snapped.

"The man who has naught to live for is not the most dangerous to his foes," said Mananaan. And then quickly he took his harp and sang one of the old war-songs of the Sidhe. Strangely did it ring in the vastness of waves and sky and wind. For a while Skafloc thought he saw cloudy hosts bound to battle, the sun aflame on plumed helmets and ranked forests of spears, banners flying and horns shouting and scythe-bladed chariot wheels rumbling over heaven.

They sailed steadily for three days and nights. Ever the wind blew behind them, and the boat rode the waves as a swallow does the air. They stood watch and watch, sleeping in their bags under the little foredeck, and lived on stockfish and cheese and hardtack and whatever else was aboard, with spells to get fresh water out of salt. Few words passed between them, for Skafloc was in no mood for chatter and Mananaan had an immortal's satisfaction in his own thoughts. But respect and friendliness, each for the other, grew with hard work; and they joined in singing the powerful songs that got them across the marches of Jötunheim.

And swiftly went the boat. They felt the cold and gloom deepen almost by the hour as they sped north into the heart of winter.

The sun lowered until it was a far pale disc on a sullen horizon, briefly seen through hurried stormclouds. The cold grew relentless, gnawing through clothes and flesh and bone into the soul. Spray hung in icicles on the rigging, and golden Fand on the prow was clad in rime. To touch metal was to peel skin from fingers, and breath froze in the moustache.

More and more did it become a world of night, where they sailed over black, dimly silver-sparked seas between moon-ghostly mountains that were icebergs. The sky was an utter murk holding uncounted bitter-bright stars, among which leaped northern lights that brought the howe-fire back to Skafloc's mind. Only the drone of wind and rush of sea were heard in that stupendous lifelessness.

They did not come into Jötunheim as into some kingdom on Midgard. It was just that they sailed farther than mortal ship would have gone ere sighting land, into waters that grew ever more chill and dead and pitchy, until at last they had nothing but stars and moon and shuddering aurora for light. Skafloc thought this realm could not lie on earth at all, but in strange dimensions near the edge of everything, where creation plunged back into the Gap whence it had arisen. He had the notion that this was the Sea of Death on which he sailed, outward bound from the world of the living.

Now, after those three days when they saw the sun, they lost track of time. Somehow moon and stars were wheeling awry; and there was no time in wind and waves and deepening cold. Mananaan's spells began to fail .He had gone beyond the realm where his powers held good. Foul winds came, against which few craft other than his could have sailed. Snow and sleet blew blindingly. The boat rolled and pitched in the gales, shipped water of numbing chill, flapped her sail and fought her rudder. Icebergs loomed monstrous out of blackness, and barely did the travellers save themselves from shipwreck.

Belike the fogs were most terrible—windless, soundless grey damp that dripped and froze, cut off eyesight half an arm away, soaked through clothes to skin and ran down into boots until teeth clattered. The boat would lie moveless, rocking ever so little to unseen wavelets, and the only sounds were their muffled slap and the fog dripping from ice-sheathed tackle. Groping, cursing, shivering, Skafloc and Mananaan sought to break such weather with charms—to scant avail. They had the feeling that Powers crept through the blindness overside and stared hungrily inboard.

Then a storm might come, like as not from the wrong direction, and unease would be lost in struggle. Mast groaned, sheets ripped hands, combers brawled under rails, and the boat mounted a wave toward the raving sky merely to slide down its trough as if into hell.

Quoth Skafloc:

> Black and cold, the breakers
> bellow, thunder inboard.
> Ropes and helm turn rebel.
> Roaring winds are sleet-cloaked.
> Seamen curse and stumble,
> sorry they upped anchor.
> Bitter is the brew here:
> beer of waves is salty.

But he did not stop working. Mananaan, who thought a grumble betokened better health than a lament, smiled into the crazy skies.

And the time came at last when they raised land. They saw it by unwinking stars and by northern lights that leaped and flickered high over gaunt mountains and greenly flashing glaciers. Surf boomed on cliffs behind which the land climbed steeply, a dead huge world of crags and ice-fields and wind screaming over ancient snow.

Mananaan nodded. "Yonder is Jötunheim," he said, his words already half lost in those noises. "Utgard, nigh which you say the giant bides, should by my reckoning lie to the east of here."

"As you say," muttered Skafloc. He had long since lost

his way, nor did any elf know much more than frightened rumours about these coasts.

He felt weariness no longer, he was past that. It was as if he went on like a ship with the steering oar lashed, because there was nothing else to do and no one to care if it foundered.

But it came to him, as he stood there looking on the terrible face of Giant Land, that Freda could not be less unhappy than he. More so, perhaps; for he could lose himself in the quest of the sword and know she was safe, while she knew only that he was on a deadly search and must have little to do but think about it.

"That had not struck me before," he whispered in astonishment, and of a sudden he felt tears freezing on his cheeks. Quoth he:

> Late will I the lovely
> lost one be forgetting.
> Ways that I must wander
> will be cold and lonely.
> Heavy is my heart now,
> where she sang aforetime.
> Greatest of the griefs that
> she gave me is her sorrow.

And he fell again to brooding. Mananaan let him be, having learned it was no use trying to hasten his arousal from such fits, and the boat ran eastward on the harrying wind.

Naught seemed to stir in this waste of rock and ice, save the tumbling breakers and the snow-devils awhirl in the mountains and the flapping auroral fires. But he felt there were presences not far off. Here was the spawning ground of those who threatened the viking gods—Asa-Loki, Utgard-Loki, Hel, Fenris, Jörmungandr, Garm who at the end of the world will devour the moon.

By the time Skafloc had shaken off his glumness, the boat had sailed a long ways, and Mananaan was steering close to every fjord in search of their goal. The sea king had grown uneasy, for he could almost smell the lairs of Utgard, and not he himself cared to come near that dark town.

"Bolverk dwells in a mountain, I was told," Skafloc said. "That would mean a cave."

"Aye, but this cursed land is riddled with caves."

"A big one, I should think. With signs of smithery about."

Mananaan nodded and made for the next inlet. As he neared the sea-cliffs, Skafloc began to understand the size of them. Up they went, in such a cataract of height that he grew dizzy trying to see their tops. A few aurora-lit clouds sailed over them, and he had the feeling that those walls of rock were toppling on him—now the sides of the world fell asunder as it sank beneath the sea!

Antlike, the boat crawled under the cliffs and peered into the fjord. It ran past sight, a maze of holms and skerries and crags jutting high enough to block out stars. But Skafloc's nostrils tingled to a faint scent borne on the wind—smoke, hot iron—and he heard the far-off banging of a hammer.

There was no need for words. Mananaan headed into the fjord. Soon the cliffs had shouldered all wind aside and the sailors must scull. They went right swiftly, but so long was the fjord that they scarce seemed to move.

Deeper grew the stillness, as if sound had frozen to death and the northlights danced on its grave. Some dry snow-flakes drifted out of the great starry sky. The cold ate and ate. It seemed to Skafloc that the quiet was that of a beast of prey waiting to pounce, with greedy eyes and switching tail. He knew somehow that he was being watched.

Slowly the boat won around the many twists and out-thrusts of the fjord, on into the stark land. Once Skafloc heard a slithering inshore, that kept pace. The wind yowled over the clifftops, so high that it might almost have been blowing between the stars.

Strange was it to see the image of Fand, dancing ever farther into Jötunheim.

At last the boat came to a place where a broad rough slope cut down from a mountain whose top was crowned with the Lodestar. A glacier ran along that slope, glimmering in the uneasy half-light, to end at the water. "This looks to be our landing spot," said Mananaan.

Something hissed from the tumbled blocks of ice piled beneath the glacier's side.

"Methinks first is a guard to get by," said Skafloc. He and his companion busked themselves, putting on helm and byrnie, with furs above against the tearing cold. Each took a shield on his arm and girded a sword at his waist. Skafloc had yet another sword in his gloved hand, while Mananaan bore his great spear whose head gave back what light there was in a ripple like moonglade.

The boat grounded gently on ice and shale. Skafloc could jump ashore without going into the slurried water. He drew the hull up and made fast while Mananaan stood watch, straining into the gloom beyond. Thence came a grinding sound, as of a heavy weight dragging over stones.

"Our way is dark and has an evil smell," remarked the sea king; "however, we grow no safer by dawdling."

He started off between and over the house-sized chunks of ice and rock. Blackness thickened until the seekers must grope ahead by what few ragged patches of stars showed between the heights. The stench waxed around them, with something altogether cold about it, and the stirring and hissing got louder .

Passing a ravine that led toward the glacier, Skafloc saw the long pale shape within. His grip tightened on the haft.

The thing slid out and towards them. Mananaan's battle-cry rang between the steeps. He drove his spear into the looming form. "Out of the way, white worm!" he shouted.

The thing hissed and struck at him. Its coils scraped on the stones and sent them rattling. He darted aside, and as the flat head smote near, Skafloc hewed. The shock of the blow rammed back into his shoulders, and the worm turned gape-jawed on him. Barely could he see the creature in this dark, but he knew that mouth could swallow him whole.

Mananaan thrust his spear into the pallid neck. Skafloc cut again at the snout. The charnel smell made his throat seize up; he gasped for air and rained blows. A drop of blood or venom splashed on him, ate through his coat, and seared his arm.

He cursed, and hewed more strongly at the weaving head. Then he felt his sword crumple, corroded by that blood. He heard Mananaan's spearshaft break as it went in.

Drawing their sheathed blades, he and the sea king pressed forward afresh. The worm withdrew, and they followed it up onto the glacier.

Grisly to see was the thing. Its coils writhed halfway to the peak, leprous white and thicker than a horse. The snake head swayed high above, drooling blood and poison. Mananaan's broken spear was in one eye; the other glittered balefully down. Its tongue flickered in and out, a blur to the sight, and it hissed like sleeting gale.

Skafloc slipped on the ice. The worm hacked down at him. Yet swifter was Mananaan, to hold his shield above the fallen man and smite with his sword. That blade gashed open the puffed throat. Skafloc scrambled to his feet and swung likewise.

The worm brought a coil lashing around. Skafloc rolled aside into a snowdrift. Mananaan was caught in a loop, but ere it could crush him his glaive had slotted between two ribs.

At that the worm fled, plunged past them like a snowslide into the sea. Gasping and trembling, the wayfarers sat for a long while under the northlights before they took up their journey anew.

"Our second blades are pitted," said Skafloc. "Best we go back for new weapons."

"Nay, the worm might be lurking for us by the shore, or if not that, then sight of us may re-awaken its wrath," answered Mananaan. "These arms will serve till we have the rune sword."

They climbed slowly along the slick, mysteriously shimmering glacier. Black ahead, the mountain blotted out half the sky. Dimly, the wind brought noise of a beating hammer.

Onward they went, until hearts fluttered and lungs gasped. Often they must rest, even sleep a little, there on the back of the glacier, and it was well they had brought food along; for the ice was sharply canted and treacherous.

Naught stirred, naught seemed to live in the cold, but always louder came the ringing of the hammer.

Until in the end Skafloc and Mananaan stood at the head of the glacier, halfway to the top of the mountain crowned with the Lodestar. A narrow trail, broken and boulder-strewn, hardly to be seen in the murk, went off leftward. Sheer cliffs dropped from it to whittering depths. The travellers roped themselves together and crept along it.

They came, after many falls where one saved his partner by clawing himself to the rock, out on a ledge that fronted a cave mouth. From the deeps behind rolled the sound of iron.

A great red dog was chained in the opening. It howled and flung itself at them. Skafloc half raised his sword to kill it.

"No," said Mananaan. "I have the feeling that seeking to slay this beast would bring the worst of luck. We had best try to slip by it."

They held their shields overlapping and went in crabwise, right arms to the rock. The hound's weight slammed against them and its teeth dented the rims. The howling shook their skulls. Barely could they win past the reach of the chain.

Now they came into lightlessness. They held hands and groped along a downward-slanting tunnel, feeling ahead for pits and often crashing into fanged stalagmites. The air was less cold than outside, but its dankness made it seem more so. They heard the noise of mighty waters and thought that this must be one of the sounding rivers that flow through hell. Louder and nearer clamoured the beat of the hammer.

Twice came a yelping that made echoes fly, and they stood braced for battle. Once they were set upon by something big and heavy, that bit chunks out of their shields. Blind in the dark, they yet made shift to slay the thing. But they never knew what shape it had had.

Soon afterwards they saw a red glow, like that star which is in the Hunter. They hastened forward and came, more slowly than they would have thought, to a vast frosty chamber. And into this they stepped.

Dimly was it lit by a wide but low forge-fire. In that light, the hue of half-clotted blood, they could make out vague gigantic things that might belong in a smithy. And at the anvil was a Jötun.

Huge he was, so tall they could scarce see his head in the reeky gloom, and so broad that he nonetheless was squat. He wore only a dragonskin apron on his hairy body, which was gnarled like an old tree bole and muscled like a snake-pit. Black hair and beard hung matted to his waist. His legs were short and bowed, the right one lame, and he was hunch-backed, bent over till his arms touched the ground.

As the seekers entered, he turned a terrible face on them, broad-nosed, wide-mouthed, scarred and seamed. Under the heavy brow ridges were twin hollownesses; his eyes had been plucked from the sockets.

His voice carried the boom and hiss of those rivers that flow through hell. "Oho, oho! For three hundred years has Bolverk toiled alone. Now the blade must be hammered out." And he took that on which he had been working and flung it across the room. The clang when it struck flew back and forth between the walls for a long while.

Skafloc stood boldly forth, met the empty glare, and said: "I bring new work that is also old for you, Bolverk."

"Who are you?" cried the Jötun. "Mortal man can I smell, but there is more than a little of Faerie about him. Another I can smell who is half a god, but he is not of

Æsir or Vanir." He groped around him. "I am not easy about either of you. Come closer so I can tear you apart."

"We are on a mission you will not dare hinder," said Mananaan.

"What is it?" Bolverk's question rolled through the caverns until it was lost in the inner earth.

Quoth Skafloc:

> Asa-Loki,
> angry, weary
> with his prison,
> wishes sword-play
> Here the weapon
> for his wielding:
> Bolverk, take
> the bane of heroes.

And he opened his wolfskin bundle and flung the broken sword clashing at the giant's feet.

Bolverk's hands fumbled over the pieces. "Aye," he breathed. "Well I remember this blade. Me it was whose help Dyrin and Dvalin besought, when they must make such a sword as this to ransom themselves from Svafrlami but would also have that it be their revenge on him. We forged ice and death and storm into it, mighty runes and spells, a living will to harm." He grinned. "Many warriors have owned this sword, because it brings victory. Naught is there on which it does not bite, nor does it ever grow dull of edge. Venom is in the steel, and wounds it gives cannot be healed by leechcraft or magic or prayer. Yet this is the curse on it: that every time it is drawn it must drink blood, and in the end, somehow, it will be the bane of him who wields it."

He leaned forward. "Therefore," he said slowly, "Thor broke it, long ago, which none but he in the Nine Worlds had strength to do; and it has lain forgotten in the earth ever since. But now—now, if Loki calls to arms as you say, there will be need of it."

"I did not say that," muttered Skafloc, "though I meant you to think I did."

Bolverk heard him not. The Jötun stared sightlessly ahead, rapt, while his fingers stroked the sword. "So it is to end," he whispered. "Now comes the last evening of the world, when gods and giants lay waste creation as they slay each other, when Surt scatters flame which leaps to the cracking walls of heaven, the sun blackens, earth sinks undersea, the stars fall down. It ends—my thralldom, blind beneath the mountain, ends in a blaze of fire! Aye, well will I forge the sword, mortal!"

He went to work. The clamour of it filled the cave, sparks flew and bellows gusted, and as he worked he called out spells which made the walls shudder. Skafloc and Mananaan took shelter in the tunnel beyond.

"I like this not, and wish I had never come," said the sea king. "An evil is being waked to new life. None have named me coward, yet I will not touch that sword; nor will you, if you are wise. It will bring your weird on you."

"What of that?" answered Skafloc moodily.

They heard the seething as the blade was quenched in venom. The fumes stung where they touched bare skin. Bolverk's doom-song bellowed through the caverns.

"Throw not your life away for a lost love," pleaded Mananaan. "You are young yet."

"All men are born fey," said Skafloc, and there the matter stood.

Time dragged—though they did not understand how the giant could be done as soon as he was, blind and without help—until he shouted: "Enter, warriors!"

They came into the bloody light. Bolverk held forth the sword. Brightly gleamed the blade, a blue tongue about whose edges little flames seemed to waver. The eyes of the dragon on the haft glittered, the gold glowed as with a shiningness of its own.

"Take it!" cried the giant.

Skafloc seized the weapon. Heavy it was, but strength to swing it flowed into him. So wondrous was the balance that it became like a part of himself.

He swept it in a yelling arc, down on a rock. The stone split asunder. He shouted and whirled the blade about his head. It shone in the murk like a lightning flash.

"Ha, halloo!" Skafloc yelled. And he chanted:

Swiftly goes the sword-play!
Soon the foe shall hear
the wailing song of weapons.
Warlock blade is thirsty!
Howling in its hunger,

hews it through the iron,
sings in cloven skullbones,
slakes itself in bloodstreams.

Bolverk's laughter joined his. "Aye, wield it in glee," said the Jötun. "Smite your foemen—gods, giants, mortals, it matters not. The sword is loose and the end of the world comes nigh!"

He gave the man a scabbard bedight with gold leaf. "Best you sheathe it now," he said, "and draw it not hereafter unless you wish to kill." He grinned. "But the sword has a way of getting drawn at the wrong time—and in the end, never fear, it will turn on you."

"Let it strike down my enemies first," Skafloc answered, "and I care not overly much what it does later."

"You may ... then," said Mananaan under his breath. Aloud: "Let us be off. Here is no place to bide."

They left. Bolverk's eyeless face stared after them.

When they had won out—the hound on the chain shrank whimpering aside—they set swiftly down the glacier. As they neared the bottom they heard a loud rumble and looked back.

Black against the stars, higher than the mountain, loomed three who strode down upon them. Mananaan said, scrambling for the boat: "I think Utgard-Loki has somehow learned of your trick and wishes not that you should fulfill whatever plans the Æsir have. Hard will it be to get quit of this land."

XXIII

The war which Mananaan Mac Lir and Skafloc Elven-Fosterling waged on Jötunheim would be well worth the telling. One should speak too of the struggle with berserk gale and windless mist, with surf and skerry and ice floe, with a weariness which grew so deep that only the image of Fand, bright against the undying night, gave cheer. That best of boats should have been honoured with golden trim and a song.

Many were the enchantments whereby the Jötuns sought to do away with their visitors, and hard luck did these two suffer on that account. But they worked out spells they could use here and wrought mightily in return, not alone warding off the worst of the giant magic but also turning storms loose to scourge the land and singing mountainsides down on Jötun garths.

They never sought to stand in open fight against the giants, though twice when one alone fell on them they killed him; but they coped with monsters of land and sea raised against them. Often their escapes from pursuit were narrow, especially when they went foraging inland during the long times of foul winds, and each would make a story in itself.

It should be told of their raid on a great steading to steal horses. In the end they left it ablaze and made off with a booty of which the steeds were not all. The beasts they took were the smallest of ponies in that land, but in the outer world would be reckoned the hugest and heaviest among stallions, shaggy black hulks with fiery eyes and devil hearts. Yet they took well to their new masters and stood quietly in the boat, which barely had room for them. And they feared neither daylight nor iron, even Skafloc's sword, nor did they ever grow tired.

Not every Jötun was a giant, or hideous or hateful. After all, some of this blood had become gods in Asgard. A lonely crofter might welcome guests who bore new faces, and not ask too closely what they were about. No few women were of human size, well favoured and well disposed. Mananaan of the glib tongue found the outlaw life not wholly bad. Skafloc did not look twice at any woman.

There is much else to tell, of the dragon and his golden hoard, of the burning mountain and the bottomless chasm and the quern of the giantesses. It should be told of the wayfarer's fishing in a river that ran from hell, and of what they caught there. The tales of the everlasting battle and of the witch in Iron Wood and of the song they heard the aurora hissing to itself in the secret night—each is worth telling, and would make a saga in itself. But since they are not in the main thread of the story, they must be left among the annals of Faerie.

Suffice it to say that Skafloc and Mananaan got out of Jötunheim and sailed south on the waters of Midgard.

"How long have we been gone?" wondered the man.

"I know not. Longer there than here." The sea king smelled the fresh breeze and looked up into a clear blue sky. "And it is spring."

Presently he went on: "Now that you have the sword—and have already blooded it well—what will you do?"

"I will seek to join the Erlking, if he still lives." Skafloc looked grimly ahead, over the racing waves to the dim line of horizon. "Put me ashore south of the channel and I will find him. And let the trolls dare try to stop me! When we have cleared mainland Alfheim of them, we will land in England and regain that. Finally we will go to their home grounds and lay their cursed race beneath our heel."

"*If* you can." Mananaan scowled. "Well, you must try, of course."

"Will the Sidhe lend no help?"

"That is a matter for the high council. Surely we cannot until the elves are in England, lest our country be ravaged while its warriors are elsewhere. But it may be we will strike then, for the battle and glory as well as to clear a menace from our flank." The sea king's proud head lifted. "However that goes—for the sake of blood shed together, toil and hardship and peril in common, and lives owed each to the other, Mananaan Mac Lir and his host will be with you when you enter England!"

They clasped hands, wordlessly. And soon Mananaan set Skafloc and his Jötun horse off, and sailed for Ireland and Fand.

Skafloc rode his black stallion toward the distant Erlking. The horse was gaunt, still stepping high but with hunger in his belly. Skafloc did not look rich himself, his clothes were ragged and faded, his armour battered and rusty, the cloak he wrapped around his shoulders was worn thin. He had lost weight in his farings, the great muscles lay just under the skin and the skin was drawn tightly over the big bones. But he kept haughtily straight. Lines were graven deeply in his face, which had lost all youth and become like the face of an outlaw god—its softest showing a faint mockery, and most times a harsh aloofness. Only the fair wind-tossed hair was young. So might Loki look, riding to Vigrid plain on the last evening of the world.

He went over hills, the reborn year around him. It had rained in the morning and the ground was muddy, pools and rivulets glittering in the sunbeams. The grass grew strongly, a cool light green to the edge of sight; and the trees were budding forth, a frail tint of new life across their boughs, the vanguard of summer.

It remained chilly; a strong wind gusted across the hills and whipped Skafloc's cloak about him. But this was a wind of spring, frolicking and shouting, lashing the sluggishness out of winter blood. The sky stood high and altogether blue, the sun struck through white and grey clouds, lances of light smote the wet grass in gleams and sparkles. Thunder rolled from the darkened southeast, but against that smoky cloud-mass shone a rainbow.

The honking of geese came from overhead, the wander-birds were homeward bound. A thrush tried out his song in a dancing grove, and two squirrels played in a tree like little red fires.

Soon would come warm days and light nights, green woods and nodding flowers. Something stirred within Skafloc as he rode, the unfolding of a buried and almost forgotten gentleness.

O Freda, if you were with me—

Day slanted towards the west. Skafloc rode straight forward on his tireless horse, taking no pains to stay unseen. He went at an easy pace for the Jötun breed, so that the black stallion could snatch food on the way; but earth quivered beneath those hoofs. They were entering Faerie lands, the middle province of Alfheim, bound for the mountain fastnesses where the Erlking must be if he yet held out. They passed signs of war—burnt garths, broken weapons, clean-picked bones, all crumbling away with the speed of Faerie things. Now and again a fresh troll spoor showed, and Skafloc licked his lips.

Night rose, strangely warm and well lit after the realms whence he had come. He rode on, at times dozing in the saddle but never ceasing to listen. Well before the enemy horsemen crossed his path he heard them and buckled on his helmet.

They were six, dark powerful shapes in the starlight. He puzzled them—a mortal, in clothes and mail half elven and half Sidhe, on a steed akin to theirs though even bigger and craggier. They barred his path, and one shouted forth: "In the name of Illrede Troll-King, halt!"

Skafloc spurred his stallion and drew the sword as he lunged ahead. The blade flared hell-blue in the night. He rode full tilt in among that squad, and clove a helmet and skull and lopped another off ere the trolls were aware of it.

Then one struck at Skafloc from the left with a club, another from the right with an axe. Guiding horse with knees, he held shield between him and the first. His sword leaped to meet the second, tearing through the axe haft and the breast behind. Slewing the glaive about, Skafloc split the troll on his left from shoulder to waist. He plucked with one finger at the reins. His monster horse reared and struck out with forefeet that crunched the skull of the fifth troll.

The last screamed and sought to flee. Skafloc threw his sword in a gleaming bolt that went in the troll's back and came out of his breast.

Thereafter he rode on, seeking the beleaguered Erlking. Near dawn he halted by a river for a short sleep.

He woke to the rustle of leaves and a faint shiver in the ground. Two trolls were stealing on him. He sprang to his feet, drawing sword though with no time to busk himself otherwise. They rushed. Through the shield and shoulder and heart of the first he hewed. At once he raised his dripping blade and the second troll could not stop fast enough to keep from spitting himself on it. Against that hard shock Skafloc held steady, braced by the unearthly strength that flowed from his weapon.

"This was nigh too easy," he said; "but no doubt better sport will come along."

He rode on through the day. About noon he found a cave where several trolls lay asleep. He killed them and ate their food. It mattered little to him that he was leaving a trail of corpses for anyone to follow. Let them!

Near dusk he reached the mountains. High and beautiful they reared, snowpeaks afloat in the sunset sky. He heard song of waterfalls and sough of pines. Strange, he thought, that such peace and loveliness was a place for slaughter. By rights, he should have been here with Freda and their love, not with a grim black horse and a sword of doom.

But so it went, so it went. And how went it for her?

He rode up the steeps and across a glacier on which his steed's hoofs rang. Night spread across heaven, clear and cold at these heights, a rising near-full moon to turn the peaks into ghosts. A while later Skafloc heard, far and weird in the still spaces around him, the lowing of a lur horn. His heart jumped and he spurred the horse to a gallop, from crag to crag and over windy abysses. The air hooted in his ears and the echoes of iron horseshoes toned between the mountains.

Someone fought!

The harsh bray of a troll horn reached him, and soon the distance-dwarfed shout of warriors and clatter of weapons.

An arrow zipped past. He snarled and crouched low in the saddle. No time to deal with the archer; bigger game was at hand.

He burst over a ridge and looked across moonlit white up-and-down to the battlestead. Men might have seen only a peak on which whirled snow-devils, and heard only a curious note in the wind. Skafloc's witch-sight pierced beneath. He saw the mountaintop as a high-walled, frost-bedecked castle whose towers climbed for the stars. Ringed about it on the upper slopes were the black tents of a great troll army. One pavilion was of more than ordinary size, with a dark ensign over it; and from the highest turret of the castle flew the banner of the Erlking. The overlords had met.

The trolls were storming the fortress. Like dogs they yelped under the walls, they raised ladders and sought to climb, they hid the foundations with their numbers. Many engines of war did they have, mangonels that cast fireballs over the parapets, wheeled towers trundling ahead full of armed men, rams beating on the gates, trebuchets to hurl boulders against masonry. The shouts, trampling of feet and hoofs, clash of metal, roar of drums and horns, filled the night with a storm of sound that started avalanches grinding and smoking downward and made the ice-fields ring an answer.

The elves stood on their battlements and fought the trolls off. Swords gleamed, spears and arrows darkened the moon, boiling oil gushed from cauldrons, ladders were upset—but the trolls came on, and the elves were few. This siege was drawing to an end.

Skafloc pulled out his sword. The blade hissed through the scabbard and poured moonlight over its length in cold ripples. "Hai-ah!" he shouted, spurred his horse and went down the slope before him in a cloud of snow.

He did not toil through the ravine that barred his way. At the brink, his thighs felt the stallion's muscles bunch, and then he was soaring through the middle of the sky with stars everywhere around him. He struck the farther side with a shock that slammed his teeth together; but at once he rushed up the mountainside.

The troll camp was almost empty. Skafloc reined in, his horse pawing the wind, and leaned over to snatch a brand from a fire. The speed of his gallop whipped it to a full blaze as he rode around setting tents aflame. In a short while many were burning and sparks were spreading to the rest. Skafloc hastened on toward the castle gates, busking himself fully while he did.

As before, he carried shield on left arm, sword in right hand, and steered the horse with knees and words. Ere the trolls at the main gate were aware of him he had struck down three and his beast had trampled as many.

Then the outermost of that mass turned on him. His sword leaped and whirred and shrieked, clove with a belling through helm and hauberk, flesh and bone, to rise streaming. Never did its death-dance halt, and Skafloc mowed trolls like ripe wheat.

They surged around him, but none could touch the iron he wore and few of their blows landed. Those that did, he seldom felt—not when the sword was in his grasp!

He swung sideways and a head rolled off its shoulders. Another swing, and he had opened a horseman's belly. A third blow shore through helm and skull and brain. A warrior on foot stabbed at him with a spear, scraping his arm; he leaned down and struck the troll to earth. But most of those afoot died under the kicks and bites of the Jötun horse.

Clang and screech of outraged metal rose beneath the moon. Blood steamed in the trampled snow, corpses wallowed in its pools. The black stallion and his rider and the blade of terror rose high over all, carving a road to the gates.

Hew, sword, hew!

Panic fell on the trolls and they scrambled to get clear. Skafloc shouted: "Hai, Alfheim! Victory-Father rides with us tonight! Sally forth, elves, come out and kill!"

A ring of fire, the burning camp, walled in the battlefield. The trolls saw and were dismayed. Also, they knew a Jötun steed and a haunted sword when they met them. What manner of being fought against Trollheim?

Skafloc rode his rearing stallion back and forth before the gate. His mail gleamed wet with blood in the light of moon and fire. His eyes flung back a blue like that of his blade. And he taunted his foes and called on the elves to sally.

The frightened whisper ran among the milling trolls: "*—It is Odin, come to make war—no, he has two eyes, it is Thor—it is Loki, risen from his chains, the end of the world is nigh—it is a mortal possessed by a demon—it is Death—*"

Lur horns blew, the gates swung wide, and the elves rode forth. Fewer by far than the trolls were they, but a new hope lit their haggard faces and gleamed from their eyes. At their head, on a milk-white charger, his crown aglitter in the moonlight and his hair and beard flowing hoar over byrnie and dusk-blue cloak, came the Erlking.

"We had not looked to see you alive again, Skafloc," he called.

"Nonetheless you have," replied the man, with no trace of his old awe—for nothing, he thought, could frighten him who had spoken with the dead and sailed beyond the world and had naught left to lose anyhow.

The Erlking's weird eyes rested on the rune sword. "I know what weapon that is," he murmured. "I do not know if it is good for Alfheim to have it on our side. Well—" He raised his voice. "Forward, elves!"

His men charged the trolls, and bloody was that battle. Swords and axes rose and fell and rose afresh dripping, metal cried out and shattered, spears and arrows clouded the sky, horses trampled the dead underfoot or screamed with wounds, warriors fought and gasped and sank to earth.

"Hola, Trollheim! To me, to me!" Illrede rallied his folk and got some of them into a wedge that he led to split the elves. His ebon stallion snorted thunder, his axe never rested and never missed, and elves began to shy away from him. Above the dragonskin coat, his face was icy green in the moonlight, a maelstrom of rage; the tendrils of his beard writhed, the lamps of his eyes burned black.

Skafloc saw him and uttered a wolf-howl. He brought his Jötun horse about and pressed toward the troll-king. His sword screamed and crashed, hewing enemies as a woodman hews saplings, a blur of blue flame in the night.

"Ha!" roared Illrede. "Make way! He is mine!"

They rode at each other down a suddenly cleared path. But when the troll-king saw the rune sword, he choked and reined in.

Skafloc's laughter barked at him. "Aye, your weird is upon you. Darkness comes for you and your whole evil race."

"The evil done in the world was never all troll work," said Illrede quietly. "It seems to me that you have done a deed more wicked than any of mine in bringing that blade to earth again. Whatever his nature, which the Norns and not himself gave, no troll would do such a thing."

"No troll would dare!" sneered Skafloc, and rode in upon him.

Illrede chopped valiantly out. The axe caught the Jötun horse in the shoulder. It did not go deep, but the stallion screamed and reared. While Skafloc fought to stay in the saddle, Illrede cut at him.

The man got his shield in between, but it split, though it kept the edge from him; and Skafloc rocked in his seat from that blow. Illrede pressed closer, to smash at the man's head. The helmet was dented, and only the uncanny strength lent by the sword kept Skafloc from swooning.

Illrede raised his axe anew. Dizzily, Skafloc smote at him. That was a weak blow. Yet sword and axe met in a shower of sparks, and with a loud noise the axe burst asunder. Skafloc shook his head to clear it. He laughed and cut off Illrede's left arm.

The troll-king sagged. Skafloc's blade whined down and took off his right arm. "It does not become a warrior to play with a helpless foe," gasped Illrede. "The sword is doing this, not you."

Skafloc killed him.

Now fear came upon every troll, and they backed up in disorder. The elves pushed furiously against them. Din of battle rang between the mountains. In the van of the elves, the Erlking fought even while he egged them on. But it was Skafloc, riding everywhere, harvesting men with a blade that seemed to drip blue fire as well as blood, who struck the deepest terror.

At last the trolls broke and fled. Hotly did the elves give chase, cutting them down, driving them into the burning camp. Not many escaped.

The Erlking sat his horse in the first thin dawnlight and looked over the death heaped about the castle walls. A cold breeze ruffled his unhelmeted hair and the mane and tail of his horse. Skafloc rode to him, gaunt and weary, painted with blood and brains, though with no look of lessened revengefulness.

"That was a great victory," said the Erlking. "Still, we were almost the last elf stronghold. The trolls have riddled Alfheim through and through."

"Not for long," answered Skafloc. "We will go forth against them. They are spread thinly, and every free elf now skulking as outlaw will join us. We can outfit from the trolls we kill, if naught else. Hard will the war be; but my sword bears victory.

"Also," he added slowly, "I have a new standard to raise in the forefront of our main army. It ought to shake the foe." And he lifted a spearshaft whereon was impaled the head of Illrede. The dead eyes seemed to watch and the mouth to grin with menace.

The Erlking winced. "Grim is your heart, Skafloc," he said. "You have changed since last I met you. Well, let it be as you wish."

XXIV

At winter's dawn, Freda stumbled into Thorkel Erlendsson's garth.

The landholder was just arisen and had come out to look at the weather. For an eyeblink he did not believe he saw aright—a shield maiden, with arms and armour of an unknown coppery metal and clothes of altogether outlandish cut, groping ahead like one gone blind—it could not be.

He reached for a spear he kept behind the door. His hand dropped as he looked more closely on the girl and knew her: worn out, emptily staring, but Freda Ormsdaughter come back.

Thorkel led her inside. Aasa his wife hastened to them.

"You have been long gone, Freda," she said. "Welcome home!"

The girl sought to reply. No words would come out. "Poor child," murmured Aasa. "Poor lost child. Come, I will help you to bed."

Audun, Thorkel's next oldest son after the slain Erlend, came into the house. " 'Tis colder outside than a well-born maiden's heart," said he, and then: "Who is this?"

"Freda Ormsdaughter," answered Thorkel, "returned somehow."

Audun stepped over to her. "Why, this is wonderful!" he said gladly. He clasped her waist, but ere he could kiss her cheek the mute woe of her fell on his heart. He stood aside. "What is the matter?" he asked.

"Matter?" Aasa snapped. "Ask what is not the matter with the poor sorrow-laden lass. Now go, you heavy-footed goggle-eyed men, get out and let me put her to bed."

Freda lay awake for a long time, gazing at the wall.

When at last Aasa brought her food and made her eat, and murmured to her and stroked her hair like a mother with a babe, she began to weep. Long was that flow of tears, albeit oddly noiseless. Aasa held her and let her cry them out. Thereafter Freda fell asleep.

Later, at Thorkel's bidding, she agreed to make her home there for the time being. Though she soon recovered herself, she was not the glad girl folk remembered.

Thorkel asked her what had happened. She lowered a whitening face. He added quickly: "No, no, you need not speak it if you do not want to."

"No reason for hiding the truth," she said, so low he could scarce hear. "Valgard bore Asgerd and myself east-ward over the sea, meaning to give us to a heathen king whose good will he would have. Hardly had he landed when . . . another viking fell on him and put his men to flight. Valgard escaped, and Asgerd was killed in the strife. This other chief took me with him. At last, though, having . . . business whereon I could not go . . . he left me at my father's garth."

"That is strange gear you carried."

"The viking gave it to me. He had it from somewhere else. I often fought by his side. He was a good man, for a heathen." Freda looked into the hearthfire of the room wherein they sat. "Aye, he was the best and bravest and kindest of men." Her lips twisted. "Why should he not be? He came of good folk."

She rose and walked quickly outdoors. Thorkel looked after her, tugging his beard. "Not all the truth has she told," he muttered to himself, "but I think it is all we will ever hear."

Even to the priest by whom she was shriven, Freda said no more than that. Afterwards she went off alone and stood on a high hill looking skyward.

The winter was fading and this was a bright day, not overly cold. Snow glistened white on the silent earth, while overhead reached a cloudless blue.

Freda said quietly: "Now I have done a mortal sin, in not confessing who he was that I lay with unwedded. Yet I put the burden on my own soul and will bear it to the grave. All-Father, You know our sin was too dear and wonderful to be besmirched by the ugliest of names. Lay what punishment You will on me, but spare him, who knew no better." She flushed. "Also, I think I may be bearing under my heart what you, Mary, must remember—and *he* shall not bear an evil name for the sake of what his parents did. Father and Mother and Son, do what You will with me, but spare the innocent child."

When she came down she felt somewhat eased. The cool air kissed the blood into her cheeks, the sunlight ran in bronze and copper across her hair, and her grey eyes were bright. There was a smile on her lips when she met Audun Thorkelsson.

Though hardly older than she, he was tall and strong, a skilled husbandman and promising in weapon-play. His curly fair locks gleamed about a face blushing and shyly smiling in return, like a girl's, and he ran to join her.

"I . . . was looking for you . . . Freda," he said.

"Why, was I wanted?" she asked.

"No, save—well—yes, I wanted—to talk with you," he mumbled. He walked by her side, now and then stealing a glance from downcast eyes.

"What will you do?" he blurted at last.

The blitheness faded from her. She cast one look into the sky and another across the fields. The sea was not visible from here, but the wind was such today that its voice came faintly to her ears, tireless, relentless.

"I know not," she said. "I have none left—"

"Oh, you have!" he cried. His tongue locked and he could say no more, however much he cursed himself for it.

Winter bled away under the joyous weapons of spring. Still Freda dwelt in Thorkel's house. None held it against her that she carried a bastard; something would have been wrong with her had she not, after what was past! Because of health and strength, if not some lingering elven-breath, she suffered little from morning sickness. Thus she could work hard, and when there was no more work to do could go for long walks, alone by choice though Audun often came along. Aasa was glad of help and of a talk-friend, having no daughters and few working girls; this household was nothing like what Orm's had been. But she did most of the talking. Freda answered in well-bred fashion when spoken to, if she heard.

At first, time had been her torturer, less by the weight of her sin and the loss of her folk—those she could bear, and the new life within her was some cheer for them—than by the loss of Skafloc.

No sign, no word, no sight since that last stricken gaze by Orm's howe in the winter sunrise. He was gone, ringed in by his foemen, off into the grimmest of lands for a prize that must bring doom on him. Where was he this day and that day? Did he live yet, or did he lie long and stiff on the ground with ravens picking out the eyes which had shone for her? Did he yearn for death as once he had yearned for Freda? Or had he forgotten what he could not stand to remember and left his humanness for the cool forgetting that was in Leea's kisses—? No, that could not be, he would not cast his love adrift while he lived.

But lived he yet—and how, and for how long?

Now and again she dreamed of him, as if he stood living before her, their hearts throbbed together and his arms were both hard and tender around her. He murmured in her ear, laughed, spoke a love-stave, and play became love . . . She awoke in the darkness and thick air of the shut-bed.

She had changed. The life of men seemed a dull and niggling round after the glamour of the elf court and the mad, yes, glad days of their troll-hunt through a winter wilderness. Thorkel having been christened merely so the English could deal with him, she rarely saw priest—and, knowing her heart sinned, was glad of that. Dreary was a church after the woodlands and hills and sounding sea. She still loved God—and was not the earth His work, and a church only man's?—but she could not bring herself to call on Him very often.

Sometimes she could not keep from slipping out in the middle of the night, taking a horse, and riding a ways northward. With her witch-sight she might catch a glimpse of Faerie—a scuttering gnome, an owl hatched from no egg, a black ship coasting by. But those she dared hail fled her, and she could get no word of how the war went.

Even so, that briefly seen world, weird and moonstruck, was Skafloc's. And for a short miraculous time it had been hers.

She kept herself too busy for overmuch brooding, though, and her young healthy body bloomed. As the weeks passed into months, she felt the same stirring within her that brought back the birds and called forth buds like clenched baby fists. She saw herself in a pool and knew she had become woman rather than girl—the slim shape fuller, the bosom rising and swelling, the blood coursing steadier just beneath the skin. She was becoming a mother.

Could he see her now—*No, no, it must not be. But I love him, I love him so.*

Winter went in rain and pealing thunder. The first soft green spread over trees and meadows. The birds came home. Freda saw a pair of storks she knew, wheeling puzzled above Orm's lands. They had always nested on his roof. She wept, quietly as the rains of late spring. Her breast felt empty.

No, not that, it was filling again, not with the old boundless joy but with a stiller gladness. Her child was growing within her. In him—or her, it mattered not—all burnt-out hopes rose new.

She stood in twilight with the blossoms of an apple tree overhead, drifting down on her at each mild breeze. The winter was gone. Skafloc lived in the springtime, in cloud and shadow, dawn and sunset and high-riding moon, he spoke through the wind and laughed through the sea. There would be winter, and winter again, in the great unending ring-dance of the years. But she bore the summer beneath her heart, and every summer to come.

Now Thorkel made ready for a trading voyage to the east (with maybe a little viking work, should the chance come along) that he and his sons had long planned. Audun was no longer happy about it, and at last he said to his father: "I cannot go."

"What is that?" cried Thorkel. "You, who have day-dreamed of this more than any of us, would stay behind?"

"Well, I—well, someone is needed here."

"We have good housecarles."

Audun looked uneasily away. "So did Orm."

"This is a smaller farm than Orm's, thus has nearer neighbours. And have you forgotten how the folk hereabouts decided on keeping watchers out this year, after what happened?" Thorkel's shrewd eyes stabbed his son. "What ails you, lad? Speak the truth. Are you afraid of fighting?"

"You know I am not," flared Audun, "and unblooded though I be, I will kill whoever says I am. It is not my wish to go this time, and there is an end of that."

Thorkel nodded slowly. "Freda, then. I thought as much. But she is without kindred."

"What of that? Her father's lands must be hers. I myself will get money when I sail out *next* summer."

"And the child she bears, by this wanderer of whom she does not speak but always seems to think?"

Audun looked angrily at his feet. "Again, what of that?"

he mumbled. " 'Twas not her fault. Nor the child's, for that matter, whom I would right gladly set on my knee. She needs someone to help her—yes, and to help her forget the man who wantonly cast her off. Could I find him, you would see whether I fear to do battle!"

"Well—" Thorkel shrugged. "I can command you, but not your will. Stay behind if you feel you must." After a while he added: "You are right, those broad acres should not lie fallow. And she ought to make a good wife, with many strong sons in her." He smiled, though his eyes were troubled. "Woo her, then, and win her if you can. I hope your luck is better than Erlend's."

After the grain was planted, Thorkel sailed with his remaining boys and other young men. Since they meant to seek more than one land on the far side of the North Sea, their homecoming was not awaited before late fall or early winter. Audun gazed wistfully after their ship. Yet when he turned and saw Freda beside him, he felt well repaid.

"Did you really stay just to oversee the harvest?" she asked.

His ears were hot, but he answered brashly: "I think you know otherwise."

She glanced away and said naught.

The days lengthened and earth burst into its fullness. Warm winds, shouting rains, birdsong and deer and fish silvery in the rivers, flowers and light nights— More and more Freda felt her babe stirring.

Ever oftener, too, was Audun by her side. Now and again, in a rush of unhappiness, she bade him begone. Always his sorrowful mien brought remorse to her.

His wooing went with lame words to which she scarcely listened. She buried her face in the fragrance of the flower-bunches he gathered for her, and through the petals she saw him smile, shy as a puppy—strange, that so big and sure a youth was weaker than she was.

If they wed, it would be him that was given to her. He was not Skafloc, only Audun. *O unforgotten beloved!*

But the memory of Skafloc was becoming a summer that was past, recalled in a new year. He warmed her heart without searing it, and her longing for him was like a still tarn whereon sun-glints had begun to dance. To mourn without end was to be weak: unworthy of what they had shared.

She liked Audun. He would be a stout shield for Skafloc's child.

There came an evening when they two stood on the shore, the waters murmurous at their feet and the sunset red and gold behind them. Audun took her hands and said with a lately learned steadiness: "You know I have loved you, Freda, from before that time you were taken away. In these past weeks I have frankly sought your hand. First you would not listen and later you would not reply. I ask for an honest answer now, and if it is your wish, I will trouble you no more. Will you wed me, Freda?"

She looked into his eyes and her voice was low and clear: "Yes."

XXV

In late summer the northland weather turned rainy. For days and nights on end, wind scourged the elf-hills and veiled them in lightning-blinking grey. The trolls seldom dared leave Elfheugh; bands of their homeless enemies had grown too big, well-supplied, and cunning at ambush. They slouched and slumped about, drinking, gaming, quarrelling, and drinking again. In their sullen, fearful mood, the lightest word might lead to a death-fight. Meanwhile their elf lemans had gotten so perverse that hardly a day went by without friendships broken and often lives lost over a woman.

Rumours were muttered along the dim corridors. Illrede—aye, he had fallen, and his grinning head lay in a cask of brine until battle, when it became the standard of the foe. The new King Guro could not hold the troll armies together as the old had done, and each time he made a stand he was driven back. A demon on a giant horse, with a sword and a heart from hell, led the elves to victory over twice their number.

Wendland had fallen, whispered someone, and the elves' terrible chieftain had ringed in trolls there and spared not a one. It was said you could walk on troll corpses from end to end of that wide field.

Strongholds in Norway, Sweden, Gothland, Denmark were stormed, said another, and—somehow, though they were elf castles and built with elf skill to withstand assault—they fell as quickly as they had earlier surrendered to the trolls, and their garrisons were put to the sword. A fleet was taken in a Jutish bay and used for raids on Trollheim itself.

Allies and hirelings, such of them as survived, were falling away. A company of Shen was said to have turned on its troll companions in Gardariki and butchered them. A goblin uprising wiped out three towns—or five or a dozen—in Trollheim.

The elves were thrusting into Valland with the trolls in retreat before them . . . a retreat that became a rout and finally, caught against the sea under the cromlechs and menhirs of the Old Folk, a slaughter. Tales went around the castle of that dreadful horse which trod out warriors' lives, that weapon manyfold worse which sheared through metal as if through cloth, with never a blunting of its twin edges.

Valgard, gaunter and grimmer and curter of speech as the months wore on, sought to raise flagging spirits. "The elves have rallied," he said. "They have gained certain powers. Well, have you never seen a man thresh about just before he dies? They spend their last strength, and it is not enough."

But this the trolls knew: that fewer and fewer ships came from across the channel or the eastern seas, and what word they brought got worse and worse until Valgard forbade his warriors to talk freely with their crews; that the outlaw elves under Flam and Firespear grew nightly bolder, until a whole army was not safe from their sniping arrows, their swift forays on horse or by water; that the Irish Sidhe were arming as if for war; that weariness, despair, and hatred of one's fellow spread among themselves, fed by the elf women's sly minxiness.

Up and down the castle Valgard prowled, from its highest towers where chough and merlin nested to its deepest dungeons where toad and spider lurked, snarling, sometimes smiting and even killing in bursts of blind rage. He felt hemmed in, trapped by these misty-blue walls, by the outlaws beyond, by the waxing hosts of the Erlking, by his whole life. And naught could he do about it.

No use leading men forth. That was like fighting shadows. The slinkers would be gone; from somewhere a shaft would thunk into a troll's back, a noose tighten around a troll's neck, a pit with sharp stakes at the bottom open beneath a troll's horse. Even at the table one was never sure; now and again someone died, clearly poisoned, and no bland servitor offered any clue and it *might* have been done by a troll with a grudge.

Cunning and patient were the elves, turning their weaknesses into strengths, biding their time. The trolls could not understand them and came slowly to fear this race they thought they had beaten.

Who were now beating them, thought Valgard bleakly. But this he kept from his men as much as possible, though he could not stop the whispers or the wrangling.

Naught could he do, save sit in Imric's high seat draining cup after cup of fiery wine. Leea tended to him, and his beaker was never empty. He sagged in silence, eyes blurring toward blindness until he slid to the floor.

Often, however, when he was not yet too drunk to walk, he would slowly lift his great frame. Reeling a little, he made his way through the hall where the troll chiefs sprawled in spilth and vomit. He took a torch and fumbled down a rough-hewn stair. Leaning on the cold slippery wall, he got to one dungeon door and opened it.

Irmric's white body, streaked and blackened with clotted blood, glimmered in the gloom by the light of the coals below his feet. The imp tending that fire kept it ever hot, and the earl hung by his thumbs without food or drink. His belly was sunken in, his skin was taut over the arching ribs, his tongue was black, but he was an elf and this was not enough to let him die.

His slant cloudy-blue eyes rested on Valgard with the unreadable stare that, somehow, always chilled the changeling's heart. The berserker put a grin on that fear.

"Can you guess why I have come?" he said. His voice was thick and he swayed on his feet.

No word spoke Imric. Valgard struck him in the mouth, a blow that sounded very loud in the stillness here and set him swinging to and fro. The imp shrank aside, eyes and fangs agleam in the murk.

"You know, if your brain has not shriveled in your skull," said Valgard. "I have come before. I will come again."

He took a whip from a bracket on the wall and ran the thongs through his fingers. His eyes glittered; he wet his lips.

"I hate you," he mouthed. He brought his face close to Imric's. "I hate you for bringing me into the world. I hate you for stealing my heritage. I hate you for being what I can never be—nor would, cursed elf! I hate you because of your evil works. I hate you because your damned fosterling is not at hand for me and you must do instead—now!"

He lifted the whip. The imp huddled as far into a corner

as he could get. Imric made no sound or movement.

When Valgard's one arm tired, he used the other. After it was also weary, he threw down the whip and left.

The wine was working out of him; only a coldness and headache remained where it had been. As he came by a window he heard the roar of rain.

The troll-hated summer for which he had longed, thinking to lie out in green vales and beside clucking rivers, and which he had spent in futile sallies against the elves or caged between these walls—the summer was waning at last. But so was Trollheim. There was silence from Valland. The last word thence had been of a field stark with slaughter.

Would the rain never end? He shuddered at the wet breath through the window. Lightning glared blue-white and his bones shook to the thunder.

He stumbled upstairs to his chambers. The troll guard sprawled in sottish sleep—ha, were they all drunks and murderers of their own kin? Where in this stinking, brawling horde was one to whom he could open his heart?

He came to his bedroom and stood huge and stoop-shouldered in the doorway. Leea sat upright on the couch. She at least, he thought dully, she had not played the bitch like the other elf women; and she gave him comfort at times when he trembled for himself.

Lightning blazed anew. Thunder sent quiverings through the floor. Wind screamed and dashed rain against glass. Tapestries fluttered and candles flickered in a cold draught.

Valgard sat heavily down on the edge of the bed. Leea slid arms about his neck. Her gaze rested moon-cool upon him; her smile and silkiness and the odour of her were luring though somehow they had no warmth. She spoke, sweetly beneath the storm: "What have you been doing, my lord?"

"That you know," he muttered, "and I wonder why you have never sought to keep me from it."

"The strong do as they please to the weak." She slipped a hand beneath his clothes, making plain what he might do to her; he paid no heed.

"Aye," he said, and clenched his teeth. "That is a good law when one is strong. But now the trolls are breaking; for Skafloc—by every word I hear, it must be Skafloc—has come back with a weapon that carries all before it. What now is the rightful law?"

He turned to look darkly at her. "Though what I can

183

least understand," he said, "is the fall of the great strong-holds. Even an elf army victorious in the field should have broken itself to bits against such walls. Why, some few have never been out of elf hands despite everything we could bring against them. A few others we starved out; most yielded to us with no fight, like this one. We had them fully manned, well supplied—and they were lost as soon as a troop of the Erlking's got to them." He shook his unkempt head. "Why?"

Seizing her slim shoulders in rough hands: "Elfheugh shall not fall. It cannot! I will hold it though the gods themselves take the field against me. Ha, I hanker for battle —naught else would so cheer me and my weary men. And we will smash them, you hear? We will fling them back and I will raise Skafloc's head on a pike above these walls."

"Aye, my lord," she purred, still smiling and secret.

"I am strong," he growled, deep in his throat. "When I was a viking, I broke men with my bare hands. And I have no fear, and I am crafty. Many victories have I won, and I will win many more."

His hands fell slackly to his lap and his eyes darkened. "But what of that?" he whispered. "*Why* am I so? Because Imric made me thus. He moulded me into the image of Orm's son. I am alive for no other reason, and my strength and looks and brain are—Skafloc's."

He climbed to his feet, gaped before him like a blind man, and screamed. "*What am I but the shadow of Skafloc?*"

Lightning leaped and flamed, hellfire loose in heaven. Thunder banged. Wind hooted. The rain flung itself down rivering panes. A gust within the walls blew out the candles.

Valgard swayed and groped through the lightning-raddled gloom. "I will kill him," he mumbled. "I will bury him deep under the sea. I will kill Imric and Freda and you, Leea— everyone who knows I am not really alive, that I am a ghost conjured into flesh moulded after a living man's—cold flesh, my hands are cold—"

The thunder-wheels rumbled down the sky. Valgard howled. "Aye, throw your hammer around up there! Make your noise while you can! I will put my cold hands about the pillars of the gods' halls and pull them down. I will tread the world beneath my feet. I will raise storm and dark-ness and glaciers grinding out of the north, and ashes shall whirl in my tracks. I am Death!"

Someone beat frantically on the door, scarcely to be

heard above the weather. Valgard made a beast noise and opened it. His fingers sought the neck of the troll who stood wet and weary before him.

"I will begin with you," he said. Foam flecked his lips. The messenger struggled, but troll strength was too little to break that hold.

When he sprawled dead on the floor, the berserkergang left Valgard. Weak and trembling, he leaned against the doorjamb. "That was unwise," he breathed.

"Perhaps he had others with him," said Leea. She stepped out on the landing and called: "Ohé, down there! The earl wants to speak with any who lately arrived."

A second troll, likewise spent and reeling, a bloody gash in his cheek, shambled into sight, though he did not try to climb the stairs any farther than that. "Fifteen of us set out," he groaned. "Hru and I alone are left. The outlaws dogged us the whole way."

"What word were you bearing?" asked Valgard.

"The elves have landed in England, lord. And we heard, too, that the Irish Sidhe, led by Lugh of the Long Hand himself, are in Scotland."

Valgard nodded his gaunt head.

XXVI

Under cover of an autumn storm, Skafloc led the best of the elf warriors across the channel. He was chief of that host, for the Erlking stayed behind to command the rest in driving the last trolls from mainland Alfheim. To take England, the king warned, would be no light task; and if the trolls should repulse the invaders, Britain would be a rallying point for them, later a base for counter attack.

Skafloc shrugged. "Victory goes with my sword," he said.

The Erlking studied him before answering: "Have a care about that weapon. Well has it served us hitherto; nevertheless it is treacherous. Sooner or later it is fated to turn on its wielder, maybe when he is most sorely needed."

Skafloc paid scant heed to this. He did not outright wish to die—there was, after all, much to do in the world—but who knew if he would not be spared for many years yet? However that might be, he did not mean ever to try to get rid of the sword. It gave him what nothing else could. Wielding it in battle, he did not go berserk; indeed, his awareness was never more keen, his wits never more swift and sure. But he flamed upward, out of himself, no longer alone, altogether one with what he was doing and that which he did it with. So might it feel to be a god. So, in different wise, had it felt to be with Freda.

In hidden Breton bays he gathered ships, men, and horses. He slipped word to the elf chiefs in England, that they should start hosting their scattered folk. And on a night when gales cloaked the northern world, he took his fleet across the channel.

Sleet-mingled rain drove out of a sky that was black save when lightning split it open; then each last drop on the wind and grassblade on the earth stood forth starkly white. Thunder rolled and roared through the clamorous, battering air. The waves seethed white with foam and spindrift, booming out of the west and snarling far up onto every shore. Not even the elves dared raise sail; they rowed. Rain and sea dashed in their faces and drenched their garb. Blue fire crawled over the oars and the reeling dragon heads.

Out of the dark reared England. The elves pulled until it seemed their thews must snap. Surf bawled on beach and reef. The wind caught at the ships and sought to hurl them onto rocks or against each other. Skafloc grinned and said aloud:

> Cold and lustful
> are the kisses
> which Ran's daughters,
> white-armed, give us:
> laughing, shouting,
> shaking tresses
> hoar and salt-sweet,
> high breasts heaving.

From the bow of his rolling longship he saw the headland which was his goal; and for a moment longing overwhelmed him. Quoth he:

> Home again the howling,
> hail-streaked wind has borne me.
> Now I stand here, nearing
> ness of lovely England.
> *She* dwells past that shoreline.
> Shall I ever see her?

Woe, the fair young woman
will not leave my thinking.

Then he must give his whole mind to the struggle to round the cape.

When the fleet had done this, it found sheltered waters for landing and a small troop of elves waiting to help. The ships were grounded, dragged ashore, and made fast

Thereafter the crews busked themselves swiftly for war. A captain said to Skafloc: "You have not told us who is to stay and guard the ships."

"No one," he answered. "We will need our men inland."

"What? The trolls might come on the fleet and burn it! Then we would have no way of retreat."

Skafloc looked about the lightning-lit strand. "For me," he said, "there will be no retreat. I will not leave England again, alive or dead, till the trolls are driven out."

The elves regarded him with more than a little awe. He hardly seemed a mortal, tall and iron-clad as he stood, the demon sword at his waist. Wolf-greenish lights flickered far back in the ice blue of his eyes. The elves thought he was fey.

He swung into the saddle of his Jötun horse. His call struck through the wind: "Sound the lur horns. We ride after prey tonight!"

The army set off. About a third of them were mounted. The rest hoped soon to get steeds. Like French or Normans, rather than English or Danes, elves on land fought by choice as cavalry. Rain sluiced over them, fallen leaves scrunched soddenly under them, lightning cracked, the wind thrust cold with the first breath of a new winter.

After a while they heard the remote brassy bellow of troll battle-horns. The elves hefted their weapons and smiled in the flickering glare. Rain-streaming shields came onto arms and the lurs dunted again.

Skafloc rode at the head of the wedge. He felt no joy just then. The thought of more slaughter wearied and sickened him. Yet he knew it would be otherwise when he unsheathed his blade, and so he could hardly wait for battle.

The trolls appeared, a darkling mass on the great rolling down. They must have sensed the newcomers and gone out from a nearby castle, belike Alfarhöi. Their force was to be reckoned with, albeit smaller than the elves'. A full half of it was mounted, and Skafloc heard someone behind him say merrily, "Here is where I get four legs under me."

The chief on his right was less high-hearted. "We outnumber them," he said, "but not by enough to roll over them. This would not be the first time brave warriors have beaten a bigger host."

"I do not fear they will defeat us," replied Skafloc; "still, it would be bad if they killed very many, for then the next fight might indeed be our last." He scowled. "Curse it, where is the main body of England's elves? They were to meet us erenow. Unless the messengers were caught on the way—"

The troll horns sounded to battle. Skafloc drew his sword and swung it above his head. Lightning made it flare blindingly, dripping blue fire.

"Forward!" He spurred his horse. And the glory of power surged upward in him.

Spears and arrows arced overhead, unseen and unheard in the storm. The ripping wind made it hard to aim, and so the clatter of weapons was quickly begun.

Skafloc leaned forward in his stirrups and hewed. A troll struck at him. His sword bit through both those arms. Another rode close, axe lifted. The blade screamed around into that one's neck. A pikeman jabbed; the point glanced off Skafloc's shield, he cut the shaft in twain, his horse trampled the troll into the mud.

Axe and sword! Clang and spark-flash! Cloven metal, rent flesh, warriors sinking to earth, devil-dance of lightning!

Through the clangour rode Skafloc, smiting, smiting. His blows shuddered in byrnie and bone, shocks that slammed back into his own shoulders. Weapons lashed at him, to be stopped by shield or shorn across by sword. The hawk-scream of his blade sounded through wind and thunder. None could stand before him, and he led his men through the troll lines and turned on the foe from the rear.

Nonetheless the trolls fought stubbornly. They re-formed into rings that held firm. From these, arrows flocked. Charging horses ran into braced spears. Elves toppled under axe and club. Where was help, where was help?

As if in answer, a horn blew—and another, and another —a war-cry, a hail of missiles, a sweep of ragged hundreds out of the night!

"Ha, Alfheim!" Firespear rode in the van. Blood streamed from his lance like the rain from his helmet. Glee shone from his face. By his side, battle-dinted axe dripping, came Flam of Orkney. And other elf chiefs were in the fight, rising as if out of the earth to cleanse it of its despoilers.

Now it became no great task to clear away the foe, and erelong only corpses kept the down. Skafloc held saddle-council with Firespear, Flam, and their fellow lords.

"We came as fast as we could," said Firespear. "We had to stop at Runehill and secure it, since the gates stood open for us and few trolls were left. Well had the women done their work! I think they will have everything finished for us in Alfarhöi, seeing that most of its garrison is lying here."

"Good," nodded Skafloc. Battle past and sword sheathed, he felt a return of weariness. The storm was dying overhead in wink and grumble, the wind sank and rain washed heavily out of a lightening sky.

"The Sidhe of Erin go to war too," Flam said. "Lugh has landed in Scotland, and Mananaan drives the trolls from the northern waters and isles."

"Ah—he kept his word." Skafloc showed a little cheer. "A true friend is Mananaan. He is the only god I would trust."

"And that only because he is a half-god, stripped of most of his powers and brought down to Faerie," muttered Firespear. "Unwise is it to have any dealings with gods ... or giants."

"Well, we had best move, so we can be inside ere dawn," said Flam. "Today we sleep in Alfarhöi. Oh, long since I slept in an elf burh beside an elf woman!"

Skafloc's mouth writhed, but he did not speak.

Though fall that year had come in with such rage, it soon turned mild and stayed thus uncommonly long. It was as if the land were welcoming back her lovers of old. Some lay down with her for ever, and the maples remembered them in the colour of their leaves. Other trees rustled in a thousand hues of gold and bronze, wide across hazy hills under dreaming heaven. Squirrels bustled about, bringing in their little harvests; stags shook antlers and belled forth pride; the lonesome cry of southbound geese drifted downward with the leaves. At night the stars gleamed untellably many, so bright that it seemed one could reach up and pluck them from that crystalline blackness.

And the luck of the elves rode high. North and south, east

and west, their enemies broke before them with small loss to themselves. For not only did they have dread allies, they were better supplied and got more reinforcements weekly as the Erlking cleared the mainland; and they took back their castles with ease. The trolls, on the other hand, were altogether cut off after Mananaan drew tight his blockade. Toward the end of that season, elves were heard to complain about how hard they must search to find any who could give them a fight.

There was no gladness in this for Skafloc. First, he knew what lay behind it. Once Valgard saw that his troops would be cut down piecemeal in the field, he began withdrawing them as fast as might be toward Elfheugh; knots of them stayed behind, making too much trouble for the elves to get at the larger bodies. While Skafloc had no doubt he could overrun their last stand, the cost might be high.

That did not really grieve him, but it did offend a certain sense of workmanship, and he weighed different schemes for ending the matter more handily. His thinking was slower than of yore, because of the second thing which gnawed at him.

And that thing sprang from the very peace he was bringing. Pitched battles dwindled to skirmishes, to chivvyings, to naught. For days, finally weeks on end, his sword slept. Then memory awoke. He had hoped the wound within him was somewhat healed. He found that it was not. He could not say whether his long lyings awake hurt the more, or his dreams.

In such wise did his autumn fade toward a new winter. The end of it came one night in the Danelaw, when Firespear—to whom Skafloc had told no more than he told anyone else, leaving them to suppose he had either grown tired of his human girl or left her among men for safekeeping—sought him out and said: "You may like to know, I was riding at dusk by a garth not far hence and saw a young woman who might well be Freda Ormsdaughter. She was great with child, though to me she looked as if she also bore sorrow."

Skafloc rode alone through evening. The black stallion went at a walk, no faster than a mortal steed. Strewn leaves crackled under his hoofs and danced before him on a cool wind. Such of them as were left on the boughs were still bright, as if to make a crown for his rider. Twilight closed hazily in as he went through woods that the man remembered.

Skafloc was unbowed by the weight of helmet, byrnie, or dragon-hilted sword. His hair blew long and light from under a cap coif. His face, strong blunt lines of it standing out beneath weather-darkened skin, was set unbending. Yet his heart knocked and knocked, blood beat in his ears, his hands were wet and his lips dry.

Dusk became a rustling dark. He splashed across a brook which purled icy clear, and by witch-sight spied dead leaves floating seaward like small brown boats. He heard an owl hoot and the trees creak—but underneath all was a singing silence wherein only his heart lived.

O Freda, Freda, are you really so near?

Many stars had twinkled forth when Skafloc rode into Thorkel Erlendsson's yard. He hissed a word that made the dogs run off without barking; and the hoofs fell softly. The steading was dark save for a weak glow of firelight from under the front door of the house.

He dismounted. His knees shook. It took a surge of will for him to walk over to that door. The bolt was in place, and he stood for a moment readying the spell that would slide it back.

Thorkel was a yeoman of worth but no chieftain; so his main room was not big, and no one slept there when he did not have guests. Freda sat late by a low hearthfire as was her wont. Audun came in from the rear. His eyes were brighter than the flame-glow. "I could not sleep," he said. "The others can—how they can!—so I put my clothes back on hoping we could talk without being stared at."

He joined her on the bench. The light sheened ruddily from her hair. She did not go with it covered in the manner of a wife, but she had braided it. "I can hardly believe my luck," he said. "Any day now, my father comes home and we shall be wed."

Freda smiled. "First I must have my babe, and get well from that," she said, "though it could likewise come any day."

She grew grave. "And have you in truth naught against me—or him?" she asked slowly.

"How could I?" said Audun. "How often must I tell you? It is your child. That is enough for me. It will be like my own."

He laid his arms about her.

The bolt slid free. The door opened and the night wind blew in. Freda saw the tall form limned athwart the dark. She could not speak. Rising, she crept backwards until she was stopped by the wall.

"Freda," croaked Skafloc above the faint hiss and crackle of the fire.

It was as if an iron band tightened around her breast. She lifted her arms, but wide apart with the hands turned inward.

Like a sleepwalker, Skafloc came toward her. And she took a step toward him, and another.

"Hold!" Audun's voice crashed across the silence. His shadow wavered huge before him. He snatched a spear that leaned in a corner, and pushed himself between those two.

"Hold . . . I, I, I tell you hold!" he stammered. "Who are you? What will you?"

Skafloc traced a sign and spoke a stave. Those in the rear of the house would not awaken while he was inside. He did it without thinking, in the way that a man brushes off a fly. "Freda," he said again.

"Who are you?" cried Audun. His tone cracked in the middle. "What will you?" He saw how those two looked at each other, and though he did not understand, he whimpered in pain.

Skafloc looked over the boy's shoulder, hardly aware of him. "Freda," he said. "My darling, my life. Come away with me."

She shook her head, wrenchingly, yet still she reached for him.

"I went to Jötunheim, I came back to war, thinking Time and swords might cut me loose from you," Skafloc said raggedly. "They could not. This deathbringer I carry cannot do it, nor law nor gods nor aught that is in the Nine Worlds. Then what are they to us? Come with me, Freda."

She bent her head. Her face was wrenched out of shape with what fought behind it. She sobbed, with hardly a noise though her ribs seemed about to be torn loose; and tears broke forth.

"You hurt her!" screamed Audun.

He stabbed unskilfully with the spear. It glanced off the broad, byrnied chest and furrowed Skafloc's cheek. The elf lord spat like a lynx and reached for his sword.

Audun thrust again. Skafloc leaped aside, unhumanly

swift. The sword went *s-s-s-s-s* as it rose from the scabbard. It clove the shaft over. "Get out of our way!" grasped Skafloc.

"Not while my bride lives!" Audun, beside himself with rage and terror—terror not of death but of what he had seen in Freda's eyes—felt his own tears run. He snatched forth his dagger and lunged for Skafloc's throat.

The sword flamed high, whistled down, and sang in bone and brain. Audun skidded across the floor and crashed into a wall, where he crumpled gruesomely limp.

Skafloc stared at the reddened blade in his hand. "I did not mean that," he whispered. "I only wanted to beat him aside. I forgot this thing must drink each time it is drawn—"

His glance lifted to Freda. She gaped at him, shuddering, mouth stretched open as if for a scream.

"I meant it not!" he shouted. "And what does it matter? Come with me!"

She fought for a voice. It came at last, half strangled: "Go. At once. Never come back."

"But—" He took a stiff step forward.

She stooped and picked up Audun's dagger. It gleamed in her hand. "Get out," she said. "Any nearer and I drive this into you."

"I wish you would," he answered. He stood swaying a little. The blood coursed down his gashed cheek and dripped on the floor.

"Or I will slay myself if I must," Freda told him. "Touch me, murderer, heathen, who would lie with your own sister like a beast or an elf, touch me and I will sheath the knife in my own heart. God will forgive me the lesser sin if I escape the greater."

Rage flapped up in Skafloc. "Aye, call on your god, whine your prayers!" he said. "Is that all you are good for? You were ready to sell yourself for a meal and a roof, whoredom no matter how many priests snivel over it . . . after what you vowed to me aforetime." He lifted the sword. "Better my son die unborn than he be given to that god of yours."

Freda stood stiff before him. "Strike if you will," she jeered. "Boys and women and babes in the womb—are they your foes?"

He lowered the great blade, and suddenly, without cleaning it, he clashed it into the scabbard. As he did, the fury drained from him. Weakness and grief rose in its stead.

His shoulders sagged. His head bent. "Do you really disown me, then?" he said low. "The sword is accursed. 'Twas not I who spoke those foul things or slew that poor lad. I love you, Freda, I love you so that the whole world is bright when you are near and black when you are gone. I—like a beggar, I ask you to come back."

"No," she gasped. "Leave. Go away." A scream: "I do not want to see you ever again! Go!"

He turned toward the door. His mouth trembled. "Once I asked you for a farewell kiss," he said most quietly, "and you would not give it to me. Will you now?"

She went to Audun's huddled form, knelt down and touched her lips to those. "My dear, my dear," she crooned, stroked the bloody hair and closed the dulled eyes. "God take you to Him, Audun mine."

"Then farewell," said Skafloc. "There may come a third time when I ask you for a kiss, and that will be the last. I do not think I have long to live, nor do I care. But I love you."

He went out, closing the door behind him against the night wind. His spells faded away. The folk of the garth were awakened by barking dogs and hoofbeats that drummed off toward the rim of the world. When they came into the front room and saw what was there, Freda told them an outlaw had tried to steal her.

In the darkness before morning her time came upon her. The child was big and her hips were narrow. Though she made scant noise, her pains were long and hard.

With a murderer about, there could be no sending after a priest at once. The women helped Freda as best they could; but Aasa's face was grim.

"First Erlend, now Audun," she muttered to herself. "Orm's daughters bring no great luck."

At daybreak men went forth to seek for spoor of the killer. They found nothing, and by sundown returned home saying that tomorrow it ought to be safe for one or two to ride to the church. Meanwhile the child had come forth, a well-shaped, lustily howling man-child whose mouth was soon hungrily at Freda's breast. In the early evening she lay, worn out and atremble, in the offside room they had given her to herself, with her son in her arms.

She smiled down at the little body. "You are a pretty babe," she half sang; she had not altogether come back from that shadow land where she had lately been, and nothing seemed wholly real save what she held. "You are red and wrinkled and beautiful. And so you would be to your father."

Tears flowed, mild as a woodland spring, until her mouth was salt. "I love him," she whispered. "God forgive me, I will always love him. And you are the last that is left of what was ours."

The sun burned bloodily to darkness. A gibbous moon swept through clouds blown on a sharp wind. There would be storm tonight; the long fall of elven-welcome was past and winter came striding.

The garth huddled under heaven. Trees groaned around it. The noise of the sea beat loud.

Night deepened and the wind rose to a gale, driving troops of dead leaves before it. Hail rattled now and again on the roof, like night-gangers thumping their heels on the ridgepole. Freda lay wakeful.

About midnight, far away, she heard a horn. Something of its scream ran cold through her. The child cried out and she gathered him to her.

The horn sounded again, louder, nearer, through skirling wind and grinding surf. She heard hounds bay, like none that she knew. Hoofbeats rushed through the night, filling the sky with their haste. Earth rang an echo.

The Asgard's Ride, the Wild Hunt—Freda lay in a shroud of fear. How could it be that no one else stirred? Her babe wailed at her breast. The wind rattled the shutters.

There came a mighty tramping of hoofs in the yard. The horn sounded again, a blast to which the house shook. The clamour of hounds went around the walls, music of brass and iron.

A door led from Freda's chamber to the outside. Someone knocked on it. The bolt flew back and the door swung wide. The wind flew around the room, billowing the cloak of the one who trod in.

Though no light burned, she could see him. He must stoop beneath the rafters. His spearhead flashed like his single eye. Wolf-grey hair and beard streamed down from under the hat that shadowed his face.

He spoke with the voice of wind and sea and the hollow sky: "Freda Ormsdaughter, I have come for that which you swore to give me."

"Lord—" She shrank back, under no shield but a blanket.

If Skafloc were here—"Lord, my girdle is in yonder chest."

Odin laughed in the night. "Think you I wanted a sleeping draught? No, you were to give me what lay behind; and already you bore that child."

"*No!*" She hardly heard her own scream. She thrust the crying babe behind her. "No, no, no!" She sat up and snatched the crucifix they had hung over her head. "In the name of God, of Christ, I, I bid you flee!"

"I need not run from that," said Odin, "for you swore away their help in this doing. Now give me the child!"

He thrust her aside and took the little one in the crook of his free arm. Freda crawled from the bed to crouch at his feet. "What do you want with him?" she moaned. "What will you do to him?"

The Wanderer answered from boundlessly far above her: "His weird is high and awful. Not yet is this game between Æsir and Jötuns and the new gods played out. Tyrfing still gleams on the chessboard of the world. Thor broke it lest it strike at the roots of Yggdrasil; then I brought it back and gave it to Skafloc because Bolverk, who alone could make it whole again, would never have done so for As or elf. The sword was needed to drive back the trolls—whom Utgard-Loki had been secretly helping—lest Alfheim be overrun by a folk who are friendly to the foemen of the gods. But Skafloc cannot be let keep the sword, for that which is in it will make him seek to wipe out the trolls altogether; and this the Jötuns dare not allow, so they would move in, and the gods would have to move against them, and the doom of the world would be at hand. Skafloc must fall, and this child whom I wove my web to have begotten and given to me must one day take up the sword and bear it to the end of its weird."

"Skafloc die?" She clasped his feet. "Him too? Oh, no, oh, no!"

"What has he further to live for?" asked Odin coldly. "If you should go to him at Elfheugh, whither he is bound, and make whole again what was broken at the howe, he would gladly lay down his weapons. Then that which is would have no need of his death. Otherwise he is fey. The sword will kill him."

With a swirl of his cloak, the Wild Huntsman was gone. His horn blew, his hounds yelped and howled, hoofbeats rushed away and were lost in the night. Then the only sounds were the empty whistle of wind, shout of sea, and weeping of Freda.

XXVII

Valgard stood in the topmost room of the highest tower in Elfheugh and watched the gathering of his foes. His arms were folded, his body was rock-still, and his face was as if carved in stone. Nothing but his eyes seemed altogether alive. Beside him were the other chiefs of the castle and of the broken armies which hid in this last and most powerful stronghold. Weary and downcast were they, many wounded, and they stared fearfully at the hosting of Alfheim.

On Valgard's right, Leea shimmered in the rays that struck through the unglazed windows from a sinking moon. Thence also came the breeze that blew her spidery gown and pale hair about her. A half smile was on her lips and her eyes shone twilight blue.

Below Elfheugh's walls, the slopes lay white with rime and moonlight. There moved the elf army. Weapons rattled, ringmail chimed, lur horns lowed, horses stamped ringingly on the frosty earth. Shields flung back the moonbeams, and the heads of spears and axes gleamed cold under the stars. The elves were setting up their camps; tents ringed the castle and fires blossomed ruddy. To and fro flitted the shadowy forms of the warriors.

A rumble rolled through the hills. Into sight came a war chariot, bright almost as a sun. Flames flickered about the swords on its hubs. Four huge white horses drew it, arching their silken-maned heads and snorting like storm winds. He who stood spear-armed behind the driver towered over all others. Dark locks blew about a countenance of majesty and grimness. The eyes burned with a light of their own.

A troll said unsteadily: "That is Lugh of the Long Hand. He led the Tuatha De Danaan against us. He reaped us like wheat. The Scottish ravens darkened the earth, too gorged to fly, and not a hundred trolls escaped."

Still Valgard spoke no word.

Red-cloaked, silver-byrnied, Firespear pranced his steed around the castle walls. Bright and handsome was his face, though cruel in its mockery, and his lance reached aloft as if to impale stars. "He led the outlaws," muttered someone else. "Their arrows came from everywhere. They rose out of the night against us, and left fire and death behind them."

Valgard stayed moveless.

In the moongladed bay, hulks of troll vessels smouldered or lay driven on to the strand and broken. Elven longships rode at anchor, gleaming with shields and weapons. "Flam of Orkney captains those, which Mananaan Mac Lir took back from us," said a troll chief harshly. "The seas are bare of our craft. One got through, to tell us how the coasts of Trollheim are plundered and ablaze."

Valgard might have been graven in dark stone.

The elves ashore began to raise a pavilion bigger than the others. A man rode thither on a black horse of monster size and planted his standard—a spearshaft atop which leered the shrivelling head of Illrede. The dead eyes stared straight at those in the tower.

A troll's voice broke as he said: "That is their leader, Skafloc the Mortal. Naught can stand before him. He drove us northward like a flock of sheep, slaughtering, slaughtering. The sword he wields goes through stone and metal as if through cloth. I wonder if he is indeed a man, and not a fiend risen from hell."

Valgard stirred. "I know him," he said softly. "And I mean to slay him."

"Lord, you cannot. That weapon of his—"

"Be still!" Valgard turned to rake the troll with his eyes and lash them with his words. "Fools, cowards, knaves! Let any who fear to fight go out to yon butcher. He will not spare you, but you will die quickly. As for me, I am going to break him, here at Elfheugh."

His tones deepened, rolling like those war-wheels below: "This is the last troll stronghold in Britain. How the others were lost, we know not. Our folk have only seen elf banners flying over them as they retreated hither. But we do know that this castle, which never yet fell to storm, is now packed with warriors to a number greater than that outside. It is bastioned alike against magic and open assault. Naught but our own cravenness can take it from us."

He hefted the great axe that never left him. "They will pitch their camp tonight and do no more. Soon comes dawn. Tomorrow night they may begin siege, more likely storm. If it is storm, we will cast it back and sally forth in pursuit. Otherwise we will make the attack ourselves, having the fortress behind us for withdrawal should things go wrong."

The teeth gleamed in his beard. "But I think we will carry them before us. We are more than they, and man for man stronger. Skafloc and I will seek each other out; there is no love between us twain. And I will kill him and get his victorious sword."

He stopped. The lord from Scotland asked: "And what of the Sidhe?"

"They are not all-powerful," snapped Valgard. "Once we have mowed enough elves to make it plain their cause is doomed, the Sidhe will handsel peace. Then England will be a troll realm, guarding the homeland from attack until we have gathered might to fare afresh against the Erlking."

His darkling gaze slanted down to meet Illrede's. "And I," he muttered, "will sit on your throne. But what use is that? What use is anything?"

Some time after the noise in the night had ended, a house-carle plucked up the heart to leave his bed, light a lamp from the hearth-coals, and search out how it stood in Thorkel Erlendsson's home. He found the outer door open in the room of Freda Ormsdaughter, her child gone, and she lying swooned and bleeding on the threshold. He carried her back. Thereafter she tossed in a fever, crying out things which caused the priest, when he came, to shake his head and cross himself.

None could get sense out of her. Twice in the following days she tried to slip away, and each time someone saw her and led her back. She had no strength to fight them.

But there came the night when she awoke alone, her mind clear—or so she believed—and a little health returned to her. She lay for a while making plans. Then she crept from her bed, clenching her jaws lest teeth clatter in the cold, and found the chest where her clothes lay. Fumbling in the dark, she put on a wollen gown and long, hooded cloak; she carried shoes in hand and went in stockinged feet to the kitchen for bread and cheese to take with her.

On the way back through her room, she stopped to kiss the crucifix above the bed. "Forgive me if You can," she whispered, "that I love him more than You. Evil am I, but the sin is mine, not his."

She went out beneath the stars. They were very many, unwinking and sharp. The night was quiet, save where frost crackled under her feet. The cold bit at her. She walked toward the stable.

The castle remained dusky and still while day waned toward sunset. Leea put her hands about Valgard's arm, where it was thrown across her bosom. Slowly, carefully, she lifted it and laid it on the mattress, and slid herself out on to the floor.

He turned, mumbling in his sleep. The vigour of his wakefulness was gone, leaving a skull over which a scarred hide was drawn tight, save that it sagged at eyes and chin. Leea looked down upon him. A dagger from off a table sheened in her grasp.

Easy to slash his throat—No, too much depended on her. If she should make a slip—and he had a werewolf's alertness, even when asleep—everything might yet be lost. She turned away, no louder than a questing shadow, drew gown and girdle over her nakedness, and left the earl's chambers. In her right hand she held the knife, in her left the castle keys, lifted from the hiding place she had suggested to Valgard.

She passed another elf woman on the stair. This one carried swords from the armory. Neither spoke.

The trolls tossed in uneasy slumber. Now and again Leea flitted by a watchman, who paid her no heed beyond a lickerish glance. Elf women were often sent on errands by their masters.

Down into the dungeons she went. She came to the cell door behind which was Imric, and undid the triple lock.

The imp stared at her through the restlessly reddened dark. Leea was on him in a single pounce. His wings rattled, but ere he could cry out he was flopping with his gullet slit across.

Leea scattered the fire. Reaching up, she cut the ropes that bound Imric. He fell heavily into her arms and lay corpse-like when she had lowered him to the floor.

She carved healing runes on bits of the charred woods and put them under his tongue, on his eyes and burnt feet, on his lame hands. She whispered spells. The flesh writhed as it grew back. Imric gasped with pain but made no other sound.

Leea put certain keys off the ring beside him. "When you have recovered," she said low, "free the elf captives. They have been placed in the dungeons for safety's sake. Weapons will be hidden in the old wellhouse behind the keep. Do not go after them until the fighting is at a peak."

"Good," he muttered out of his parched throat. "Also I

will get water and wine and a haunch of meat...and everything else the trolls owe to me." The gleam in his eyes came near to frightening Leea herself.

On soundless bare feet, she followed an underground passage to a tower for astrologers, now unused, which overlooked the outer walls on the east side. Up the stairs she wound until she stood among the great brass and crystal instruments. From there she stepped forth onto the encircling balcony. Though she was shaded, the sinking sun well-nigh blinded her with glare and stabbed her with rays of a more terrible, invisible light. She barely saw one who stood tall and brightly byrnied outside the wall, as had been asked in the message which a bat carried for her through the last dusk.

She could not tell who it was. A warrior of the Sidhe, belike, though maybe—her heart stumbled—maybe Skafloc himself.

She leaned over the rail and flung the ring of keys upward and outward in a glittering arc. It looped on his spear; and those were the keys to unlock and unbolt the castle gates.

Leea hurried back into grateful dimness. Like a skimming bird she raced for the earl's chambers. Hardly had she doffed her clothes and gotten back into bed than Valgard blinked awake.

He clambered to his feet and peered out the dusking window. "Almost sundown," he said. "Time to arm for battle."

Taking a horn off the wall, he opened the door to the stairs and blew a long blast. Watchmen who heard it passed the signal on, down and down the reaches of the castle... not knowing it was the call for every elf woman who was able to plunge a knife into the heart of the troll who had her.

Freda kept fainting, and rousing in a whirl of red-spattered darkness just as she was about to fall off her horse. It was pain, swordlike through her half-healed body, that brought her back to awareness, and she thanked it with dry lips.

She had taken mount and remount, and flogged them on unmercifully. Hills and trees wavered past, like stones seen through a swiftly running river. Often they struck her as unreal, things of dream; nothing was real except the tumult that filled her head.

She remembered her horse stumbling once and throwing her into a brook. When she rode on, the water froze in her dress and hair.

Many eternities later, when the sun was again sinking as red as the blood in her trail, her second horse fell. The first had already died; nor did this one get up. She took to her feet, crashing into trees because her eyes could not place them, pushing through bushes whose twigs clawed at her.

Ever more high and loud rose the clamour within her. She could not think who she was, nor care. Nothing mattered save that she keep moving north toward Elfheugh.

XXVIII

At sundown Skafloc let sound the battle horns. His elves came forth from their tents, into the dusk, with a clashing of metal and a great revengeful shout. Horses tramped and whinnied, chariots rolled brazen over the frosty ground, and a forest of spears lifted behind the flying banners and the head of Illrede.

Skafloc mounted his Jötun stallion. The sword called Tyrfing seemed almost to stir of itself at his hip. Beneath the helmet his face might have been the mask of a forgotten war-god, worn thin in everything but ruthlessness.

Of Firespear he asked, "Do you also hear a racket behind the walls?"

"Aye," grinned the elf. "The trolls have just found out how it was that the other castles fell so easily. However, they will not catch the women, with the hiding places there are in that burh, ere we have caught them."

Skafloc gave him a key off the ring at his belt. "Do you lead the attack on the rear, with a ram," he reminded needlessly. "When we open the front gate, it should draw enough defenders for you to get at the hind one. Flam and Rucca will lead diversionary assaults to right and left, which will swing to help us when we enter. I will go with the Sidhe and those guardsmen the Erlking sent, against the forward portal."

The full moon rose enormous out of the eastern sea. Its light fell glittery on metal and eyes, ghostly on banners and white horses. The lurs dunted and the host raised another shout that rang between crags and cliffs, up toward the stars. Then elves and allies moved to do battle.

A twanging sounded through the night. Shaken the trolls might be, with a third of their number murdered in sleep and the killers loose somewhere in that maze of a castle; yet they were doughty warriors and Valgard roared them on to their tasks. From the walls their archers sent a steady rain of arrows down on the elves.

Shafts rattled off shields and mail; but some struck deep. Man after man toppled, horses screamed and bolted, dead and wounded littered the uphill way.

That was a rugged tor, and only one narrow road led to the main gate. Elves needed no path, they sprang over rattling talus and frost-slippery rocks, from crag to next higher crag, war-cries ringing from their throats. They threw hooks that caught the tops of cliffs and swarmed up ropes tied to these, they rode their horses where no goat would have dared to go, they stormed to the flat ground under the walls and sped their own arrows aloft.

Skafloc took the road, so that he could lead the chariots of the Tuatha De Danaan. Frightfully they rumbled behind him, wheels sparking and crashing on stones, bodies glowing as if the bronze were still molten. Though arrows rattled off helms, hauberks, and shields, neither warriors nor drivers suffered hurt. Nor did he, thundering on his dark horse along a path of shadow and tricky moonlight.

Thus the elves won to the walls. Boiling water and blazing oil and ice-slick vitriol gushed down at them, spears and stones and the lurid fire of the Greeks. Elves shrieked when the flesh peeled from their bones, and their comrades drew snarling back.

Skafloc shouted, wild to draw his sword. To him the elves dragged a testudo, a shed on wheels, and covered by this he rode to the gate.

On the battlement above, Valgard signed to his men at the war engines. Long before those brazen-bound doors gave way to a battering ram, the shelter would be crushed under huge hurled stones.

Skafloc put the first key in place and turned it, calling out the rune words. A second key, a third—Valgard helped load a ballista with a boulder beneath whose weight it groaned. Trolls wound it up.

Seven keys, eight—Valgard grasped the lever. Nine keys, and the gate was unbarred!

Skafloc reared back his horse. The pawing forefeet clashed

on the doors. They swung open, and Skafloc galloped the tunnel thickness of the wall and burst out into the moon-silvery courtyard. Behind him, the passage echoed to the wheels of the chariots of Lugh, Dove Berg, Angus Og, Eochy, Coll, Cecht, Mac Greina, Mananaan, the whole host of the Sidhe, to hoofs of horses and running feet. The gateway was taken!

Guards beyond struck out with their weapons. An axe smote the leg of the Jötun horse. The stallion neighed and kicked, trampled, trod warriors into bloody smears.

Skafloc's sword wailed forth. The blade flamed icy blue in the half-light, sang its killing-song, rose and fell, striking like an adder. Clamour and clangour of metal belled at the stars, shouts, whistle of blades, earthquake rumble of wheels.

Back and back went the trolls. Valgard howled, his eyes glowing wolf-green, and led a rush down from the wall to the courtyard. Mightily he smote at the flank of the invaders. An elf fell to his axe, he twisted the edge loose and struck at another, smashed the face of a third with its beak—hewing, hewing, he waded into battle.

At the rear gate rose the drumbeat of Firespear's ram. The trolls cast stones at it, pots of burning oil, spears and arrows and darts—until from behind them leaped a crew gaunt and bloody and tattered, but with weapons hungry in their hands—Imric's gang of freed prisoners. The trolls turned to fight them, and Firespear opened the gate.

"To the keep!" Valgard trumpeted. "To the keep, and hold it!"

Trolls carved a way to where he loomed. They made a shield-wall against which elf swords clattered, and brought it by sheer weight and force to the front door of the keep.

It was locked.

Valgard hurled himself at it. The door cast him back. He chopped out the lock and swung the door open.

Bowstrings sang in the darkness behind. Trolls fell. Valgard lurched back with an arrow through his left hand. Leea's voice jeered at him: "The elf women hold this house for their lovers—better lovers than they have lately had, O you ape of Skafloc!"

Valgard turned away, wrenching the arrow from his hand. He howled and frothed. Back into the courtyard he went, axe whirring and belling, striking at anything that was before it. The berserkergang was on him.

Skafloc fought in that colder glory which the rune sword lent him. It was fire in his hand. Blood and brains spurted, heads rolled on flagstones, guts were slippery under his horse's hoofs—he fought, he fought, icily aware and thinking, yet whirled high out of himself so that he and the killing were one. He scattered death as a sower strews grain, and where ever he went the troll lines broke.

The moon climbed from the waters whereon it had built a bridge—strange they should be so quiet—and over the castle walls. Its light fell upon ghastliness. Swords flew, spears thrust, axes and clubs beat, metal and men cried their pain. Horses reared, trampling, whinnying, manes clotted with blood. The struggle swayed back and forth over its own corpses and stamped them into meaningless meat.

The moon rose further, until from the courtyard it was as if an eastern watchtower pierced its heart. Then the trolls broke.

Few of them were left. The elves harried them about the like animals.

Few of them were left. The elves harried them about the castle grounds and out onto the white hillside, hunting them lik animals.

"To me, to me!" Valgard's voice boomed over the waning battle. "Hither, trolls, and fight!"

Skafloc heard and wheeled his horse around. He saw the changeling stand huge in the gateway, smeared with blood from helm to shoon, a ring of elven dead before him. A dozen or so trolls were trying to reach him and make a death-stand.

And he was the worker of every harm—It might have been the sword Tyrfing that laughed with Skafloc's lips. Valgard, Valgard, your weird is upon you! And Skafloc spurred his horse forward.

Riding, he thought for an eyeblink that he saw a hawk lift from somewhere seawards and wing toward the moon. A chill struck into his bones, and he knew with a part of him that he was fey.

Valgard saw him coming and grinned. The changeling braced back against wall and raised his axe. The black stallion bore down on him. He swung as never before. The weapon clove the horse's skull.

That weight could not be stopped by anything less than the wall itself. When the stallion crashed, the stones shook.

Skafloc flew from the saddle. Elf-lithe, he twisted in midair to land on his feet. But he could not keep from striking the wall and rebounding into the gate passage.

Valgard wrenched his axe loose and ran to make an end of his foe. Skafloc had crawled away, out of the tunnel to the moonlit hillside beyond, at the foot of which were bay and sea. His right arm hung broken. He had cast aside his shield and gripped the sword left-handed. Blood dripped from his torn face and flowed down the blade.

Valgard stalked close. "Many things end tonight," said he, "and your life is one of them."

"We were born nigh the same night," answered Skafloc. Blood ran from his mouth with the words. "There will not be long between our deaths." He sneered. "When I go out, how can you, my shadow, stay?"

Valgard screamed and struck at him. Skafloc brought up the sword. The axe Brotherslayer hit that blade, and in a clang and crash and sheeting of sparks burst asunder.

Skafloc staggered back, caught himself, and lifted the sword anew. Valgard stalked empty-handed toward him, growling deep in his throat.

"Skafloc! Skafloc!"

At that cry Imric's fosterling turned about. Up the road came Freda, stumbling, worn, bloody, in rags, but his Freda coming back to him. "Skafloc," she called. "My dearest—"

Valgard rushed in and wrenched the sword from the hand of his unseeing foe. He swung the blade aloft and brought it down.

Howling, he raised the sword anew. Beneath the blood, it ran with unearthly blue fires. "I have won!" he shouted. "I am lord of the world and I tread it under my feet! Come, darkness!"

He hewed at the air. His hand, slippery with what it had been shedding, lost its grip. The sword twisted around and fell point foremost on him. That great weight knocked him from his feet, drove through his neck and into the earth. There he lay pinned with the blade gleaming before his eyes and his life rivering from his throat. He tried to haul it loose, and the edges opened the veins in his wrists. And that was the end of Valgard the Changeling.

Skafloc lay with cloven shoulder and breast. His face was wan in the moonlight. But when Freda bent over him, he could smile.

"I am sped, my darling," he whispered. "You are too

good for a dead man. You are too lovely to weep. Forget me—"

"Never, never." Her tears fell on him like the rain of a morning in spring.

"Will you kiss me farewell?" he asked.

His lips were already cold, but she sought them hungrily. And when she had opened her eyes again, Skafloc was dead in her arms.

The first cold streaks of light were in the eastern sky when Imric and Leea came out. "Why heal the girl and take her home?" No joy of victory was in the elf woman's tones. "Better send her in torment to hell. It was she who slew Skafloc."

"It was his weird," answered Imric. "And helping her is the last thing we can do for him. If we elves do not know the thing called love, still, we can do that which would have gladdened a friend."

"Not know love?" murmured Leea, too softly for him to hear. "You are wise, Imric, but your wisdom has its bounds."

Her gaze went to Freda, who sat on the rime-white earth with Skafloc cradled in her arms. She was singing him to sleep with the lullaby she had thought to sing to their child.

"Happier was her fate than mine," said Leea.

Imric misunderstood her, wittingly or otherwise. He nodded. "Happier are all men than the dwellers in Faerie— or the gods, for that matter," he said. "Better a life like a falling star, bright across the dark, than a deathlessness which can see naught above or beyond itself." He looked to the sword, still flashing in the throat of its prey. "And I feel a doom creeping upon me," he breathed. "I feel that the day draws nigh when Faerie shall fade, the Erlking himself shrink to a woodland sprite and then to nothing, and the gods go under. And the worst of it is, I cannot believe it wrong that the immortals will not live forever."

He trod over to the blade. "As for this," he told the dwarf thralls who followed him, "we will take it and cast it from us, well out to sea. I do not think that will do much good, though. The will of the Norns stands not to be altered, and the sword has not wreaked its last harm."

He went with them in a boat to see that they did their work aright. Meanwhile Mananaan Mac Lir took away Freda and the body of Skafloc, that he might himself see to the welfare of the one and the honouring of the other. When Imric came back, he and Leea walked slowly into Elfheugh, for the winter dawn was about to break.

Here ends the saga of Skafloc Elven-Fosterling.